"Do you need help for a day or two?" Whitney asked. "Because I have some free time."

Somehow Tanner managed to keep his jaw from dropping.

Did he need help? He had tens of miles of fence to ride before turning his steers out on ranch pasture and his cow-calf pairs on the grazing allotment near Old Timber Canyon.

He gave her a frowning look, which she met with an open expression. She was obviously serious in her offer, but that didn't keep him from looking for ulterior motives. Why would she offer to help him?

"Do you have any skills?" She'd been born and raised on a ranch, as he'd been, but he doubted her father had worked her as hard as his father had worked him.

Whitney fixed him with a steady blue gaze, giving him the impression that she was very sure of her skills. "I can probably out-cowboy you."

He laughed. "That I'd like to see."

Dear Reader,

When I was in high school, my career goal was to be an actress. Real life interfered and instead I studied geology, then graduated during a time when jobs in the field were scarce. Then to make things interesting, I married a fellow geology student. We both ended up with teaching careers, which turned out to be very rewarding.

My heroine, Whitney Fox, exchanged her dream of raising and training horses for a safe career in the city. She never questioned her decision until she got laid off and needed to head back to the family ranch. She assumes that she'll return to the business world, but ranching life appeals to her, as does the cowboy next door, who is also dealing with some life changes and figuring out a path forward.

I enjoy writing books where the characters are certain about what they want, only to slowly discover that perhaps they should choose a different course. That awakening process is so much fun to plot and plan.

The Cowgirl's Homecoming is the third book in my Cowgirls of Larkspur Valley series. I hope you enjoy reading it, and that you'll check out the adventures of Whitney's friends Kat and Maddie in *Home with the Rodeo Dad* and *A Sweet Montana Christmas*.

Best Wishes,

Jeannie Watt

HEARTWARMING

The Cowgirl's Homecoming

—

Jeannie Watt

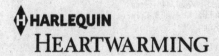

HARLEQUIN
HEARTWARMING

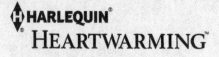

ISBN-13: 978-1-335-47565-7

Recycling programs for this product may not exist in your area.

The Cowgirl's Homecoming

Copyright © 2024 by Jeannie Steinman

For questions and comments about the quality of this book, please contact us at CustomerService@Harlequin.com.

Harlequin Enterprises ULC
22 Adelaide St. West, 41st Floor
Toronto, Ontario M5H 4E3, Canada
www.Harlequin.com

Printed in U.S.A.

Jeannie Watt lives on a smallish hay and cattle ranch in southwest Montana with her husband and parents. When she's not writing, Jeannie keeps herself busy sewing, baking and feeding lots of animals. She grew up in north Idaho, graduated from the University of Idaho with degrees in geology and education, and then spent the next thirty years living in rural northern Nevada. Twenty-two of those years were spent off the grid, which gave her a true appreciation for electricity when she moved to the family ranch in Montana after retiring from teaching. If you'd like to contact Jeannie, please visit her Facebook page at Facebook.com/jeannie.watt.1.

I dedicate this book to my dad.

CHAPTER ONE

"Do you believe bad things happen in threes?" Whitney Fox pulled a rose-pink satin bridesmaid dress out of its packing material and shook out the folds as she spoke. If things did happen in threes, she was afraid of what might happen next.

"Me? Oh, come on." Maddie Kincaid, one of Whit's best friends and the owner of Spurs and Veils Western Bridal Boutique, made a face as she took the dress from Whit and slipped it onto a hanger for steaming. It was mid-May, and the bridal season was ramping up, one reason that Whit had volunteered to help. The other was that she needed to talk to someone other than her dad and job recruiters.

"Thinking that way sets you up for the next bad thing to happen," Maddie added as Whit opened another giant cardboard box, this time to reveal pale blue dresses.

"Fine." Whit started pushing aside thin

plastic. "I'm on the cusp of something good. A new beginning."

An unexpected, scary new beginning. One door had slammed shut and now she had to pry another one open. Which door would it be? And how long would it take to find it? Her stomach tightened at the silent questions.

"That's better." Maddie tended to look on the bright side and right now that was exactly what Whit needed. Someone to tell her things would work out, because for the first time since the trauma of losing her mom nine years ago, Whit was floundering.

She needed to come up with Life Plan Number 3, and so far, she had nothing.

Life Plan Number 1, developed during middle school, had been to become independently wealthy, buy the ritzy Hayes Ranch next door to her family ranch, and raise and train champion Quarter Horses there.

That plan had not panned out.

Life Plan Number 2, formulated during high school while her mother had been ill, had been to get a sensible college degree, save money in a sensible manner and work her way into a lucrative, sensible corporate position. Her dream of becoming a horse trainer had been pushed so far aside that she knew it was never going to happen, although she'd never officially broken the news to her friends Kat and Maddie. The three of them had formed their middle school dream pact together, and Kat and Maddie had achieved their dreams. Kat now owned a small farm and Maddie had her bridal shop. Whit did not have her ritzy ranch and horse training facility. Nor did she want it.

The final few years of her mom's life had taught Whit a hard lesson about ranch economics. Medical bills had sapped them during a time of drought and low cattle prices, and while her dad had been able to pull the ranch out of the red eventually, those nip-and-tuck years had convinced Whit that she needed security. Maybe even some luxury. She needed to become a city girl.

Which she had done. Missoula wasn't exactly a megacity, but it was more urban than Larkspur, and she'd landed a well-paying job there, managing regulations and permitting for a renewable energy company. She'd worked long hours and some months spent more time on the road than she did in the office, but the rewards had been worth it—job security, stellar benefits and a healthy paycheck.

Then the axe fell.

Corporate buyouts were rarely good for the employees of the purchased company. Whit's case had been particularly painful—she'd worked her butt off to get the promotion that (a) allowed her to splurge and pay cash for a luxury car—the symbol of her success, and (b) put her in the direct path of the axe. Her job had been meshed with another position that an employee from the purchasing company now filled. The one bright spot was that the yearly lease on her property was close to renewal, thus allowing Whit to move from Missoula back to the home ranch without paying penalties. It was a pretty dim bright spot, but the only one she had.

"You know," Maddie said, as she began running the steamer over the dress, "you can fill in here until you find something."

"Probably best if I don't," Whit replied before pulling a dress out of the box and removing the protective tissue and plastic. "At least not in the front part of the store."

Maddie murmured something that sounded a lot like, "You make a good point," and Whit laughed as she stripped off the last of the tissue from a blue silk slip dress. Maddie was a master at gently directing people to flattering fits and colors. Whit, not so much.

"I'm going to sell my car." She tried to sound matter-of-fact, but it was hard to keep regret from coloring her voice.

"Sorry." Maddie knew how much Whit loved her first major splurge.

Whit and the Audi TT had seen three thousand miles together before she'd received the layoff notification. They'd been good miles, too, but Whit needed to recoup as much money as possible to provide herself with a cushion until Life Plan Number 3 came to fruition. She'd sunk her entire promotion bonus plus a chunk of her savings into the car. It hadn't seemed risky at the time, but now Whit would dearly love to have a do over. She and her coworkers had not seen the buyout coming or she wouldn't have made her splurge. One day, security. The next day, pink slip.

"After you sell the car, then what?"

"I don't know." A difficult admission, but an honest one. Whit felt like next steps should be obvious, as in, get a new job in her field

ASAP, but other factors were coming into play. Like a sense of inertia. She felt freaking paralyzed. Why?

Maddie lowered the steamer head and it spit hot water at the floor before she brought it back up to horizontal. "So your entire plan is to sell the car?"

"Sad, huh?" Whit was determined to put on a brave face while she sorted things out. She hated when people worried about her, having had enough of that after her mother died.

"You need time to regroup," Maddie said sympathetically. "Anyone would, given the circumstances. Maybe you can get something temporary here until you find your next real job."

Whit searched her brain. "I can't imagine what that would be, although—" she made a face "—I can play the banjo."

"Not that well."

Whit tossed a wad of plastic at Maddie. "I'm a great banjo player." Her expression sobered. "I'll figure something out."

"I know you will. Just please—no 'Foggy Mountain Breakdown.'"

"But it is foggy in here." Whit, thankful for the change of subject, fanned the moist air, wondering why the old hardwood floorboards weren't warped, considering the amount of steaming that went on over the years as garments were unpacked and hung.

Maddie turned the dress to tackle the back while Whit unpacked the rest of the shipment. After pulling the last gown out of the box, she smoothed a hand over her hair. The long blond strands that usually behaved nicely were starting to frizz.

"Have you ever watched *The Fog*?" Maddie shot her a frowning look and Whit shrugged. "Just wondering if anything sinister ever appeared out of the swirling mist back here."

"Nothing sinister, unless you count my former business partner." Who'd secretly hooked up with Maddie's now-ex-fiancé. "Steam is great for the skin."

"So that's your secret," Whitney murmured as she retrieved the plastic wad and tossed it into the trash. Maddie did have beautiful skin.

"Lots of steam and the love of a cranky cowboy."

Whit grinned. "I don't find Sean cranky."

"He tries, but yeah, he's missing the mark more and more." Maddie's lips curved into a gentle smile that made Whit want to smile in return. After breaking up with her cheating fiancé, Maddie had found a guy who truly loved her for who she was, and vice versa. Heartwarming, but not what Whit was looking for.

What are you looking for?

Not a man. She was doing fine on her own, thank you very much. But other than that parameter, she felt uncharacteristically lost and she hated it.

Whit busied herself gathering packing materials and stuffing them into the box for recycling while Maddie emptied the steamer tank. She returned to the room and stood a few feet away from the rack, admiring the shiny, smooth rose-pink satin dresses hanging next to pale blue silk gowns. A few bars of the wedding march played in the main part of the shop, indicating that a customer had entered the store, and a familiar voice called, "Where are you guys?"

"Back here," Maddie replied.

A few seconds later Kat, the third member of their decades-long friendship triad, came into the room carrying a box that made suspicious scratching noises.

"Kittens," she said. "They were giving them away at the grocery store, so I took them all."

"As one does," Maddie said.

"I had to. They're very young, and I'm of the opinion that you can't have enough kitties." Kat set down the box and opened the lid. Maddie and Whit both made an automatic "aw" sound as the three little black-and-white kitties inched their way along the cardboard on their bellies.

"I think they need to be bottle-fed for a while," Kat said. "I guess the mama just disappeared."

"I'd take one off your hands, but I don't know what my situation looks like yet," Whit said as Maddie reached in the box to pull out a kitten. Whit did the same, tucking the squirming baby against the warmth of her neck.

"But you have a plan, right?" Kat replied, stroking her kitten's head with a single finger as it lay in her palm.

Whit's stomach tightened again, but thankfully Kat's phone chimed before Whit had to confess that she had no plan at all. "Oops," Kat said while reading the screen. "Troy is ahead of schedule and waiting in the back lot, so I guess I'd better collect my kitties and go."

"What kitties?" Maddie asked innocently,

pulling the collar of her blouse over the kitty she held.

"Livia's kitties," Kat replied, Livia being the one-year-old daughter of Troy, Kat's fiancé.

"I will not deprive her," Maddie said with a sigh. She set the kitten back in the box alongside the other two and Kat gently closed the lid.

"I'll be in touch," she said as she lifted the box, holding it in front of her with both hands. "Good luck with the job hunt," she said to Whit. "Keep me posted."

At a tick after six o'clock, Whit and Maddie stepped out of the shop and into the crisp late-spring air. It appeared that everyone from shop employees to the patrons of the nearby bar whose happy hour had just ended were headed to their vehicles at the same time. Doors slammed; engines started.

Whit led the way across the lot to her car. She'd parked the luxurious dark gray vehicle in a far corner to protect it from parking lot dings and dents. She felt a little pang as she beeped the lock open, then gestured to Maddie to climb inside the plush interior.

"It's beautiful," Maddie said, running her

hand over the leather console that separated the bucket seats.

"Nicest vehicle I ever owned." Whit buckled in, then pressed the start button and the engine turned over, purring so gently that it was hard to tell that it was running. Soon she'd be driving the Corolla again, a car so old that she'd parked it on the ranch rather than trade it in for the negligible amount it would have brought.

Thank goodness she had.

A line of vehicles had formed at the parking lot exit and Whit nosed her car in behind a Corolla similar to the one she'd be driving in the future, moving forward a few feet at a time as the vehicles ahead of her waited for breaks in the traffic. When her turn came, a long open stretch appeared and she swung out into her lane, glad to have made a quick escape. She glanced in her rearview mirror and saw a big truck follow her out, its grill just a little too close for comfort.

"Look out!" Maddie cried, and Whit jammed on the brakes, barely missing the dog that had darted in front of her. Less than a second later a crash from the rear snapped her head forward and then back, rattling her brain, but thankfully not deploying the airbag.

She shot a dazed look at Maddie, and then they twisted in their seats to stare out the back window.

"Son of a—" Whit wrenched her door open and stepped onto the pavement. She ignored the passersby approaching from various directions as she strode to the rear of her car. Her bumper and one taillight had been smashed, and there was a big crease in the trunk.

"No, no, no," she muttered, taking in the damage and trying to calculate the impact this would have on her already limited plan. Of course the truck had a deer guard on the front, and the damage to it was negligible.

"Why did you stop so fast?" a deep voice growled from behind her.

She turned to find a tall guy in a cowboy hat staring at her with an outraged look on his face. She was having none of it. She drew in a breath and fired back.

"What were you thinking riding my bumper like that?" The words were barely out of her mouth when recognition struck.

Tanner Hayes. It'd been years since she'd

seen the man, but there was no mistaking those chiseled features when he tipped his hat back. He, in turn, gave her the once-over, looking like he couldn't quite place her.

"Whitney Fox," she said drily. "Your neighbor."

"I know who you are."

Maddie cleared her throat and they both turned to look at her. "I'll see if anyone saw anything." She spoke to Whit, pointedly ignoring Tanner.

"Please do," Whit said in a grim voice. She turned back to the man, thinking that her one saving grace was that the Hayes family was swimming in money, so he should have no problem handling the repairs.

But repairs took time and would bring down the resale value of her car. The only concrete part of her plan had just taken a massive blow.

"This is your fault." They needed to get that much straight here and now. Whit gestured at the damage. "You hit me."

"You stopped dead in the middle of a turn." His voice was low and not one bit apologetic.

"Because I didn't want to hurt a dog."

"I didn't see a dog," Tanner said stubbornly.

"Well, a dog ran out in the road in front of

me. Anyway, it doesn't matter," Whit replied. "You rear-ended me. The law is on my side."

"Not necessarily."

Whit propped her hands on her hips, noting that a crowd was edging in. Fine. Maybe public shame would do some good.

"Right. Because if you're the guy with the money, then the law tends to be on your side."

"Now wait a minute."

"All I'm saying—" she poked a finger at his chest "—is that you're not buying your way out of this like your dad bought his way out of everything."

His expression went stony, which meant that she'd struck a nerve. Good. She wanted to strike more than a nerve but had to make do with what was legal and available.

"Don't bring my father into this."

Whit felt a small wave of shame. Tanner's father had recently passed away, but the man had never been close to anyone, not even his two sons, who'd left home before Whit was out of high school. But, yeah, she shouldn't have brought his dead father into this.

She lifted her chin, but didn't mutter the apology that teetered on her lips. Something told her not to and she listened. "All I'm saying is that, often, in cases like this, money talks."

Her head came up as the deputy sheriff's vehicle turned onto the street and parked opposite. Bill Monroe got out of the cruiser and crossed the street. He looked over the damage as he approached, giving a low whistle, then he tilted his hat back as he recognized Tanner.

"Hey, Tanner. It's been some time. Some homecoming."

"It was his fault," Whit said stonily.

"That remains to be seen," Tanner said.

The deputy propped his hands on his hips. "That's for me to decide."

Whit rolled her eyes. Bill and Tanner were old high school buddies, but she knew she was in the right here. "I stopped to avoid a dog. He—" she pointed at Tanner "—was following too closely and smacked me from the rear, and I want that in your report."

Maddie appeared out of nowhere to touch her arm and Whit gave her friend a quick look. Fine. She would allow law enforcement to do their job.

She stepped back and watched as Bill commenced taking measurements and speaking to people who'd witnessed the accident. She gritted her teeth as Bill noted various conflicting eyewitness accounts in his book.

Yes, there had been a dog...

No, Tanner hadn't been following too closely. She'd stopped too abruptly...

Yes, he was too close. She'd done the only thing she could...

They were both at fault...

Neither was at fault...

And all the while this was going on, Tanner stood silently watching the proceedings like the heir to a throne would do—the throne being a sprawling ranch in this case—confident that things would work out in his favor.

And they probably would.

Once Bill had gathered his information and allowed them to move their vehicles, Tanner jerked his head to the side of the street, as if he expected Whit to follow. She frowned at him, and he exhaled and decided to speak where he stood.

"This was unfortunate, but insurance will cover it, and your car will be as good as new—regardless of whose fault it is."

"No," she said grimly. "It won't be as good as new. Its value has now decreased. Some of us don't have the ability to buy a new car on a whim."

"And you think I do?"

Whit sensed Maddie moving beside her, as if trying to signal to her that it was time to drop the matter and leave. Normally, Whit would have done that. She would have taken the hit in stride and moved on. But these weren't normal circumstances. Her vehicle was now worth less than it had been a few minutes ago, through no fault of her own. And the Hayes family had always rubbed her—and most of the community—the wrong way. But money talked and the townspeople listened, regardless of their feelings.

Tanner was watching her, waiting for a reply to his question, which Whit had no intention of giving. It appeared that he had no intention of speaking, either. In the end, Whit was the first to blink.

"I think that when you grow up wanting for nothing, it twists your sense of reality," she said tightly. His mouth went even flatter than it had been before. The crowd that had gathered on the sidewalk was still good-sized, probably because most were patrons from the nearby pub who'd come out to see what the ruckus was about.

And who didn't want to watch a fiery verbal face-off between two people who'd just been involved in a collision?

Maddie gave Whit's arm a yank, and as she gave in and allowed her friend to steer her to the car, she was surprised to find herself guided to the passenger side.

"I'm driving," Maddie said in a no-nonsense voice. "You've had a shock. You can take over after you drop me at my place."

"Fine," Whit muttered, opening the door and getting in without a backward glance— although that part was hard.

Maddie adjusted the mirror and then pulled away before Tanner did. Whit sat back in the ridiculously comfortable seat. "Guess it'll be a minute before I sell my car."

"But you will."

Spoken like the positive-thinking soul her friend was.

"Whose fault was it, Maddie?" Bill had taken witness statements, but so had Maddie in an informal way.

"He was too close behind, but you stopped abruptly. He probably would have hit you even if he'd been farther behind." Maddie stopped at the light. "It was the dog's fault, actually. And whoever allowed him to run."

Whit leaned her head against the window. Her friend was right. It was done, and now it was a matter of mitigating damages, not flinging blame. The blame-flinging had made her feel good in the moment, but it wasn't going to fix her car. It was annoying that she was going to struggle after this, and Tanner Hayes would throw money at the problem and it would, no doubt, go away.

CHAPTER TWO

THE SUN WAS just setting when Tanner pulled his truck to a stop in its parking place beside the barn, out of sight of the main house.

Habit.

His father had been all about appearances, which was pointless because his superior attitude made the ranch an unfriendly place to visit—and to live, which was why Tanner had left home the day after high school graduation, one month before his eighteenth birthday. He'd half expected his dad to insist that he stay until he was officially of age, but Tanner had hurt his dad's enormous pride by making it known he intended to follow his brother Grant's lead and leave home as soon as possible.

They'd eventually worked out a relationship that appeared relatively congenial to the outsider looking in, and he and his brother dutifully returned home for holidays and to help with the larger ranch events, such as branding and moving the cattle to high pasture, but he could never describe his relationship with his dad as anything but strained.

They'd gone through the motions and a part of Tanner wanted their interactions to be genuine, instead of always feeling like they were playacting, and he sensed that on some level, his father did, too. But his dad had been unwilling or unable to drop his pride and admit that there was work to do between them. If there was a problem, it was on Tanner and Grant. Carl Hayes was the patriarch and infallible.

Such was life with a narcissist.

But while his relationship with his dad was troubled, his relationship with the ranch he'd grown up on was not. He loved the land, the work, the animals, which was why, despite the revelation about the state of the ranch finances, he'd disagreed with Grant about selling and they'd worked out a deal. Or so he hoped.

Grant had a tendency to shake hands on an agreement, then attempt to wheedle small changes. Tanner hoped that this time things would play out differently. In return for a healthy sum of money—divided into two payments, a year apart—Grant had signed a paper agreeing to give Tanner three years to turn the ranch around. If he didn't, they would sell.

Coming up with the money had been a stretch for Tanner, who'd never made a whopping salary working for the wheat farm. But he'd managed to secure the funds, so now he'd only be fighting time, instead of time and his brother.

A joyous bark sounded from the yard, and Rose, his yellow Labrador retriever, bounded across the driveway, poking his leg with her nose as he unloaded the groceries he'd bought for his injured foreman.

"Hey, girl." He ruffled her ears and then shut the truck door. He walked around the front of the vehicle, taking in the minor damage to the deer guard, and shook his head. The law probably was on Whitney Fox's side regardless of how abruptly she'd stopped, and his insurance would be the one with the rate hike. Yet another financial worry to add to the stack.

He and Rose headed to the small house across the driveway. Len Anderson, Tanner's ranch manager, had been injured two weeks ago in an ATV accident, and now they were both holding their breath as they waited to see how quickly the old man would regain mobility. Len insisted he'd be good to go with modifications by the middle of June.

That was a fantasy, but Tanner played along, mainly to make the older man feel better.

Len had a daughter who was urging him to come live with her, but Len did not want to go. Not because he didn't love his daughter, but because she lived in a two-bedroom house in bustling Boise, Idaho, and Len was not the bustling city kind of guy. He said he would rather gnaw his foot off than live in a city, and Tanner, even though he barely knew the man, believed him.

Len was a tough old bird. He'd had to be to put up with Tanner's dad. Tanner recalled a long line of employees coming and going from the ranch because of his dad's habit of finding fault with even a job well done, but Len had hired on shortly after Tanner left home and he'd lasted.

Outlasted, actually.

As he and Rose crossed the lawn to Len's front porch, he marveled at how the old man found the time to keep his yard looking so immaculate, in addition to all his other duties. The grass needed to be mowed, which Tanner would tend to, but the flowers along the fence and the honeysuckle vine that climbed the trellis attached to the porch were pruned and well-tended.

Tanner knocked, then opened the door when Len called for him to come in.

"Hey," he said, holding up the bag of frozen dinners. "I got two weeks' worth."

"Let me find my wallet." Len shifted in his chair, reaching for the side table.

"We'll settle up later," Tanner said.

Len gave him a sour look. The guy was clearly unhappy, but he'd seemed unhappy before the accident that had put him first in the hospital, then in the easy chair. Tanner shrugged it off, assuming that only an unhappy guy could have worked with his father for so long. Because any happy guy working for the late Carl Andrew Hayes would have eventually ended up unhappy, unless he was remarkably thick-skinned.

Then again, maybe Len's temperament was the result of a decade of being harangued.

"Any luck finding help?" the older man asked, not quite meeting Tanner's eyes.

"Not yet. It's a bad time of year. But I think that with a little patience we'll get someone temporary to help Wes." He'd sent an email to the local high school guidance counselor to see if she knew of any kids looking for summer work, in addition to posting ads on social media and the local job boards. He was dealing with his father's unfortunate legacy. Carl Hayes had lifted alienation to an art form. It was as if he'd gotten some twisted satisfaction from one-upping people, even if he suffered consequences because of it.

Len let out a huff of breath. "Wes and I can handle things if push comes to shove."

Total lie. Wes was the worst worker ever, needing constant supervision and, according to what Tanner had learned while chatting with the guy at the hardware store, very likely to disappear when the whim struck him, leaving Tanner high and dry.

"Your dad was hard on help." Len spoke bitterly, possibly more bitterly than he intended, because he gave a slight shrug after speaking.

Was he hard on you?

Tanner didn't ask because he didn't know how the answer could be anything but yes.

Why would his dad treat anyone differently than he'd treated his own sons?

"That doesn't make the search for help any easier," Tanner agreed.

"Are you riding out tomorrow?"

"I have more bookwork, then I'll get a couple of hours in." Tanner had miles of fence to check, and he was doing it himself instead of sending Wes. He loved being on horseback, allowing fresh air and spectacular views to help him gain perspective, which he sorely needed.

His dad, never one to admit defeat or ask for help, had indulged in increasingly desperate means to keep up appearances. Tanner wondered if Carl had ever acknowledged to himself how much trouble he was in. He'd never done so with Tanner the few times he'd asked about finances—which he'd done only because of a few odd rumors floating around resulting from delays in payment. Tanner had spent the days since taking control of the ranch going over the books. It had been a gut-wrenching experience.

He should have been more cautious and not quit his day job managing a farming operation in central Washington State, but he'd wanted out, and it was too late to change things now. He had to turn the ship around. No easy task, but he had a few sources of income tentatively lined up—water and pasture leases being the most promising, if he could firm up some deals. No one, it seemed, had a clue as to the actual state of the ranch, and for that he was grateful. It made negotiating so much easier when the other party didn't know that they had the advantage, and he wasn't letting on that he was eager for a deal.

He talked for a few more minutes with Len, and when it became apparent that his injured foreman wanted to be left alone, he obliged, heading back to the house to unpack the few groceries he'd bought for himself. Skimping on food wasn't going to save the ranch, but discovering the extent of the financial quagmire he was in made splurging on anything other than the basics feel obscene. His one extravagance, good whiskey, was covered, because his dad had a cellar full of the stuff to impress people he'd done business with.

He'd barely gotten the groceries unpacked when there was a knock on the back door. Wes stepped into the kitchen, looking apologetic.

"Heifers are out again."

An excellent end to the day.

"Did you double-latch the gate?" One of the young cows had figured out how to bang the gate just right to open it. After the second escape, Tanner had determined what was going on, but not who the gate-opening culprit was.

"I did," Wes said stoutly. His demeanor said otherwise. He was young, and green, and bristled at anything that smacked of criticism.

Tanner knew it was a pain to remember to do more than slip the chain into the slot when closing gates, but it didn't take that long to fasten a second latch.

"They're close," Wes said. "And they're not heading for the county road." He cleared his throat. "Yet."

A black cow on a dark road was no fun for anyone, the cow included. And it would be dark in short order, so they had best get the girls rounded up while they still had light.

Rose got to her feet. For a Lab, she was a decent cow dog, but she was getting older, and Tanner didn't want her to get hurt. "You stay here," he told her.

She gave him a sad look, then settled under the table. He grabbed his hat and followed Wes out the door. His errant ranch hand was already aboard his four-wheeler, ready to give his impression of a motocross contestant.

"Be easy with them," Tanner said.

Wes nodded and roared off to get behind the herd while Tanner grabbed a cow-sorting stick and headed to the gate. Thankfully, the heifers hadn't gone far, and Wes soon had them heading to the open gate that Tanner flanked, gunning the ATV engine and generally terrorizing the escapees. Yes, a frightened cow moved faster, but they also sometimes lost it and ran through fences.

Tanner stood several yards away from the gate, in the center of the driveway, creating a barrier. The heifers took one look at him and cut toward the gate. Only one animal refused to go in, but Wes roared up on it and it jumped the fence to get away from the ATV.

Tanner tightened his jaw. Better over than through, but now he had a fence jumper, the worst kind of cow to try to contain.

Tanner secured both latches, then rattled the gate just to make sure it was secure before turning to Wes, who sat beaming on his four-wheeler.

"I asked you to be easy on them."

Wes gave him a hurt look that shifted into indignation.

"I didn't hurt them."

"I don't want them afraid of the four-wheeler," Tanner replied in a voice that was only slightly strained by irritation. Although it might be too late for that. Wes had been with the ranch for four months, having been his father's last hire—and he was very fond of the ATV.

"But you wanted them in. Quick-like, right?"

"Yes, but in the future, don't treat the four-wheeler like a weapon against them."

"Right." Wes tipped back his hat. He looked like he wanted to say something, but ultimately decided against it.

He's going to quit.

Tanner shook off the thought. He couldn't afford to have Wes quit, but he also couldn't afford to have his heifers riled. Cattle were smart and if they associated the four-wheeler with attacks, then it was going to make his job more difficult in the future, especially if he was trying to move them alone.

"Are we good?" he asked.

"Yeah. We're fine." Wes gunned the ATV engine and headed for the barn. Not long after, as Tanner was on his way to the house, Wes's truck roared by. He shifted down as he crossed the cattle guard, his pipes shooting out exhaust.

Not a good sign. Tanner watched the Chevy barrel down the long driveway toward the county road with a sinking feeling in his gut. If the guy was going to quit because of what had just transpired…well, that was ridiculous. But then again, Wes wasn't the brightest crayon in the box, so there was no telling. Tanner headed on to the house, telling himself that he'd apologize in the morning when Wes showed up for work.

If he did.

WHIT WOKE UP with a headache, which she attributed to Tanner Hayes smashing her car the day before. The crash hadn't hurt her physically, but it had taken a mental toll. She'd tried to put the matter aside and get some sleep, but had woken up time and again wondering how much of an effect it would have on the asking price of her Audi. She was going to lose money. That was a given.

She rolled onto her back and flopped an arm over her face trying to think of something besides her smashed up Audi and the cowboy who'd done the damage. Lying in bed, be-grudging reality, wasn't helping matters. She pushed back the covers just as her dad rapped on the door.

"Whit?"

"Yeah, Dad?"

"I'd like to talk to you before I head out for the day."

"I'll be down in a minute." She heard his footsteps receding down the hall and won-dered at his tone. It was his get-to-the-bottom-of-things tone, but there was nothing for him to get to the bottom of, unless he'd seen her car and was wondering what had happened.

That was it. Protective father mode was probably kicking in. She'd simply explain that she'd seen no reason to burden him with the mishap when she'd returned home the previ-ous evening. He'd been sleeping in his chair, and she'd retired to her bedroom to do a lot of mental math instead of sleeping.

She headed to the bathroom, showered, changed into her jeans and T-shirt, braided her hair into a single plait that was a touch shorter than the one she'd worn in high school, then headed to the kitchen to explain to her dad how her car had gotten damaged.

When she walked into the room, her dad had two mugs and a carafe of coffee on the table. He always made coffee, then poured it into a vacuum jug to keep it from getting bitter during the day. He loved his coffee, but this morning, he was staring morosely into his mug.

"Dad?"

He looked up and Whit became cognizant of a sinking sensation in her midsection. Before she could ask, he said, "What happened yesterday evening?"

"I got rear-ended."

She expected a look of paternal concern, but instead her father nodded, telling her that he not only knew what had happened, he'd probably already inspected the damage. "And did you happen to say some things to the guy who rear-ended you?"

"Maybe?"

Where on earth was this going?

Whit pulled out a chair and reached for a mug. She filled it to the brim and took a sip as she waited for her dad to explain.

Ben Fox blew out a breath. "I took coffee with the guys this morning at the café."

A regular occurrence since she'd been a little girl. The ranch was only five miles from town, and it wasn't unusual for her dad to meet with his fellow farmers and ranchers several mornings a week at an unearthly hour.

"And?"

"And I heard that you got rear-ended by Tanner Hayes."

"I did." She nodded to punctuate the admission.

"You told him a thing or two after it happened?"

"It was his fault, and he was trying to blame me. I defended myself."

Ben stared at the table between them with a hard expression. "I was in the middle of making a deal with the guy for water rights. It's a tricky negotiation. He's teetering on the bubble between yes and no, and my only child tells the guy that he's not going to buy his way out of the situation the way his dad bought his way out of things." He fixed his daughter with a grim look. "Or so I heard."

Whit's stomach gave a sick twist. There had been a bit of a crowd, and whoever had reported to whoever reported to her dad was pretty accurate.

"I didn't know you were negotiating."

Ben brought his big hand down on the table. "Didn't you want him to buy his way out of it? Fix your car and all?"

Whit pushed a few wisps of hair off her forehead as she tried to come up with the right words to explain herself. "Dad, what I wanted was for him to take responsibility for the accident so that my insurance rates wouldn't go up. And—" her mouth tightened "—I was pretty mad. I was just about to list the car for sale, and he smashes into the back of it and pretends it's my fault, like he expects to weenie out because of who he is. How was I supposed to let that ride?"

Her dad met her gaze in a way that told her that he really wished she had figured out a way.

"I would appreciate it if you would make it better."

"How?"

"Apologize. I can't afford to lose this water lease. If I do, then the expansion we've talked about is not going to happen."

He gave her another long look and Whit swallowed. Her father had wanted to expand his fields to the west forever, had worked so hard to increase the value of the ranch after her mother had passed away, but had lacked the water to do so. Carl Hayes was too much of a megalomaniac to work with, but apparently, his son had been more amenable to a deal.

Of all the people who could have followed her too closely, thus making the accident his fault, it had to be him.

Drat.

"Fine. I'll call him." She had his cell number from the exchange of information.

"See him in person."

"Why?"

Her dad sighed. "So that he can see your face and see that you're sincere. Very, very sincere."

Whit planted her palm flat on the table. "Fine. I'll go see him. I'll make it better." She didn't know that she would apologize, unless she really had to, but she would do what she could to iron this out.

"Whit?" She looked up and saw her dad fighting an inner battle. One corner of his mouth quirked into a rueful grimace. "I get it. Why you were angry. I might have said something along the same lines."

But he still needed her to make it better. Whit reached out and patted her dad's rough hand. "I'll get right on that apology."

CHAPTER THREE

HUMBLE PIE. Her least favorite food.

But Whit was determined to make things better as her dad had asked. Thankfully, she was a fairly good actress, having played the corporate game for many years. In the beginning of her career, there'd been times when she'd done herself more harm than good by pointing out things her bosses didn't want to see or hear, but after a few incidents, she'd learned when to keep quiet and when to speak up. More importantly, she'd learned *how* to speak up in a way that didn't put up backs. Now she was going to draw on her experiences and make this right for her dad.

The Hayes Ranch bordered her family land and had been the ranch she, in her fantasies, had wanted to purchase and use as a horse training facility. Why not? If she was going to dream, it only made sense to dream big. The Hayes Ranch was older and larger than her family ranch, and covered both bottom land and mountainside. Her family had not indulged in fancy gates and archways, thinking such things were a little pretentious, but she had to admit that the gate she'd just driven through, with stone pillars and wrought iron scrollwork, was something to behold.

She rounded a corner, then slowed as a yearling Angus lifted her head from where she was grazing along the roadside. The sound of the engine seemed to startle her because she took off at a dead run, dodging Whit's borrowed ranch truck and heading toward the county road. Not good. Whit looked in the side mirror and saw that the heifer had slowed to a walk maybe twenty yards away, but was still heading for the road. Having nearly hit a cow a few months ago while visiting her dad, Whit wasn't going to be party to that happening to anyone else.

She pulled her truck to the side of the road, got out, closed the door and studied the cow who studied her back, head high, waiting to see what this predator was about to do.

Whit started down the fence line that bordered the opposite side of the road, staying as far away from the cow as possible. Once she eased her way by, she'd start moving the animal in the direction of the ranch.

Easier said than done.

The heifer was nervous. She wanted to eat, but she wasn't going to let Whit get close to her. Finally, Whit crawled through the barbed wire fence and walked in the field, far enough away from the cow to keep from spooking her. Once she was between the cow and the county road, she waved her arms and started the cow running back for the safety of the herd…which had just ambled around the corner where she'd parked the truck.

Holy moly. What kind of outfit did Tanner Hayes run?

Whit waved her arms and continued walking forward. The cow herd stopped as they spotted their leader and Whit coming at them. Heads came up. Danger was assessed, and moments later the herd was galloping back in the direction from which it had come, tails high, bucking comically as they ran. Whit got into her truck and followed behind them. The animals seemed to be afraid of engines, because once hers started, quiet as it was, they ran harder.

Once around the corner, past the trees lining

the road, the ranch buildings came into sight. The main house, a rock-and-timber structure with a lot of glass, sat in the middle of what had once been a hayfield. Spruce and pine trees surrounded the house, offering shade and protection from the wind, and the meadow behind was a riot of blooming wildflowers, planted no doubt by some landscaping expert.

Opposite the wide driveway that ran beside the house was a gorgeous wooden barn, a smaller house that probably housed workers or the manager and various sheds and outbuildings, all sided with rough timber to give that true Montana ranch look that Whitney's place, also a true Montana ranch, didn't have.

At the far side of the field behind the barn, she caught sight of a man on horseback heading for the gate near the barn at a fast trot. The heifers milled against the fence that separated the driveway from the pasture and an older man on crutches came out of the small house.

"Hey," she called. "I brought these gals home for you."

"Thank you." The man spoke in a clipped voice, maybe due to pain. "They go in there." He pointed to an open gate.

As he spoke, the guy on horseback arrived at the back of the barn, disappeared from sight, then a moment later reappeared on foot in the corral where the heifers were supposed to be contained. He marched through the corral to the main driveway and then called, "Can you move them my way?"

Tanner Hayes, not the hired man as she'd expected.

She waved her understanding, then circled to get behind the herd. She was a stranger and if there was one thing a cow hated, it was a stranger, and these girls seemed spookier than most, leading her to wonder about the animal husbandry on the Hayes Ranch.

Stranger danger worked, and she'd barely gotten behind them when they raced toward their safe place—the pasture they'd busted out of. Once the last heifer had galloped through the gate, shooting a kick in Tanner's direction, he swung the gate closed, double-latched it, then shook his head as if angry at the herd.

Cows will do what cows will do, and while Whit understood the man's irritation, she once again wondered what kind of rancher

Tanner Hayes was. Did he expect his cows to kowtow to him because he was wealthy, too?

"How in the heck?" the old man shouted as Tanner approached.

Tanner shook his head as he walked. He looked different in his ranch clothes. When Whit had confronted him after their fender bender, she'd taken in his expensive boots, expensive hat and perfectly worn-in jeans, which had given off wannabe vibes to her.

He no longer looked like a wannabe. A legitimate cowboy strode toward her wearing worn everything, from the battered palm hat that covered his dark hair to his manure-kicking round-toed boots.

Whit felt a strange little flutter go through her. She'd expected to apologize to the slick rich guy from yesterday. But instead she was talking to someone who looked like he was closer to the land than she was.

She cleared her throat, realizing that she'd studied the man for a few seconds longer than necessary. "I found them on the driveway, heading west."

Tanner gave a grim nod, then shot a look at the old man still balancing on his crutches. "I've got this, Len."

Len's mouth pulled tight before he turned and maneuvered the door open with a crutch, and then made his way into the small house.

"My foreman had an ATV accident," Tanner said when he turned back to her.

"Must have been a doozy."

"He rolled it on a hill. I hate those things," Tanner said.

So did she, but she wasn't going to say that aloud, because it would look too much like sucking up. When she delivered her apology, she didn't want to look like it came from a place of desperation.

"Somebody left the gate open?" She was trying to make small talk, not accusations, but she wasn't sure she'd succeeded.

She was about to explain what she meant when Tanner said, "I think someone opened the gate on purpose."

"Really?" That sounded just plain weird.

"Yeah. I had a guy quit today."

No longer so weird-sounding. "He must have quit at the beginning of his shift," she said.

"He showed up at sunup. Got his tools, pounded on my door and as soon as I answered, he told me he was done."

Whit gave what she hoped was a sympathetic nod. "And you think he opened the gate?"

Tanner ran a hand over the back of his neck. "I'm not making any accusations." But he did think that. It was clear from his expression.

You must be some kind of boss.

Whit pushed the thought aside. Sour thoughts were not going to help the sincerity of her apology.

"I'm here about yesterday."

Tanner cut a look her way, as if he'd forgotten about yesterday.

"Here's the thing." She bit her lip and shifted her gaze sideways before meeting his hazel eyes dead on. "I was about to sell my car. I was literally going to start advertising today, so when you hit me…well, I might have overreacted and—" she sucked a breath in between her teeth "—said some things."

"You're apologizing for comparing me to my dad?"

No…but if that was what had caused his indignation, then she'd go with it. "I didn't mean that your dad was a jerk or anything." Even though he was. "Just that, well, people fell over themselves to kiss up to him because of his money. He really could buy his way out of most anything."

Whit gave a mental eye roll as she heard the words come out of her mouth. What she'd said just now was almost as bad as what she'd said the day before.

"And he did. You're right."

Tanner stepped closer, hands on his hips and Whit's heart started to beat a little faster as his hazel gaze grew shrewd. He was putting two and two together.

"You think what you said might affect the deal I'm working with your dad?"

"Yes." Why hedge?

Tanner nodded, not speaking, making her wish that she'd been less honest. Maybe she should have remembered to use her corporate-ese and finessed the situation by telling the guy that she'd been unaware of a deal. That she'd simply stopped by to apologize for being a jerk—which she hadn't been, but that was how corporate-ese worked sometimes.

"You didn't know about the deal yesterday, but you know about it now."

The guy was clearly sharp, or her face had given her away. "Dad told me this morning. The rancher coffee club told my dad what happened. He's afraid…" She pushed back the wisps of hair on her forehead.

"That I'll call off the deal."

"Pretty much."

"So you aren't really here to apologize."

Whit squared her shoulders, determined not to let on how easily the man was reading her. "I'm here to make sure that my dad doesn't get dinged for my actions. What happened yesterday was between you and me. He has no control over me. Or what I say in the heat of the moment."

"But you still think I'm in the wrong."

"Don't you?" Whit clamped her mouth shut a split second too late. The words were out. Did she have a freaking death wish?

Tanner stared at her, then, honest to goodness, the corner of his mouth moved. Almost like he was fighting a smile. Whit narrowed her eyes, trying to get a read on the situation.

"Do you want some coffee?"

The first look she gave him was probably rife with suspicion, as in, why invite her for coffee? But she gave a mental shrug. If it helped smooth things over for her dad and got her car fixed, why not?

"Yes. That would be nice."

He jerked his head toward the main house. "I have some left in the pot."

As HE LED the way into the house, Tanner couldn't help but wonder how Whitney's last name—Fox—might have been used to describe her. Sun-streaked blond hair, clear blue eyes and a way of wearing jeans that drew the eye made him fairly certain that she'd heard the "you're a Fox" pickup line more than once. And he imagined that a woman like Whit wouldn't have simply smiled and moved on. She would have straightened the guy out.

He opened the door and stood back so that she could precede him into the spacious kitchen, keeping his gaze above her beltline.

"Wow," she said, taking a turn. "Nice."

"Nothing but the best," he said sardonically. "For my dad, I mean. He liked to surround himself with nice stuff."

"You don't?" The question sounded genuine.

"To a degree," he said. "Who doesn't?"

"My dad. He's pretty happy as long as the dishes are done, the springs don't poke through the cushions on his chair and there's plenty of beer in the fridge."

Ben Fox had struck him that way, too. Just a regular guy who was satisfied with a simple life.

"What about you?" Tanner asked. "That's a fancy hunk of machinery I ran into." He cleared his throat and amended, "After you stopped too quickly." He honestly hadn't been following that closely behind her. He'd simply had the misfortune of being the guy behind her.

"I stopped quickly this morning, too. When I kept your heifers from heading off the property."

"Touché."

He crossed the room to the granite-topped island and poured two mugs of coffee. He kept a suite of clean mugs near the machine, taking them out of the dishwasher beneath the countertop and depositing them on top. When done, he opened the dishwasher and put them back in. Saved cupboard space and steps, he told himself. A manifestation of bachelor life.

"Cream? Sugar?" he asked.

She shook her head. "Like tar."

She'd probably get exactly what she'd asked for, because the pot had been on the heater since he'd ridden out on Emily, a very sweet mare, who was now in the corral behind the barn, enjoying her downtime. "It's not the freshest," he confessed, "but it is today's."

Tanner delivered the cup, then motioned to the table. Or rather one of the tables. There was a table for casual kitchen dining, a breakfast nook table and the official dining room table, visible through the arched side door.

Once she was seated, he took a chair and watched while she sipped, made an approving face, then sipped again. He took a quick drink and decided that she'd been honest when she said she liked her coffee like tar.

He set down the cup and got straight to business. "I'm going to lease the water to your dad. You don't need to be concerned."

"I...thank you?" The thanks sounded like a question, as if she was waiting to hear what kind of condition he was about to tack on.

He leaned back in his chair, studying her over the top of his coffee cup. "Surprised?" he finally said. Whitney regarded him curiously. Obviously, she had preconceived ideas about him, which quite possibly sprang from his dad's reputation in the area. The acorn didn't fall far from the tree, after all—except in his case it actually did. Far, far from the tree.

"A little. Yes." She set her cup down. "I'm really glad that you're not letting what happened affect your deal with my dad. He doesn't deserve that."

"I guess that's because what happened is between you and me." And he needed the money from the water lease. There was no way that he was letting any source of income slip through his fingers.

Whit appeared to be considering his words, but when she spoke, it had nothing to do with the matter between him and her.

"So, if your guy quit on you, and your other guy is on crutches—" Whitney narrowed her blue eyes "—does that mean that you're it? A one-man ranch band?"

"I have never heard it put that way, but yes. I am. Until the end of May, anyway. I have summer hires coming then."

"Are you having trouble finding local help?"

He debated about how much to confess before finally replying, "Bad time of year."

An *uh-huh* expression crossed her face. She knew exactly why he had to wait for the summer help.

"You can say it if you want."

"Say what?" she asked.

"You can say that no one wants to work on the Hayes Ranch because Carl Hayes was a jerk."

"I wouldn't say that."

"Not to my face?"

Her mouth tightened briefly before she let loose with the truth. "All right. Your dad had a reputation."

"Well earned, too."

She frowned at his honest assessment.

"Why do you think I took off as soon as I graduated?" he asked.

"I guess I figured you went to some Ivy League school, followed by an internship with one of your dad's rich business associates, then, I don't know. A stellar career of some sort?"

"I went to college in Idaho. I paid my own way. I went to work at a career that had nothing to do with my dad."

Whit lifted her mug and took another drink. "What was your career?"

"I managed production for a big wheat farm in central Washington. Basically, I crunched numbers." He turned his cup in his hands. "I missed spending most of my time outdoors. I missed trees, too. Rolling farmland is pretty in its own way, but… I like being around timber."

He had no idea why he'd confessed such a thing, but Whitney seemed to understand. She studied the table for a moment, then lifted her gaze and asked, "Do you need help for a day or two? Because I have some free time."

It was all Tanner could do to keep his jaw from dropping.

Did he need help? He had tens of miles of fence to ride before turning his steers out on ranch pasture and his cow-calf pairs on the grazing allotment near Old Timber Canyon.

He gave her an assessing look, which she met with an open gaze. She was obviously serious about her offer, but that didn't stop him from wondering about ulterior motives. Why would she offer to help him? He'd already informally agreed to the water lease and would set the wheels in motion as soon as she left. As to the car, their insurance companies were already battling that one out.

Does it matter why she offered?

He had to admit it did not, unless she ended up being more of a hindrance than a help.

"Do you have any skills?" She'd been born and raised on a ranch, as he'd been, but he doubted her father worked her as hard as his father had worked him.

Whitney fixed him with a steady blue gaze, giving him the impression that she was very sure of her skills. "I can probably out-cowboy you."

He couldn't help it. He laughed. Not because he didn't believe her, but because she'd come to apologize, then drew a line in the sand. "That I'd like to see."

"Fine. Finalize the water deal, and I'll be here bright and early tomorrow morning."

CHAPTER FOUR

"YOU'RE GOING TO do what?" Ben Fox asked, tipping back his hat. The wrinkles at the corners of his eyes deepened as he studied Whit's face, clearly expecting her to say, "Just kidding."

"I am going to ride fence for Tanner Hayes for a couple days. Help him out. I start in two days, because he's visiting with his lawyer tomorrow. Something about a water lease."

Ben reached out to pat her knee in a silent thank-you. They sat on the wooden bench under the ancient elm tree that shaded their house, her dad taking a rare midday break. Leaves rustled above their heads in the gentle breeze, reminding Whit of how the sound of the leaves brushing against her bedroom window had kept her from sleeping when she was a kid. Now she found the sound oddly comforting, a reminder of how she'd stayed up late, reading *Western Horseman* and dreaming of the horses she would someday own.

Her gelding, Charley, who had stayed on the ranch when she'd headed off to college, was not the fiery steed of her youthful dreams. He was not coal black. He did not rescue her from threatening situations, nor did he come out of nowhere to win the Grand National or Kentucky Derby. He was a dependable mount with just enough attitude to make him interesting.

"How does this tie into the water lease?" Ben asked.

"It doesn't. He'd already agreed to sign when I offered."

"So it's a thank-you."

Whit considered for a moment. "No. It's a chance for me to get out into open country for a couple of days and help someone out at the same time." She gave a subtle shrug, sensing that he was about to mention that the someone was a Hayes. "It wouldn't hurt to stay on the neighbor's good side if you guys are doing business together, and it'll give me a chance to clear my head. I've got stuff to figure out."

"Like the job search?"

She needed to get on that, but she still felt that odd inertia dragging her down. She was beginning to suspect that it was latent burnout. She'd finally slowed to the point that it had caught up with her. But that didn't mean it would stay with her. She would take some time to center herself, take a mini vacation, so to speak, then hit the ground running.

"Do you like what you do?"

Her dad's question startled her. Was she telegraphing?

"Don't ask hard questions," she joked, but it was difficult to hedge with her father, so after the joke fell flat, she went with vagueness and hoped for the best. "Like any job, there were good points and bad. I gave up some stuff, gained some stuff."

"Your hours were ridiculous."

"Yes. They were." She gave her dad a pointed look. "So are yours."

"But I like what I do."

"I know." He'd lived and worked on the ranch for his entire life and while he had a lot to complain about—unruly weather patterns, drought, the price of commodities—Whit knew that he wouldn't change occupations. Devotion to the ranch had carried him through her mother's illness and passing, and now it was starting to pay off as he was able to expand, thanks to Tanner Hayes.

"You know that you can stay here as long as you want," her dad said gruffly, and when she opened her mouth, he held up a hand to stop her. "Take advantage of free rent until you find something that you *like* to do. Not something you tolerate for a paycheck."

"I can't stay, Dad." She had her pride and that meant not mooching off her father. The ranch was finally in decent shape, so her dad didn't need her help the way he had back when she was traveling home on weekends to ride fence and move cows and swath hay. And he no longer needed the infusions of cash she'd made after landing her job. The only reason he'd accepted her financial help in the first place was because he insisted on giving her a percentage of the profits, when such a thing existed.

"You own a piece of the place outright," Ben pointed out.

Not that she could sell it or anything, so it didn't matter. And if she wasn't bringing in an income, then how could she help fend off the next financial hit the ranch took?

"I'm getting back on the horse, Dad. I'm going to land a job in my field, and I don't think Larkspur has anything to offer there."

It was a discussion they'd had a few days before, and one that her dad signaled he wasn't going to have again by pulling his gloves out of his pocket, a sign that he was ready to head back to work. But instead of getting to his feet, he slapped the gloves on his thigh and focused on the toes of his boots with a faint frown.

"Something else, Dad?"

He looked up. "Thinking about this Hayes Ranch deal. Since you're in the volunteering mood…"

Red flags started waving. "Yes?"

"Will you go to the community board meeting with me? They're finalizing the Hearts of the West event and I might need backup to keep from being suckered into more than I have time for."

Like last year. He didn't say that part aloud, but Whit knew that was what he was thinking. He'd been late to the meeting last year and had gotten wrangled into soliciting prizes, which had been a train wreck. Ben couldn't ask someone for help, much less ask them to donate a prize for a community event.

He cleared his throat. "I would be grateful."

"Are Margo Simms and her minions still at the helm of the board?"

Ben nodded and Whit sighed. Margo Simms, Judy Blanchard and her sister, Debra Crane, ran the community board with a collective iron fist. And because it was a thankless job, they received little pushback, to the point that the three had become a little power mad. The community members grumbled at their dictatorial ways, but played along, because no one wanted to step up to the plate.

"I have your back," Whit assured her dad. They both wanted to do their part for the community, but it seemed as if Debra, Margo and Judy got a kick out of mismatching assignments to personalities—especially if they were late to the planning meeting. "When is this meeting, Dad?"

"Thursday. Six o'clock. Community center."

"I'll add it to my calendar." She smiled wryly. "Don't worry, Dad. I won't let them mess with you."

THE LAST THING Tanner expected at seven o'clock in the morning was for his brother, Grant, who lived hours away in Great Falls, to knock on his door. Tanner crossed the kitchen from where he'd been waiting for a second pot of coffee to brew for his thermos and opened the door. Grant stepped inside, pulled off his hat and hung it on the custom hat rack next to the door.

"Good morning." His brother looked like he'd stepped out of one of those glossy Western magazines, with dark jeans, a white Western shirt, polished boots and an expensive hat. He was capable of getting dirty, but his job in ranch insurance sales rarely called for that.

"What are you doing here?" Tanner asked. Grant had sent a text the previous day concerning an unsolicited offer on the ranch, and since Tanner had been at the lawyer's office working up the water lease, he'd simply texted back *no*, and considered the matter closed. Apparently, it was not, since Grant was now in his kitchen.

"Better question," his brother said. "Why aren't you answering my calls and texts?"

"Because I already gave my answer."

"I have business in Larkspur. I timed it so I could drop by, bring you to your senses, have some coffee and make my meeting."

Meaning that he must have started driving at 4 a.m.

"I'm not selling," Tanner said.

Grant looked around the kitchen. "This

place can't be chock-full of good memories for you."

"It's not the same place we grew up in." Tanner crossed the kitchen to the coffee maker, which was finally giving its almost-done gurgles.

Grant looked around again, but Tanner had the feeling that his brother was documenting selling points, not reliving old memories.

"It's not the same house," Grant admitted.

Their dad's second wife, Dena, who'd come into the picture after Tanner had fled home, had done a wonderful job remodeling the house into something that should have been featured in *Ranch Beautiful*. What had been a rather standard sprawling Montana McMansion with log siding and a rock chimney was now a stone, glass and cedar edifice sporting sleek lines that seemed to blend into the rocky outcrop and stand of timber a hundred yards behind the house. The massive renovation had cost Carl a pretty penny, but he'd loved the results. Unfortunately, it now appeared that he hadn't been able to afford the results.

Grant let out a heavy sigh. "It looks different, but it has the same feel."

"I burned sage," Tanner joked darkly.

"Selling would be more effective." Tanner shook his head before pulling a mug out of the dishwasher, and Grant continued, "It's a fantastic offer. Granted, we're not going to see as much profit as I'd like due to the debt, but you can use your half to get a start somewhere else." He cleared his throat. "Some place with better juju."

"I like this place." Parts of it, anyway. The other parts, the memories, he would endure until he replaced them with better ones.

"You're trying to prove something to a dead man," Grant said bluntly.

"That, too."

Grant's mouth tightened as Tanner handed him the cup. It was hard to argue with someone who wouldn't argue back, other than reiterating that a sale was off the table.

Grant tried again. "When Dad said he didn't think you were qualified to take over the place," which Tanner had offered to do when Carl started showing signs of slowing down two years ago, "it was because he was struggling with the finances. He didn't want you to know. It wasn't because he didn't think you were capable. You don't have anything to prove."

Carl had never confessed the financial realities of the Hayes Ranch, not even on his deathbed, but both Grant and Tanner had suspected that all was not well—a suspicion that was verified shortly after Carl's death from pneumonia.

His father was a difficult man in many ways. When his mom had finally fled the marriage during Tanner's sophomore year in high school, Carl had made certain that it was impossible for her to take Tanner with her. Tanner didn't know exactly what his dad had been holding over his mother's head, but he'd told his mom that he understood, that he was good staying with his dad—even though he wasn't. With Grant away at college earning his business degree, the only person left on the ranch to do things wrong—other than the constantly revolving crew—was Tanner.

The thing that saved Tanner's sanity was throwing himself into both ranch work and school, often missing meals as he stayed away from the house, working on a tractor or repairing anything that needed a fix in an effort to stay clear of his dad—which was why he was confident that Whitney Fox wouldn't out-cowboy him, but she was welcome to try.

Then along came Dena, the only person

other than Len who seemed to be able to handle Carl Hayes. Tanner believed it was because she didn't love him. If she had, then the old man would have been able to hurt and manipulate her. He tried, but his barbs just seemed to bounce off the woman, who appeared to find Carl's attempts to find fault amusing. Tanner had to give her credit—after watching her operate, he'd learned to take more of that tack himself. He'd started letting the comments slide off his back—or, at least, giving the appearance of letting them slide. The old man had a real gift for getting under the skin.

Tanner eventually learned to find satisfaction in his own opinion of what kind of job he'd done, but there'd always been a part of him that wanted his father's approval. Whenever that part stepped forward, Carl found a way to slap it back. Ironically, it wasn't until Tanner didn't care anymore that Carl began to come around. Tanner couldn't say that they'd had anything approaching a normal father-son relationship, but after Dena had taken her leave, along with a hefty chunk of change in return for her years of letting barbs bounce off her, Carl made an overture to his sons.

They then began a superficial relationship that was as close to normal as they were going to see. Went through the motions of being sons to a distant dad who was probably lonely, but unable to go beyond a certain point in his relationships. Oh, they'd played a great game of pretending. They'd even appeared together at the Larkspur Christmas parade the year after Dena had left, two years before Carl died, the make-believe happy family.

Tanner found himself wishing he hadn't done that, because it seemed to have poisoned his relationship with the community. Carl had burned innumerable bridges with his egotistical ways, and the people of Larkspur seemed to believe that the apple didn't fall far from the tree.

Carl might have brought the town to heel with his wallet, but Tanner couldn't do the same, even if he wanted to, because Carl had not only emptied the wallet, he'd put the ranch into the red with a couple of back-to-back business ventures that had gone very, very wrong.

Morals of the story: Don't dabble in crypto. Don't overextend.

Grant, having taken all the silence he could handle, put his mug on the table with a thump and leaned forward in his chair. "I know we made a deal, but I think you're making a mistake not entertaining this offer."

"There'll be others," Tanner said. And he hated to think that they had to go through this brotherly face-off with each one.

"The more money you lose, the less profit we'll see, and right now that profit is going to be slim. I don't want it to get to the place where it's zero."

Tanner pulled in a long breath, focusing on the table before raising his gaze to meet his brother's. But he didn't say a word. That way Grant had nothing to argue against except himself. The thing was that they'd be better off if he could pull the ranch out of the red and start making a profit again. Grant would get a yearly cut of the proceeds and Tanner would sink his back into the ranch.

Grant pushed back his chair. "How much of an operation do you even have left?"

Tanner figured that his brother knew the answer to that question, but he made a recitation anyway.

"I have the cattle." A hundred cow-calf pairs as opposed to the five hundred they used to run, close to another hundred steers. "I've leased out the farming. I have a summer crew—" the teenage boys who'd worked for him on the farm in Washington "—coming in a few weeks to take care of the fences and cattle." He turned his coffee mug in his hands. "The place is a shadow of its old self, but I think I can bring it back."

"If you fail, I lose, too."

"And if I succeed, you do, too."

Grant gave him a look very much like those his old man had sent his way. "I'd rather have the sure thing."

"We made an agreement," Tanner reiterated. A movement in the yard caught his attention, and he glanced out of the oversize kitchen window in time to see an older truck and trailer pull up in front of the barn. Whitney Fox got out of the truck and headed to the rear of the trailer, her long blond braid swinging from the opening at the back of her ball cap.

"Who's that?" Grant asked.

"My temporary ranch hand," Tanner said, lifting his cup to his lips to drink his rapidly cooling coffee. He felt like smiling at his brother's stunned expression. Indeed, Whitney Fox in her worn denim and flannel shirt, which seemed to accentuate her femininity instead of distracting from it, was living up to her name this morning. He saw no reason to tell his brother that temporary meant two days, which is what she'd offered, and he'd gratefully accepted.

Grant gave Tanner a look. "She's working for you?"

Tanner drained the cup. "Word has it that she can out-cowboy me."

"Shouldn't be hard. You haven't been on a horse since…?"

"Yesterday." When he'd ridden Emily to check the fences along the hayfields. "It comes back. Just like—"

"Don't say it." Grant looked out the window again, but Whitney was in the trailer, so there was nothing to see. He got to his feet. "I know you have the feels for this place, but we'd be better off out from under it."

"Not happening."

Grant could wheedle and whine, but the bottom line was that they'd made an agreement. Tanner understood that the offer Grant had received on the place was generous, but he wasn't giving up his…white whale?

It didn't matter what it was. In his gut, he knew that he needed to prove something to himself and to a dead man. He needed to hang on to the land that had kept him sane during rough times. And he would.

The horse Whitney Fox unloaded from her trailer was saddled and ready to go, as was the custom with most ranch folk in the area. She was busy tightening the cinch when Tanner and Grant came out of the house. Rose ambled out from under the porch and followed the men down the walk to the fancy gate in the low-lying stone wall that surrounded the front lawn.

"Good morning," Tanner said when Whitney looked their way. "Thanks for coming."

He didn't consider himself an expert in human nature, but he figured that Whitney would lend him a hand until she got what she wanted—a signature on the water lease and repairs to her expensive car—but all the same, he was grateful for her help. And he rather enjoyed watching his brother try to come up to speed on what was going on between them without asking questions.

"Glad to," she said, settling a hand on her gelding's rump before smiling at Grant. "Hi. Whitney Fox."

"Grant Hayes. I remember you."

Whit gave Tanner a quick look, as if to ask why it was that Grant remembered her and Tanner had not. Tanner had no answer for that, other than Grant recognized the name and was trying to gain points. Whitney couldn't have been much older than junior high age when Grant had graduated and headed off to college.

Grant's phone chimed. "Time for me to hit the road." He gave Whitney one of his patented charming smiles. "Nice seeing you again."

"And you," she said politely, but there was something about the way she watched Grant go that made Tanner wonder if she had a clearer read on his charming brother than most.

When she glanced his way, Tanner said, "It was an unexpected visit, so I'm running behind."

"You're coming with me?"

"I thought we could split up and cover more ground."

"Good idea." Whit crouched down and Rose sidled up into scratching position. Her eyes rolled upward as Whit hit the itchy spot just behind her ears. "We'll wait for you here."

Tanner went back to the house, grabbed the

saddlebags containing the lunch he'd made earlier, then headed to the barn. He snagged Emily's bridle off the wall on his way by, then continued through the barn to the back corrals where Emily and Clive, the two remaining Hayes Ranch horses, ate their morning rations. He opened the gate and Emily raised her head and then, sweetheart that she was, took a step toward him. A limping step.

Great.

She'd skidded in the mud yesterday when he'd checked the fences along the fields, and although she'd seemed fine after, it appeared that she'd injured something. He ran a hand down her leg, felt the telltale heat, then straightened and shot a look at Clive. Clive eyed him back.

His dad had once fancied himself a horse breeder, producing some excellent Rocky Mountain Horses. And Clive.

Clive was the last colt born on the property, and while being exceptionally beautiful, with near perfect conformation, a bright copper coat and lots of flashy chrome, he was also exceptionally headstrong. And he hadn't been ridden in two years.

Tanner returned to the barn, hung up Emily's

bridle and got Clive's, sighing under his breath as he considered what kind of a day he was about to have with the woman who said that she could out-cowboy him. As long as he had help, he had no problem with her showing him up, but he didn't need Clive working against him.

The one thing he couldn't afford right now was to let pride get in his way. He would ride Clive for better or worse and take advantage of Whitney's help. When he led the gelding out of the barn, Whitney gave Rose a final pat and straightened to her full height, giving both him and Clive a once-over.

"That's a beautiful animal."

"If my father was a horse, this would be him."

"Are you saying he has an attitude?"

"He thinks very highly of himself."

"I'm good with horses," she said. "Want me to tune him up?"

"I think I can handle him, but thanks."

Clive pushed him sideways with his nose, as if to contest the point, and Whitney gave Tanner a slow smile that made him forget the horse. The woman was confident, borderline cocky—or at least her smile was—and her attitude gave him the sense that today, for a few hours anyway, he might escape his own head, where he'd been spending too much time, worrying about how to save the ranch that no one knew was in trouble.

Whitney mounted her bay gelding and when she settled in the saddle, it was obvious that she and the horse were a unit. She barely twitched her rein hand and the horse responded, making Tanner hope that he didn't embarrass himself.

He did. Clive, who was taller than most Rocky Mountain Horses, sidestepped when Tanner put his foot in the stirrup, causing him to hop sideways before pushing off the ground for an awkward mount. He landed with the grace of a partially filled bag of grain. *So cool.*

"Well, that's done," he said, feeling the heat of embarrassment on the back of his neck. But the embarrassment faded as he met Whitney's gaze. She was amused, but in a good-natured way.

"We've all been there," she said. She lifted the reins and her gelding instantly moved toward the gate. When Tanner urged Clive forward, the horse pulled his nose sideways, trying to take command. He came close to winning, too.

"I'm thinking of selling him," Tanner said after riding through the gate that Whitney opened from horseback, "but we need horses."

"Horses people can ride are best," Whit said after closing the gate again.

"Is that where I'm going wrong?"

He hadn't expected to joke, but it made the humiliation of having to fight for control seem more bearable. Needing to change the subject, he said, "I called around about your car yesterday to see if anyone local could do the job. I found a guy if you want his name."

He left out the part about the people changing attitude when he mentioned *his* name. They didn't turn down his business, but there was a noticeable shift in demeanor. Voices grew cold, delivery became clipped. Schedules were suddenly full—until he'd said he needed to get a Fox Ranch car repaired. Suddenly there was an opening.

"That was nice of you."

"Well, not a lot of people work on fancy cars here, so I figured I'd save you calling around for estimates."

She glanced his way. "And the winner is…"

"Clinton Automotive. They have a sister shop in Billings that handles your make, so they can do the repairs in Larkspur. All you have to do is call to set a time. I asked about a loaner, but they said you had lots of rigs on your ranch and wouldn't need one."

Whitney laughed. "True."

Tanner didn't smile, but he felt lighter inside. As they continued across the field, he pushed Clive out of the jolting jog he'd been punishing Tanner with and into a long smooth walk characteristic of the breed.

"Does he gait?" Whit asked.

"He was bred for it, but honestly, I don't know." Tanner was just glad that the horse was no longer doing an impression of a pile driver. By the time they reached the southwest corner of the north pasture, Clive was showing signs of resignation. Tanner was not fooled. He dismounted to open the gate, then spoke to Whit from the ground, fully intending to send her on her way before doing the mounting battle again.

"I'd like you to ride the boundary heading north, then east. I'll do the opposite and meet you somewhere along the way."

"I brought my fencing tools, but they're only good for small breaks. I don't have any wire in my bags, obviously."

Tanner hadn't expected her to come prepared. "If you find a break, just let me know where it is. We'll deal with it later."

"I could do small repairs while I'm out there. It'd be faster."

"I'd like to see what needs fixed." Because he didn't know her skill level and he wanted to make certain that the fences were as tight as possible after a repair...but as soon as he'd said it, he realized it might have been a mistake. Whitney's expression did the same thing that people's voices did over the phone after he'd identified himself. "No reflection on your skills. I just—"

"No." Whitney held up a hand. "It's your ranch. Your fence."

Your need to control things.

She didn't say the words aloud, but her expression conveyed the sentiment quite nicely.

CHAPTER FIVE

DESPITE A RUGGED WINTER, the first stretch of the ranch's north pasture boundary fence was in good shape. The wire could use tightening and Whit would have done it, but she decided to take Tanner's "I want to see it first" seriously. She wondered if he micromanaged his employees on the wheat farm where he used to work, too. Were they glad to see him go?

Or did she just want to assume that since he was a Hayes he was a poor boss? His father certainly had a bad reputation in that regard. And Tanner had ticked off an employee to the point that he may have purposely left a gate open.

Whit arrived at the corner post where the east-running fence made a right-angle turn and headed into the timber. She dismounted and checked the braces that kept the fence tight. Not bad. She mounted once again and followed the fence into the trees.

It was a gorgeous day, exactly what she'd hoped for when she'd signed on to help out at the Hayes Ranch. The sun was pleasantly warm; the wind teased the tendrils of hair that had escaped her braid, but didn't blow hard enough to force her to jam her ball cap farther onto her head. She pulled in a deep breath and wondered for a moment if she *should* be trying to get a desk job.

Was that why she couldn't shake the nagging feeling that she was heading down the wrong path?

It was burnout. She'd researched the matter the night before, bringing up articles, reading about symptoms, seeing herself in the descriptions. She'd thought she was fine right up until the layoff. Stress was a way of life, as were late hours and not much time for socializing. When she went back to work, she'd have to keep an eye on herself so that burnout didn't interfere with her job.

Maybe she could settle for simply working nine to five?

That didn't lead to promotions...and she didn't know if she could settle for simply putting in her eight, then going home.

Could she?

Hard question, and because the day was so beautiful, it was one that she put out of her mind as she rode into the trees, crossing ground dappled with patches of sunlight. The spring blossoms clustered here and there. Charley stepped over a windfall, his back hooves nicking the hollow log as she crossed, making a low thudding noise. Birds flitted from tree to tree and a critter of some kind pushed its way through the brush twenty feet beyond the trail. Whit stopped, then saw a flash of white as the whitetail doe bounded out of the brush and up the hill.

The first break in the fence showed up at the edge of a small clearing that was bursting with new grass thanks to a slow-flowing spring. The spring itself was fenced with cedar rails, and a pipe led to a tank where livestock could drink without muddying the spring itself. Apparently, for all of his faults, Carl Hayes respected riparian areas.

Whit dismounted and took a look at the fence wire, which had coiled into fat loops after being broken, probably by deer. Judging from the tracks, this was a well-used trail from one feeding ground to another. She took hold of the wire and pulled. It was a clean break and would take next to no time to repair.

Whit debated, then thought, *He'll never know,* and headed to her saddlebags to get her fencing supplies. The fence had tightening ratchets close to the break, so she was able to let out enough wire to put on a clamp and squeeze it down with the special tool that took all of her strength to operate. Once reconnected, she tightened the ratchet, hammered a missing staple into a nearby post, then remounted. Easy fix.

She did two more easy fixes that morning and was pleased that there were no areas where wildlife had tangled themselves up in downed wires, creating major havoc. The sooner the wire was off the ground, the less likely that was to happen.

Whitney stopped for lunch near a small stream that headed down the mountain to join the creek that flowed through the Hayes Ranch. As she sat on a flattish slab of granite nestled among three fragrant pine trees, eating her peanut butter sandwich, it was hard not to appreciate the things that kept her father ranching. He was his own boss, worked close to nature and enjoyed the freedom of setting his own hours, except when the cattle and the hay fields set them for him.

He also froze in the winter, sweltered during the heat of summer and had to figure out how to work around the whims of nature and the commodities markets.

With a small sigh, Whitney closed her sandwich container and stowed it back in the saddlebag. She sat on the rock once again and leaned her back against the pine tree behind her, instantly realizing her mistake as she felt the nasty sensation of pitch sinking into her hair and shirt. Talk about a newbie move.

She put a hand at the back of her head above the place where she was now secured to the tree and gently eased forward, grimacing as the hair pulled free. If she put her hat back on, would it become glued to her head? Whit could honestly say that she'd never encountered a hair emergency while seated at her desk, so score one point for computer work.

After stuffing her hat in the saddlebag, she untied Charley and mounted. There were only a couple more miles to check, and if things continued as they had so far, with the exception of the few breaks she'd fixed, she'd be able to give Tanner the all-clear to release his cattle. And then, unless he had something else on the agenda, she would go home and take the pitch out of her hair.

TANNER AND CLIVE, who'd worked himself into a lather trying to assert control, had stopped near the creek that bisected the Hayes property. After drinking his fill, Clive started playing in the water, then suddenly lifted his head and whinnied, his entire body vibrating as he let out the long call. A moment later Whitney Fox rode out of the timber, the sunlight glinting off her hair as she emerged from between two tall ponderosa pines.

"Where's your hat?" Tanner asked after she'd ridden to a stop.

"I got pitch in my hair and decided I'd just as soon not glue my hat to my head." She patted the back of her head. "Thank goodness for isopropyl alcohol."

"You've done this before?"

"I grew up around pine trees."

"So did I," he said. "Yet I've never gotten pitch in my hair."

"Then you were doing things wrong."

He laughed, then said, "How'd it go, other than the pitch in the hair part?"

"Your fence is in great shape. You can turn out any time."

"No broken wires?"

"The fence is intact," she repeated, folding the reins in her hand. "How's your side?"

"A few breaks. I fixed them as I went."

She cleared her throat. "I did the same."

Like he'd specifically asked her not to. He opened his mouth to mention that small fact, but she cut him off.

"Do you know how many fences I have repaired over the years?"

She gave him a challenging look and Tanner realized that he couldn't afford to alienate either her or her father, but on the other hand, he'd expected her to have an easy day riding the fence and following directions. She'd ridden the fence, but ignored the directions.

He folded his hands on top of the saddle horn to hide his irritation. "Do you know how many people I've worked with who *thought* they knew what they were doing, but didn't?" he asked in a reasonable voice.

The look she gave him told him that he might have just talked his way out of another day of help and his stomach sank.

"Not to say that you don't know what you're

doing," he added quickly. "I was just operating in better-safe-than-sorry mode. I don't know your abilities, but I appreciate the help."

"I see your point." She didn't seem to like it, but she saw it.

Whitney turned her gelding toward the ranch without giving a reply, and he had a feeling that she was deciding whether she'd be back. Now that he'd signed the lease, she owed him nothing. Tanner let out a silent breath as he followed her to the timberline and hoped she didn't change her mind.

They rode to the ranch following the creek, a ride through mostly open country. The early spring wildflowers were starting to fade, but later blooming blossoms were taking their place and the lingering dampness from the previous evening's rain brought up scents of grass and earth as the horses made their way home. Tanner had missed these smells. Wheat and dry earth smelled good, too, but these smells brought back the joy of escaping into his own world. The security of being far from the ranch house, where his dad would always find something to judge or complain about. Yes. These were the scents of safety and freedom.

When they arrived at the ranch, Whit dismounted at the gate. Tanner wondered if she no longer had to prove her skill level by opening the gate from horseback, or if she simply wanted to feel the earth beneath her boots. He dismounted an exhausted Clive and followed Whitney through the gate.

They walked side by side to her horse trailer, where she tied her gelding, then pulled off the saddle and stowed it in the tack compartment. She laid the blanket upside down on the floor to dry, then grabbed a currycomb out of the door pocket.

"I'll take care of Clive, then we can talk about tomorrow," he said as she emerged from the trailer. "If you're coming back, that is."

"I am." She spoke to the horse's side as she applied the currycomb, loosening the caked-on dirt and letting air get to his skin.

"Good." Tanner led Clive through the barn, unsaddled him, curried his damp hair, then released him with Emily, who ambled over to see her buddy. She was still favoring the leg, but not as much as she had this morning. He'd give it another day and see how she was before calling the vet. Chances were that it would heal on its own.

When he returned to the trailer, Whitney had just set her saddlebags in the front seat of the truck. She closed the door and turned to him. "What's on the agenda for tomorrow?"

He jerked his head toward the house. "How about I get us a couple of beers and we can talk in the house?"

She shook her head, and a shaft of disappointment went through him.

She'd already said that she was coming back, so there was nothing to settle there. Was he this hungry for company?

Maybe. It wasn't like Len welcomed visitors. Tanner had left behind a solid group of friends in Washington State, but here, in the place where he'd grown up, he was a pariah. *Thanks, Dad.* He'd looked up his handful of high school friends, the kids who'd helped him ignore his home life, and who didn't hold his dad's actions against him, but with the exception of Bill Monroe, the deputy, they'd moved on. He was like a stranger in a familiar land.

So, yeah. Maybe he was justified in being disappointed.

"I wouldn't mind some cold water, though."

"I've got that."

A few minutes later, Tanner set a glass of ice water on Whit's side of the table and a beer on his own. Whit patted the back of her head experimentally, then said, "Would you mind telling me how bad it is?"

Tanner moved behind her chair, peering down at the silky blond strands that were twisted and glued together in a tangle above her braid. He caught the subtle scent of floral shampoo as he surveyed the damage.

"Do you want me to see if I can take it out?"

Whit's gaze turned thoughtful. "Scissors won't figure into your removal technique, will they?"

He grinned. "Only if you get stuck to the wall or something." She gave him a mock scowl and he said, "I have rubbing alcohol."

"Then, yes. If you don't mind, I'd love to have this stuff gone."

WHIT'S NERVES JUMPED when Tanner touched her hair, his callused fingers gently lifting the gummy knot and then pressing a cotton ball soaked in alcohol onto the strands. She'd been irritated by his assumption that she was some kind of city girl who couldn't handle a simple fence repair, but after he'd explained, she'd seen his point. Grudgingly. She hated being underestimated, but what did he know about her abilities?

"Thanks for doing this," she said as the alcohol evaporated from her scalp, making her fight a shiver. "I don't want to get pitch on the headrest."

"That truck looks like it's seen worse than pitch on a headrest."

She laughed, but it felt a little choked. Tanner was so close behind her that she could feel the heat from his body, the vibration of his chest when he spoke. How oddly intimate it was to have a neighbor she didn't know well dabbing away at her hair.

A neighbor who smelled really good.

She cleared her throat and straightened in the chair. "Just get the worst of it, and I'll do the rest when I get home."

"I can get the majority," he said. He continued dabbing and working the sticky sap out of her hair, wiping his fingers on a paper towel.

"Okay. Not perfect, but it'll do for now."

"Thanks." His hands brushed her shoulders, creating a small ripple of awareness, which in turn made Whit think, *Hmm.*

Tanner Hayes was a handsome guy. And he

smelled good. And he had a water lease with her dad that Whit simply didn't feel like jeopardizing. She hadn't read it, so she didn't know what kind of exit clause it might contain.

When he stepped back, she lightly patted the damp area on the back of her head and smiled. "That feels so much better."

"Anytime." Tanner's lips curved before he began gathering up the cotton balls that had tumbled out of the bag onto the table, but his smile seemed somewhat guarded.

"I didn't expect you to arrange for the body shop." She'd thought that she would have trouble finding someone local who would work on an Audi.

"Least I can do in exchange for some help." He capped the rubbing alcohol. "To tell you the truth, I had a rough time finding someone. Every time I mentioned my last name…" He finished the sentence by making a slashing movement across his throat.

"But Clinton Automotive was different?"

"I used your name. Totally different reaction."

"Wow," she said softly, even though she wasn't surprised. Carl Hayes had worked for his reputation of being hard on service people, despite being generous with various causes.

He shrugged. "That's my reality in this town. Guess I'll have to learn to live with it."

Whit drove home with Tanner's words playing in her head. His reality wasn't her concern, but the unfairness of being treated as if he was his father niggled at her. That said, how well did she know Tanner Hayes? Maybe he had his own way of putting people off. He'd put her off that day by stinging her pride.

It wasn't a big deal. Her objective of spending time outdoors before heading back to an office job would have been satisfied by riding the fence and noting where repairs were needed, as he'd asked. But it was difficult to ride by damage that could be fixed in less than ten minutes. Silly, really.

Enough. You're over it.

Whit's dad rode his ATV into the yard as she released Charley into the pasture. The gelding headed directly to the dusty area near the windbreak and had a good roll before climbing to his feet and shaking.

"How'd it go?" Ben shouted over the ATV engine.

Whit cupped her ear, and he turned off the noisy four-wheeler.

"How'd it go?" he repeated.

"It was a nice day out."

"Did you work alone?"

"I did. I rode that fence like I knew what I was doing," Whitney said, and her dad grinned.

"Good. I hope Hayes appreciates a seasoned employee. I did my best work training you."

Before Whit could deliver a comeback, her phone buzzed.

"Take it," her dad said. "I have stuff to do in the alfalfa field. Pivot problem. I'm going to get wet."

"Sorry about that." Whit smiled, then glanced at her phone as it buzzed again. "It's Maddie," she said.

Her dad raised his hand and then the ATV roared away.

"Did your ride go well?" Maddie asked.

"I got pitch in my hair." Which Tanner had taken out. She could still feel the careful movements of his fingers as he'd worked the alcohol into her hair.

Maddie laughed. "Of course you did. Hey, Kat wants to meet for drinks on Wednesday after I close up. Are you in?"

Whit could tell from Maddie's tone that she had more questions about the day on the Hayes Ranch, but that she would wait until they could talk face-to-face. Her friends would enjoy the part where Tanner didn't think she was capable of fixing a break on her own, considering how much fence she fixed on her own ranch.

"I'm definitely in," Whit said. "But I probably won't stay out very long." Days in the sun were wearing, and her desire to stay out until all hours had declined over the years. Corporate life had cured her of indulging in late nights followed by early mornings.

"We're getting old," Maddie said with a laugh.

"How so?" Whit asked with mock indignation.

"I was about to tell you I needed to be home by nine."

TANNER LEANED BACK in his chair and studied the computer screen as if the numbers would change if he stared at them long enough. The figures stayed stubbornly intact. He ran a hand over his forehead, then reached for his whiskey.

His dad hadn't defaulted on anything, but he wondered what would have happened in another year. Things had been coming to a head rapidly, according to the ledgers, and he'd found a rough draft of a letter to an old business acquaintance in which Carl tried to interest the guy in investing in the ranch.

That was telling, because Carl Hayes sailed his ship alone. He'd had to have been desperate to have written even a rough draft of such a letter. Tanner knew it was only a rough draft, because he'd called the man under the guise of settling his father's estate, and made certain that there'd been no deal in the works.

Carl Hayes had been thinking of asking a friend for help, but hadn't seen fit to let his own sons know the state of affairs. Pride was a rugged thing. Tanner tried to imagine his dad calling his two sons to a meeting, laying out the issues and asking for ideas as to how to rectify the financial situation the ranch had fallen into. Couldn't do it. They might have gone through the motions of looking like a family toward the end of his father's life, but that was as far as it went. Appearances were everything to the guy.

Tanner closed the computer program, stood

and stretched, then stepped over his sleeping dog as he left the office and walked into the smaller, more intimate living area on the far side of the stone fireplace where he'd left his phone. The windows of this room, which he preferred to the more ostentatious main living room with its floor-to-ceiling glass panes, looked out over the working part of the ranch.

His ranch.

If he could keep it running.

He walked around the stone fireplace to where the view was devoid of man-made anything. From these windows, it appeared that the house was isolated in a mountain valley, just as Dena had intended. The house was beautiful, yet oddly uncomfortable due to the ghosts of the past, coupled with the fact that he wasn't really a stone, cedar and glass kind of guy.

What kind of house would he build, given the chance? Easy answer. A big old farmhouse like the one his high school friend Bud Perry had lived in. He had great memories of that place, which had since been sold. When Grant had told him the Perrys had moved and that the house was on the market, he'd felt a pang of loss. Not that he and

Bud had remained close after high school, but that house, and the Perry family, had been a source of refuge for him.

He hadn't needed refuge for a long time, but returning to his family home had stirred up emotions and memories, and shopping around for a mechanic to fix Whitney's car had reminded him that in the eyes of the community, he was a Hayes.

It was probable that Carl hadn't been able to throw as much money around during the past year or two as the townspeople were used to, and without money to soften his treatment of them, they began responding differently. Why kowtow to someone if you no longer had a reason to?

Tanner got verification of his assumption the next morning, when he woke up to a stream of water heading across the kitchen floor tiles. While he had some rudimentary plumbing knowledge, it soon became obvious that he wasn't up to the task ahead of him, which involved visible pinholes in copper pipes. He could change out PVC, but copper was beyond his knowledge base, so he turned off the water main and started dialing plumbers. He'd already received two "we're too booked to help you" responses when Whitney Fox drove into the ranch. He dialed the third plumber on the list, received the same answer, then went out to tell her they might be a little late starting.

"Unless you're good with plumbing as well as fencing."

She gave him a wry look. "I have many talents. Plumbing is not one of them."

"You want to come in for a cup of coffee while I try to chase one down?"

"I've had my quota of coffee for the day." She pushed a few blond strands behind her ear and Tanner tried not to stare now that he knew how soft her hair was. "Charley and I will wait here." She cocked her head then, as if an idea had struck her. "Do you want me to saddle Clive?"

"I'll manage," he said drily.

"Just trying to save time. What's the problem with the plumbing?"

He explained the holes in the pipes, and she listened with a faint frown.

"Who have you phoned?"

He rattled off the three names and she said, "Really?"

"Yeah?"

"Huh." She pulled her phone out of the chest

pocket of the men's chambray shirt she wore over her T-shirt. "Let me try."

"Why not?"

The words came out snarkier than he'd intended, but Whitney didn't seem to notice. She'd already dialed and a few seconds later she said, "Hi, Pauline. It's Whit Fox. I'm in need of a plumber."

Tanner waited, and curiously found himself half hoping that she got the same response he did, even though it was counterproductive.

"It's pretty much an emergency," she said, meeting Tanner's gaze. He nodded. "But here's the thing. It's not at Dad's place. It's on the Hayes Ranch. I'm working here." Whit studied the ground as she listened to the short response, then said, "I'm back home now and lending a neighbor a hand."

Tanner felt his cheeks grow warm as he heard not the words, but the tone of the response on the other end of the line.

Whit laughed. "Honestly. Dad is doing some business with them."

There was another silence on Whit's end, then she said, "Really? No. I can't see that happening." She met Tanner's gaze, a slow smile forming on her face as she listened. "I'm sure

tomorrow will work. We can hold things together until then."

The "we" might have been the clincher, because Whit smiled and said, "Pauline, thank
you. Tonight would be great. I'll tell him…no,
I won't be here. I have an engagement." She
rolled her eyes. "No. Not that kind." She ended
the call and gave Tanner a cool look, as if she'd
never doubted the outcome. "Pauline's son will
stop by on his way home from work tonight, if
you don't mind a plumber arriving after five."

"I have no problem with that. I'd kind of
like to get the water back on."

"You never miss the water 'til the well runs
dry," she quipped. "Or you come home from
a dusty day's ride and have to bathe in the
horse trough."

"Have you done that?"

She gave him a *duh* look. "Haven't you?"

"My experience there is lacking." He settled his hands on his hips. "Which plumber
did you call?"

"Superior."

His first call, which had resulted in a quick,
"Sorry, we're booked," after he'd identified
himself.

"I see," he said with as much equanimity

as he could muster. The constant snubs of the community bit more than he wanted to let on. "Thank you. I appreciate your help."

WHIT HAD TO admit to feeling bad for Tanner Hayes after she'd booked the plumber who'd obviously already told him no. She almost explained to him that she and Pauline's son had gone to prom, which was true, but Tanner wasn't foolish. He knew that his father had left a legacy of bad feelings and he was paying for that. She wondered if he knew that his father had been very late to pay his last bill with Superior Plumbing. When Pauline had mentioned that, Whit had been surprised, then realized that it had most likely been lazy fiscal behavior. Carl Hayes wasn't the first wealthy person she'd encountered in her life who didn't seem to understand that small businesses depended on timely payments.

What would it be like to live in that kind of world?

She'd worked tirelessly during college and at her job in an effort to find out. She didn't aspire to be super wealthy, like the Hayeses, but she wanted to be able to live comfortably without worrying about what would happen if the ranch had a few bad years.

Yes, she'd done all the work, sacrificed her free time, and had been laid off for her efforts.

She studied the back of the man riding in front of her on the narrow trail, his sweet dog keeping pace with his gelding. Clive was behaving almost like a normal horse today. He'd tried his sidestep trick when Tanner mounted, but today the cowboy was having none of it and he'd put the gelding's far side against the fence so that there was nowhere for the horse to go when he stepped into the stirrup.

They rode across a meadow strewn with wildflowers to the area Tanner called the south pasture, where they planned to split up to ride their sections of fence. Tanner had seemed preoccupied as they rode through the meadow—possibly due to the plumber incident—but that suited Whit, who was looking forward to a day with the sun on her face and the wind in her hair. The only difference today was that when she ate lunch, she was going to avoid sitting near pitchy pine trees.

"Do you want me to ride the fence and, you know, do nothing else?" she asked as they pulled to a stop at the stream that bisected the property. She wasn't certain where they stood after the previous day's discussion about following orders. Had she prevailed? Had he? Did it matter, since this was her last day, and she could do what she wanted without repercussion?

Tanner responded by riding Clive closer to Charley, who took no offense at the gelding's presence despite Clive bumping his nose against his shoulder. Whit's awareness meter bumped up as she shortened Charley's reins.

"I want you to do what you think is best."

"Right you are." She ran a finger along the brim of her hat in a cocky salute. "It's always good to trust the cowgirl."

"Maybe so," he allowed, giving her another of those looks that made her wonder just what was what. He wasn't flirting…right? So why were her thoughts heading in that direction?

"I'll see you in a couple of hours," Tanner added, his voice all business now, leaving her to wonder what he actually thought of her.

"Yep," she agreed. They reined their horses in opposite directions and a few minutes later, Whit glanced over her shoulder in time to see Tanner disappear into the trees, looking very much the seasoned cowboy. Rose, who'd been snuffling at something in the meadow, raised her head and trotted after him.

After a single day, she didn't know what kind of boss he really was, and she probably never would. Did it matter?

Not unless she or one of her friends were working for the man, and she was almost done with what she'd promised. Now it was full speed ahead figuring out Life Plan Number 3.

TANNER DID HIS best to focus on the job at hand, pushing Clive so that they could cover some miles, but his mind kept straying to the plumbing situation. He was glad to have a plumber scheduled for later in the day, but further proof that the Hayes name was poison in the Larkspur area was gnawing at him.

This was twice that when the Fox name was substituted for Hayes the situation had changed radically. People were willing to help Whitney, while he could whistle into the wind. He didn't have the financial resources to sweeten attitudes with the promise of money, which left him either getting help out of town or convincing the locals that he was okay.

That might take years.

Or longer.

Was he being stubborn by trying to hang on to this ranch?

He'd recently left a small town where people greeted him on the street, to come back to his hometown where he was summarily snubbed. It was obvious now that by keeping to himself in high school and having only two or three close friends, he'd done himself a disservice. No one really knew him. And now they didn't want to.

But he was not his father, and he would not play the victim. There had to be a way around this.

Full-page newspaper ad? Radio spot?

Tanner Hayes is a good guy. He doesn't have a lot of money, but he's cool.

His mouth twisted into a humorless smile, then he made a grab for the saddle horn as Clive jumped sideways, startled by Rose pushing her way through thick brush at the side of the trail. Glad that Whitney wasn't there to see him scramble to stay in the saddle, Tanner pushed Clive forward with his knees. Emily's limp was abating, but he'd already decided to continue riding Clive. The gelding needed miles and he kept Tanner on his toes.

When he met Whitney a few hours later, she reported that the fence was in good condition and she'd only needed to make one small repair. He had not been so lucky, having done some for-now fixes that he'd have to address later in the summer when he had more time for real repairs. The important thing was that he'd be able to turn a herd into this pasture to graze until his start date for the Old Timber Mountain grazing allotment arrived and he'd turn the cow-calf pairs loose on the mountain.

They rode back to the ranch single file on the narrow trail leading through the trees to the meadow below. When they finally hit the grassy expanse, they waited for Rose to catch up, then began riding side by side through the knee-high grass. The air was remarkably clear due to a short rain the previous evening, and with the sun on his back and the scent of earth, pine and sweet grass filling his lungs, Tanner was struck by a sense of rightness that countered the nagging irritation that had stuck with him all day.

What was he going to do to improve public relations?

"About my car," Whitney said, scattering his thoughts of public relations.

"Yes." Tanner shot her a look, but she kept her profile to him, watching as her gelding picked his way over a fallen log half-hidden by grass.

"Do I set things up with Clinton Automotive or does your agent?" She turned to look at him then. "I've never done this before."

"Neither have I." Not until he'd had a close encounter with one Whitney Fox. "Why don't you call the place and set up what's convenient for you. I'll keep my agent apprised."

"Sounds good." She directed her attention back to the path through the deep grass, but even in profile he could see that her brow was still creased. There was no getting around the fact that the damage was going to affect the price of the car when she sold it.

He didn't know how to ask his next question, so he made it into a statement. "You said that you're selling the car."

"I have to." They rode around a residual boulder that a glacier had dumped thousands of years ago in the middle of what was now a field, then she explained, "My circumstances have changed. Temporarily." She added the word as if reminding herself of the fact. "It no longer makes sense to have a car with large insurance premiums and hefty maintenance fees." He said nothing to that, and a moment later she said, "I got laid off not long ago."

That surprised him. He gave her a quick glance, which she met with a what-can-I-say expression.

"Corporate buyout. Pretty much nothing I could have done to save myself."

"What next?"

"I'm taking a little time to settle things in my head, then I start job hunting. I don't have a fully formed plan yet, but I will."

"What kind of company did you work for?"

She explained her job with a renewable energy company, then added, "I want to live close to my dad, but that may not be possible."

After that, Whitney fell into silence, as if talking about her life situation bothered her more than she wanted to let on. And he was good with that because he knew the feeling well. As they approached the gate leading to the ranch, he glanced her way just as she looked at him. Their gazes connected. Held. Whitney was the first to look away.

They arrived at the gate leading to the last

pasture before the ranch came into sight. He dismounted from Clive and opened it, allowing Whitney through. Clive attempted to give him a shove with his nose when his back was turned, but Tanner sensed what was coming, turned and stopped the horse with a look.

At least he was making headway on that front.

By the time they reached the ranch, Whitney seemed more her usual self. She untacked her gelding, loaded him then ambled over to where Tanner had just released Clive into his corral.

"Thanks for signing the water deal with my dad," she said.

Her time on the ranch was transactional, regardless of what she'd said before. She was simply making sure that he owed her enough that he wouldn't change his mind. The thought didn't sit well, but what did he expect? He was a Hayes.

For some inexplicable reason, he'd expected her to see him as he was.

Maybe she did…but she was hedging her bets in spite of it.

"Thanks for the help," he said. He thought about extending a hand, then simply didn't. A few minutes later, when he was watching the dust from her trailer settle on the long driveway, a wave of something close to depression washed over him.

The feeling intensified two hours later after the plumber from Superior Plumbing had inspected the pipes and explained how mineral-laden water could react with copper and create the small holes that caused the leaks.

Ironic, really. His dad had wanted the best of the best in his house, so instead of PVC pipe, he'd gone copper. And the best of the best hadn't been suitable for his situation.

Now Tanner got to deal with it, just as he was dealing with the other things his dad had done for appearances, such as overextending.

"Hey, thanks," Tanner said as he walked the guy named Steve to his truck. Steve loaded his tools, then handed the handwritten invoice to Tanner, who glanced at it, then back at the man. "Thanks," he repeated.

Steve lifted his chin. "I'm going to need payment today."

Tanner blinked at the guy. It wasn't the request, but the tone, which sounded like a reprimand.

"Okay," Tanner said. "Is this a policy with

your company?" Because he hadn't encountered it in Washington State.

"Not always."

Tanner gave Steve a sideways look. Again, something in the tone. Finally, Steve looked up at the sky for a split second, then said, "Your dad left us hanging for months with a big bill. It caused some problems with our cash flow."

Tanner felt the back of his neck grow warm.

"So the policy is payment at time of service. I'm set up for digital payment." Steve held up the square payment attachment that would connect to his phone.

"Not a problem." Tanner pulled out his wallet, which he always carried, and watched silently as Steve ran the payment before handing him the card back.

"No offense. It's just business."

With a Hayes. Who hadn't paid a big bill on time.

He'd have to take another look at the finances, do some forensic digging to see who else his dad might have offended by late payments after his financial downturn.

After the plumber had left, Tanner started for Len's house, then changed his mind. Yes, the old guy might know a thing or two, but he wasn't ready to be humiliated on all fronts.

One thing was certain. If he was going to continue living in the area, he was going to have to come up with a way to rehabilitate his name.

Right now, he had no way of doing that.

CHARLEY NICKERED AS Whit approached the corral with a wheelbarrow full of weeds she'd pulled from the flower beds near the house.

"I agree," she said to the horse as she wheeled past him to the compost pile. She liked gardening, and the beds needed some serious work, but like her horse, she'd rather be riding on the mountain. The two days she'd promised Tanner Hayes on his ranch had flown by, and even though she'd let herself get caught up in worries about the future on the last day's ride, she'd felt better worrying on the mountain than she would have at home, while staring at a computer and wondering about her next act. She was not yet ready to tackle her future.

She emptied the wheelbarrow and then took a moment to look out over the fields where two tractors were at work, prepping the area where her dad would seed his new crop that would be irrigated with leased Hayes Ranch water. Funny how they had more help than they needed now that she was back home, while Tanner was struggling. He'd leased his farming, but there was still a lot to do with the cattle and the meadow hay he planned to bale.

And that was his problem. She'd lent a hand to be neighborly. In return, he'd arranged her car repair and signed the water lease with her dad.

She'd just started back to the flower bed when the phone in the house started ringing. Since her father rarely got calls, it could well be something important. She abandoned the wheelbarrow and jogged to the house, pulling off her gloves as she went, hoping to catch whoever it was before they gave up.

"Fox Ranch." She cradled the phone on her shoulder as she rubbed soil from her fingers. Her pulse gave a totally unnecessary jolt when the caller identified himself as Tanner Hayes.

"Dad's not here right now."

"I was calling for you."

"Really?" Someday she'd learn not to say

the first thing that popped into her head, but that wasn't today.

"I was wondering..." A second or two ticked by before he said, "Could we meet?"

Tanner Hayes was not his usual composed self.

She frowned. "Meet?"

"I want to ask your opinion on something that I think you have a unique perspective on." He spoke in a low voice, as if he didn't want anyone to overhear.

"You want to put a wind farm on the ranch?"

"No. I need some advice about surviving in Larkspur."

The plumbing incident shot into her head. "Ah." He didn't reply and she said, "I'm not sure what I can do."

"Would you mind letting me bounce a few things off you? Because if not you, then it'll have to be Len or his nephew Kenny, and I don't see either of them being all that helpful."

Whit had to agree. Neither were socially inclined. And maybe she needed to wrap her mind around something else after letting the reality of being unemployed get to her that day.

"Sure. Want to come here? Dad's on the trac-

tor. I don't expect him in until dark, if then."
One thing about farmwork—it didn't wait on
the convenience of the farmer.

"I'll be there shortly. Thanks."

Judging from the way he said the last word,
Whit guessed that this had not been an easy
call to make, which piqued her curiosity. She
went into the main bathroom and checked
herself out in the mirror. A little soil removal
from the cheek area, a comb through her hair,
some colored lip balm and she was ready for
guests.

She opened the fridge and realized that she
and her dad needed to up their hospitality
game, then told herself that Tanner wasn't
coming for hospitality. He was coming because he needed advice.

Would she be able to help him?

To know the answer to that, she needed to
wait for him to lay out the problem, which he
did less than a half hour later, after declining
an expired beer—her dad wasn't much of a
beer drinker—and taking a seat across from
her at the kitchen table.

"I like your house," he said.

Whit assumed he was being polite, because
the house was a sometimes-drafty farmhouse,

which had been added onto two times that Whit knew of. It was a hodgepodge type of dwelling that had seemed a touch embarrassing during her self-conscious middle school years, but Kat and Maddie had similar houses, so she'd mostly been okay with it.

"I like it, too," she said, then cut to the chase. "What's up, Tanner?"

He studied the table as if marshaling his thoughts, then tapped his finger on the oak. "I need to figure out a way to redeem the Hayes reputation. I was raised by my old man. I totally get why people avoid anything with the Hayes name on it, but I want to live here, and it's going to be difficult if I can't get a mechanic or plumber or doctor because my dad ticked them off when he was still alive."

Whit reached out to put her hand on top of his, as she would have with a close friend. Then she froze, her fingers hovering just above his.

Holy moly.

She gave the back of his hand a perfunctory pat, then settled both of her hands back in her lap, with the intention of keeping them there.

Tanner's mouth quirked up at the corner. "Did you just there-there me?"

"Maybe," she muttered, knowing that she'd totally there-there'd him. Eager to change the subject, she leaned forward in her chair, allowed her hands back on the table under the condition that they behave themselves, and said, "You're in a tough spot, Tanner. Small towns are notoriously stubborn once a judgment has been made."

"I need to stop having them judge me as if I were my dad."

"How do you propose to do that?"

Tanner met her gaze. He looked uncertain and determined and...uncertain. He cleared his throat.

"I know that you'll be busy networking and job hunting, and helping around this place, but I thought that maybe we could be seen together from time to time. And you could look happy about it, like we're friends."

Whit's pulse jumped. "Like a pretend girlfriend?"

"No."

The word burst out of his mouth and Whit felt instantly relieved. She pulled her hands back into her lap as she stared at Tanner Hayes's

handsome face. Twice he'd been turned down
for services using his name. Twice those same
services had been available to her. She saw
where he was coming from.

"Don't you think doing business with my
dad is good enough?"

"Apparently not," he said. Whit had to admit
that he had recent evidence to prove his case.
"If you don't want to do this, I understand. It
was a shot in the dark." He pushed his chair
back as if he was ready to go.

Whit made no move to stop him as she
considered the logic of his idea. All they had
to do was appear to be friends.

That would never fly.

The townspeople would assume it was something else, of course. Something more along the
lines of a romance. But instead of pointing out
the obvious to Tanner, she cocked her head in
a thoughtful way as an idea struck her.

"What?" he asked, shifting his weight after
the silence had stretched for a few seconds
too long.

"Hire me."

"What?"

"I need a temporary job. You need a temporary day hand. Hire me. Word will get around

town that I'm working for you. I'll tell people how great it is being employed by the Hayes Ranch and how different you are from your dad."

Tanner didn't answer immediately, but she could see that he was turning the idea over in his head.

"I'll tell them about the catered lunches, the after-work pool parties…" Her expression sobered and the teasing note left her voice. "All kidding aside, it could work, Tanner."

"It might," he allowed warily.

"Better than if we try to come off as instant friends. That would just turn into a spectator sport. There would be speculation about whether we're dating, and then when we part ways because I get a job elsewhere, some people will assume you did me wrong, which will not help your rep."

"That makes sense," he agreed slowly.

"This gives us a reason to be friendly that the local folk are more likely to buy because of the money aspect."

"Money," he said softly. "Right."

Whit noticed a fleeting shift in his demeanor, but she pressed on regardless. "The only caveat is that I may quit suddenly. If the right job comes along—"

"I understand." His mouth tightened as he glanced down, then he lifted his gaze. "Okay. You're hired. Can you start tomorrow? I'm riding the allotment fence up on Old Timber Mountain."

Whit felt a smile crease her cheeks. This might not be Life Plan Number 3, but it felt right. Just a little detour as she sorted out her future. "I can."

His face relaxed and Whit once again felt the tug of attraction. He was gorgeous, and he was off-limits for the simple reason that Whit needed to figure out Life Plan Number 3 before she started adding to the mix.

TANNER HADN'T GONE to the Fox Ranch with the intention of hiring help. No, he'd gone there out of desperation, getting into his truck and driving to the Fox Ranch before he talked himself out of the idea of asking Whitney to help him with his image in the community. He'd come home with a temporary hire on his books. Whitney Fox was now an employee, and every day that she showed up for work was one day closer to his summer crew arriving and him not trying to sift through the dregs of the cowboy-for-hire world to find someone reliable to work for him.

Tanner spent a few minutes loving on Rose, who'd gone out with him that day to finish some repairs on the south section fence, then fed her and headed out to tend to his horses. When he reached the corrals, Len's nephew, Kenny, came roaring in on his motorcycle, giving a happy salute as he drove by. Tanner returned the gesture, then checked on Emily's leg, which she was now putting weight on, then spent a few minutes brushing her. Clive nosed his way in, demanding equal time, and Tanner, seeing this as a good sign, also brushed the gelding. By the time he finished, the motorcycle was gone, but Len's door was open, so he headed over to rap on the door frame.

"Need help with anything?" he called into the dimly lit interior.

"I'm good." Uneven footsteps followed the words, and Len appeared from the short hallway leading to the back rooms of the house. "Kenny brought groceries."

"Nice of him."

Len gave a small grunt in reply. Tanner had yet to figure out Len's relationship with his nephew, who seemed good-natured but a little squirrelly.

"They're a bit dusty from the motorcycle, but the eggs are all whole this time," the old man said. "How'd the neighbor girl work out?"

The neighbor girl was actually a woman, but he didn't point that out.

"She has skills."

Len grunted again. "Guess it's good that you found someone to help for a couple days."

"She hired on."

Len's mouth fell open in a way that would have been comical if the old guy hadn't appeared so taken aback. "Her? You sure about this?"

"She lives close, seems to know what she's doing and she needed a job." When the old man said nothing, Tanner added, "She's gotta be better than Wes."

Len snorted. "A hot dog would be better than Wes."

And with that, the old man turned and maneuvered his way back into his house, letting the door swing shut behind him.

"YOU'RE WORKING FOR Tanner Hayes?" It was the second time Maddie had asked the question in less than thirty seconds. "You were ready to fillet him when he hit your car and now you're…"

"Neighbors," Whit said firmly. "He needs some help on his place and it just happened."

"Things don't just happen to you," Kat said.

"Not often. But there *was* that surprise layoff." She gave her friend a significant raised eyebrow look as she sipped her drink.

"Touché."

Her dad hadn't been as surprised as her friends were by the news. He'd taken it in stride, simply reminding her that the community board meeting was coming up and he'd appreciate it if she was at the meeting with him. In other words, he'd like it if she wasn't on a mountain somewhere checking a fence when the meeting began.

"It's temporary?" Maddie asked.

"Yep. Tanner has a couple people coming from Washington to work as summer hires, and I'm filling in until they get here. I get a paycheck and I can think about my future while I push cows and fix fences and, you know, enjoy the outdoors before I go back to the desk."

"Maybe you should get something more suited to your personality."

Whit smiled, then stirred her drink, thinking that Maddie made a good point. Unfortunately, the jobs she would enjoy most didn't lend themselves to high paychecks and security. She didn't want to go back to the hardscrabble life she and her dad had shared, to not knowing whether they'd be able to hang on to the ranch when one lean year led into another. Playing cowgirl was fun, but knowing that she had the means to help keep the ranch running, and that she could splurge on things like vacations and cool cars, made being chained to the desk worthwhile. Life was full of give-and-take. She'd chosen security over hardscrabble years ago, and she was making the same choice now.

"Are you attending the community board meeting?" Kat asked, apparently sensing that a change of subject was in order.

"Hearts of the West?" Maddie asked in return. "I am excused."

"No fair." Kat made a sour face.

"Well, if you were busy designing a wedding dress for Debra's daughter, you would be excused, too."

"I'm going to the meeting," Whit said. "Someone has to keep Dad out of trouble. I want to do our part, but I'd like it to be something we can do without losing sleep at night."

Kat laughed. "I remember last year."

"So do I." She'd spent a lot of time she didn't have bailing out her dad, but he was so bad at asking for anything she really had no choice but to help him solicit prizes for the various games and activities.

Maddie nudged Whit's knee and then motioned with her head. "Isn't that the other Hayes brother?"

Whit followed her friend's gaze to the bar where Grant Hayes sat talking to a man she didn't recognize.

"It is. I met him at the Hayes Ranch yesterday."

"I wonder if he's moving back, too."

"I didn't get that impression, but I don't know much about him."

"Do you know much about Tanner?"

I know that he smells good and that he's easy on the eyes. Whit stirred her drink again. "He's not giving off the spoiled rich boy vibe that I expected."

"A point in the plus column," Maddie said.

"Both brothers left home as soon as they could. Rumor has it that they didn't get along with their dad any better than the rest of the community," Kat said.

"I don't know," Maddie said. "The family seemed pretty cozy. Remember them at the Christmas parade? And the women drooling over the Hayes brothers?"

"I don't recall the latter," Whit said, wondering if she'd been able to come home that year. There'd been times when she hadn't been able to get away until Christmas Eve. "I can believe it happened, though. Grant and Tanner Hayes are lookers." She just wished she didn't notice as often as she did.

She debated with herself, then decided to let her friends know the full truth of the matter. "I'm going to help Tanner get a foothold back in the community."

"How?" Kat and Maddie asked in unison. They looked at each other, said, "Jinx," together, then laughed.

"How will you do that?" Kat said, focusing back on Whit.

"By association. I'm going to work for him, obviously, and I'm also going to make it clear that I like him just fine. Hopefully people will start looking at him differently."

She went on to explain the situation with the mechanic and the plumber, finishing with, "He's not a bad guy, and he should be judged on his own merits, not his father's."

"So—" Maddie glanced at Grant Hayes, then back at Whit "—you think the Hayes brothers are all right?"

There was a cautionary note in her friend's voice, one that Whit paid attention to. Maddie, who worked with the public, was quick to key in to people, often seeing things that others missed.

"I think Tanner Hayes is all right," Whit said. She had no evidence to the contrary, even though, in the beginning, she wanted to find something that painted him as a bad guy. "Do you know something I don't?"

"No," Maddie replied. "My only concern is that because he's doing business with your dad, and your dad really needs that water, you might have a skewed vision of things." She paused for a thoughtful moment. "Before you start paving his way into the good graces of the community, you need to be sure that he really is a good guy."

Point taken.

"He's good with his dog and his horse, and the horse is a jerk, so I think he's okay. But…" Whit's forehead creased. "If I find out he's not that way, I'll abandon ship immediately."

CHAPTER SIX

WHIT GAVE A quick glance at the truck's big side mirror as she waited for Tanner Hayes, who hadn't answered his door when she knocked. Little wisps of hair stuck out in all directions thanks to not having time to properly smooth and braid her hair, but at least the pine pitch was gone.

She was considering undoing her hair and re-braiding it when a movement in the pasture caught her eye. A horse and rider appeared over the top of the low ridge, and she could tell by the way the horse was trying to take control that it was Clive taking Tanner for a ride.

A four-wheeler appeared not far behind him, making Whit wonder how much longer Tanner might need her services. She'd been under the impression that she was his only employee for the interim, but then, as the ATV got closer, she recognized the foreman. He was riding the vehicle with one leg at an awkward angle.

"Hey," she said when Tanner reached the gate. "I didn't unload. I thought you might want to travel with me." Because it made no sense to take two trucks and two trailers for two horses and two riders.

"Sounds good," he said. He held the gate open for the ATV, and the foreman gave Whit a stern nod as he putted by. "Len has figured out how to be of use," he said. "But in a very limited capacity."

"Are you afraid that he's going to hurt himself again?"

"Totally, but some things you can't control."

"Amen to that." If she could, she'd still be working at her old job and driving the Audi with no thoughts of selling. She wouldn't be procrastinating in her job hunt while helping out the cowboy next door who, according to Maddie, may or may not be the nice guy he presented himself to be. Maddie was right—her vision could be skewed. She wanted to believe he was a guy who would continue leasing water to her dad. A guy who would be the good neighbor his father had not been.

After Tanner loaded Clive, he closed the trailer door and said, "Do you mind if I bring Rose?"

"I have a dog-friendly back seat."

"She tends to roll in the mud when she finds it."

She answered with an arch of her eyebrows. "You've seen the inside of my truck, right?"

He laughed. "I'll grab my lunch and my dog, and we can take off."

They drove with the windows down, the fresh breeze and mountain air mingling with the scent of coffee, and Tanner's soap and leather smell.

Tanner was in a lighter mood than he'd been in the day before, and Whit assumed it was because he had his foreman back on the job, albeit in a limited way. His crew was coming at the end of the next month…things were falling together for him, and now all he had to do was convince the community that he and his dad weren't one and the same.

And he might have to convince her friends. Maddie hadn't sounded certain that he was actually a good guy, but who knew what kind of gossip she'd heard about the Hayes family in her bridal shop? Whit told herself that morning that she'd keep an open mind, but so far…yeah. All signs pointed to him not being his dad.

"About my car," she said as they started down the driveway.

Tanner shot her a quick look. "Yeah?"

"I got it scheduled at Clinton Automotive, and I'd *really* like for you to pick me up after I drop it off."

"Sure," he said, not understanding what she was getting at.

"Joe Marconi works there. He's a prodigious gossip."

Tanner gave her a confused look, then caught her meaning.

Whit nodded as his expression shifted. "Joe likes me, and if he sees that I'm okay with you, then it'll be a start. You might be able to get a mechanic in a reasonable time."

"Good. I'm living in fear of something else breaking and having to call you to get it fixed."

Whit snorted at his dry response. "I guess that means you need to stay in my good graces, huh?"

Twenty minutes later, after Tanner opened and closed two wire gates on a rain-rutted road, Whit parked in the sagebrush near yet another gnarly wire gate. Tanner let Rose out of the truck, and then, as they were unloading the horses, his phone rang. He glanced at it, then put it back in his pocket.

After they'd led the horses through the gate and refastened it, his phone rang again. This time Tanner silenced it in his pocket. "My brother," he said as if that explained his actions.

Whit mounted her horse. "You don't want to talk to him?"

"Grant has a different vision for the ranch than I do."

Tanner mounted Clive, keeping his focus on the horse, but there was no missing the tension in his shoulders as the cowboy pulled his hat low over his forehead.

"Does he want to expand?" If so, then why wasn't he helping with the place?

"He wants to get out from under it. I want to keep it."

"That is a difference in visions."

Tanner gathered his reins, and she could tell by the shift in his demeanor that they would no longer be discussing his brother, but his voice was agreeable enough when he said,

"We'll ride together to the spring, then split up. I just need to warn you that the country can get rough in places. Lots of scree and talus."

"I've been in rough country."

"There are bears and rattlesnakes."

"I know," Whit said, wondering why he was stating the obvious. It wasn't like she hadn't grown up in the area.

"Most importantly, there are pine trees." His expression grew serious as he reiterated, "*Lots* of pine trees."

She sent him an uncomprehending look.

"I'm saying that I don't want to find you with your head stuck to another pitchy tree."

Whit would have smacked him if she'd been close enough. "Did you just make a joke at your new employee's expense?"

A slow smile crossed his face, which in turn caused a spiral of warmth to travel through her midsection.

"It's okay," she said with a dramatic sniff. "If you take responsibility for my car repairs, you can crack all the jokes you want."

"I am taking care of your car repairs."

"Then crack away."

He shook his head. "You've ruined it. Now I have performance anxiety."

Whit fought a smile, and he allowed himself a half smile before his expression sobered.

"I'm serious about the trail. Take care around the slumps and rockfalls. Len got hurt up here trying to use an ATV instead of a horse."

"That's why I prefer horses in the mountains."

"Me, too." He tightened his reins as Clive shied at nothing. "Except maybe this one."

Rose ran ahead of them on the trail, disappearing when she discovered an interesting scent, then reappearing. She beat them to the spring, and when they arrived, Tanner's yellow dog had dark mud encasing her legs and the lower half of her body.

Tanner grimaced. "I'm pretty sure most of it will be gone by the end of the day."

"You've seen my truck," Whit repeated before looking to the east. They'd studied a map of the area before leaving his ranch, and Tanner had shown her the distance he'd wanted to cover that day. If all went well, they'd be done with the area in two days, making minor repairs as they went.

Major repairs would be marked on the map and tended to later. It had been a heavy snow year, so Whit wouldn't be surprised to find long stretches of fencing wire lying on the ground in the areas where snow accumulation would have been higher than the fence posts.

They reined their horses in different directions, Whit heading east and Tanner north. She was almost to the tree line when Tanner shouted, "Hey!"

She looked over her shoulder, and was struck by the picture Tanner, his horse and his dog made in front of a backdrop of granite boulders and aspen.

"Yes?" she called.

"We'll meet back here at five at the latest."

She held up a thumb to indicate that she'd heard him and checked her watch, so that she could gauge time out and time back. Her phone was in the truck, due to lack of cell signal, which meant a day uninterrupted by modern communications.

No way of connecting with other human beings for at least eight hours.

She could already feel her brain begin to relax. She couldn't say that she wanted to do this kind of work forever, because for one thing it didn't pay that well, but for the moment she had to admit that it was perfect.

CLIVE SHIFTED HIS weight under the saddle as Tanner pulled the gelding to a stop in a clearing on a sloping side hill. He drew in a deep breath as he studied the valley several thousand feet below him, dotted with farms and ranches, stretching to the mountains on the west side of the river. And when he closed his eyes, he felt echoes of the same peace he'd felt as a kid when he'd ridden this fence or searched for lost cattle. Or simply hung out, riding a more reliable horse along this same trail.

This was why he was fighting to keep his ranch. This sense of peace and rightness. He belonged here. This particular parcel of land was not part of the Hayes Ranch, but they'd leased it for grazing for as long as he could remember, and it was one of his favorite places to get away from the old man's scrutiny and criticisms. He had similar places on the ranch proper, where he could disappear for a few hours while appreciating the scents, sounds and simple pleasures of being outdoors. Work had been a similar escape. He knew the fences, the infrastructure, the machinery.

Dodging his father had given him a lot of practical skills.

He turned Clive back to the trail and rode on. They'd gotten past the rocky areas and were now on softer ground surrounded by old timber and deep brush. Rose was, of course, in the brush, making noise that Clive had used as an excuse to test Tanner's boundaries and balance earlier in the ride. The gelding was too winded now to try such nonsense, leaving Tanner free to enjoy his ride.

He'd thought that this boundary fence would be the problem child, since snow tended to accumulate in ridiculously large amounts in places, but so far, other than tightening, everything was in order. When he finally found an area in need of serious repair, it was close enough to the rough track that split the property that he'd be able to bring in posts and wire with the side-by-side and a trailer.

That didn't mean there weren't more challenges ahead, but he was feeling good about the day when he checked the time on his signalless phone for the last time and turned to ride Clive to the rutted mountain road he'd follow back to the meeting area. He whistled for Rose, who pushed her way out of the underbrush and then fell in behind the horse. She was panting happily and covered with little sticky seedpods that he'd have to take care of before she hauled them home on her coat and sowed a new crop of weeds on the ranch. His dog might be getting a little older, but she could still hold her own on the mountain.

His thoughts turned to Whitney, a regular occurrence these days when he let his mind wander. What had she found on her leg of the trail? Was she going to try to fix stuff that needed two people? And was that tug of attraction going to keep growing as he spent more time around her? Or would it dissipate when the novelty wore off?

Tanner didn't see that happening.

He didn't have a firm read on her, but he liked what he saw. Desperation and the need to fit back into the community had driven him to ask for her help, and she'd not only agreed, she'd hired on. Len hadn't seemed too thrilled, but maybe the old man had sexist ideas about ranch workers.

He approached the meeting spot near the spring and felt his spirits lift when he saw her gelding grazing and then spotted her working on the pipe that fed the spring water into a trough.

She looked up as he approached and smiled

at him, and the boost to his spirits became something more.

The woman was beautiful. Wisps of her blond hair had escaped the braid she always wore, and he knew when he got closer that he would admire the freckles scattered over her nose and probably study her mouth for a moment too long. She had an effect on him.

She wiped her hands down her pants, leaving green smears, studied the palms, then wiped again.

"I fixed a blockage." She pointed to the rusty clump of mud and algae lying on the ground. The trickle that had flowed when they arrived was now a steady stream.

"You're good at this ranch stuff," he said as he dismounted and pulled the reins over Clive's head. "You should do it for a living."

Her expression shifted just enough to tell him that he'd struck a nerve, which surprised him.

What kind of nerve?

"I think I'll stick with what I trained for."

"I don't know how you could go back to working in an office," he said. "Look at this workspace."

"I love it," she agreed, but there was a guarded note to her voice.

"Any adventures today?" he asked, changing the subject to the reason they were there.

"I'm not stuck to a tree. I did see a cougar."

"Really? I've never seen one in the wild," he confessed as she picked up her gelding's lead rope, which was dragging on the ground as he grazed. Her reins were wrapped around his neck near his throat and secured so that he could eat without breaking them. "I've seen my share of bears and elk and badgers, but never a cougar."

"It was pretty much a streak in the distance. Charley took offense, but other than that, no adventures."

"The fence?"

"Nothing to address."

They fell in step, leading their horses to the trailer parked fifty yards away. Rose was already there, lying in the shadow cast by the truck.

"Amazing," Tanner said as they neared the trailer. "No flat tires."

"Were you expecting one?" Whitney asked curiously.

"I haven't had an uneventful day in weeks, so, yes, maybe I was."

She tightened her mouth grimly as she gave her head a solemn shake. "Now you've done it. Jinxed yourself."

"I don't think so." He took a chance and dropped Clive's lead rope to the ground, tempting fate while simultaneously proving Whitney wrong as he allowed the gelding to graze while he loosened the cinch. Clive played along for once in his life, and Tanner pulled the saddle off the horse's sweaty back.

Whitney knew exactly what he was doing and gave him a gentle smirk before doing exactly the same thing. The difference was that she was dealing with Charley.

After Tanner brushed the seedpods off Rose's coat, he loaded her into the back seat of Whitney's truck and then they drove down the dusty track to the main road, taking turns opening and closing wire gates. They were almost to his ranch when he said, "When we were talking about the water lease, your dad mentioned that you are part owner of the ranch."

"I am, but he has the majority. He makes the decisions."

Interesting. He knew he shouldn't pry, but her guarded response earlier had hooked his curiosity. "Is there a reason you don't work the place with him?"

"Money."

The immediate answer surprised him. It was logical, yet somehow disappointing.

"I like security and I like nice things," she said, as if sensing his thoughts. "Money helps with both."

"Nothing wrong with either of those, but what about the things money can't buy?" he asked. The cliché had merit in his book.

"I think life is better when it's well funded."

He couldn't argue with her, but was still aware of a niggling sense of disappointment at her reply. He wasn't in a place to talk about nice things, living in Dena's zillion-dollar house and trying to keep his dad's showpiece ranch running, but the Fox Ranch was nothing to sneeze at. It was well kept and orderly.

You want money, too.

He did, but it was to keep his ranch, not to indulge. A shoestring budget was fine, and while he'd been comfortable enough working for the wheat farm, he'd learned good lessons in money management during the lean years when he'd put himself through college. Money was good, but living and working in a place that brought you peace was better.

Tanner shifted in his seat and tried to force his mind elsewhere. Whitney saw things differently. It was her life.

But he still wished she hadn't said that.

THE NEXT MORNING, Whit was woken by her dad knocking on her door. "I thought you needed to be out of here by six."

She grabbed her phone, then let out a groan. Twenty minutes to get ready, catch and saddle her horse, and make lunch. She rarely overslept, but it had been a long day yesterday and it had been a minute since she'd spent the entire day in the saddle.

"I caught Charley for you." Her dad looked up from his coffee as she came into the kitchen wearing yesterday's jeans and a navy flannel shirt over a pink T-shirt, and carrying her boots.

"Thanks," Whitney said, sitting in her chair and pulling on the boots.

"I saddled him, too."

Whit raised her gaze. "Thanks." Her dad never coddled. Everyone saddled their own horses—unless they were going to be late to the job, apparently.

"Made your lunch."

Whitney narrowed her eyes. This was not normal Ben Fox behavior. Something was up.

"Why?" she asked bluntly.

"The meeting is at six tonight." He spoke as if that explained everything, which it did as soon as she recalled the threat of the community board. "If you don't show, I might end up in charge of concessions or something."

"Dad. Don't worry. I have your back. And if I don't, the word you need to practice is *no*."

"Say no to The Trio? Ha. Good one." Ben drilled her with a look that had a pleading edge to it. "Don't be late, okay?"

"Okay." She pulled on her jacket, then fastened the flaps on her saddlebags, which had a fully packed lunch in one side. After slinging the bags over her shoulder, she gave her father a reassuring pat on the arm. "I won't abandon you."

"Thank you. I don't need to be fighting these battles at my age."

"I'll be there," Whit repeated as she headed to the door. The Trio had terrified her as a teen, but she was older and wiser and not so easily buffaloed. Yes, she would do her part for Hearts of the West, as would her father, but neither of them was going to be ramrodded into doing more than they could handle. Not on her watch.

When she arrived at the Hayes Ranch fifteen minutes late, Tanner was waiting at the turnaround spot with Clive, who was saddled and ready to go. As soon as she came to a stop, he opened the rear truck door, tossed in his gear, and then led Clive to the back of the trailer.

"I overslept," she said when she caught up with him at the trailer.

"It isn't like you have to clock in." He spoke in a light voice, but she sensed a reserve and wondered if he'd encountered an event after proclaiming yesterday an uneventful day.

"I have a thing about being on time. Years in the office, I guess," she said as he tied Clive and then exited the trailer, closing and latching the door behind him.

"We were a little more free-form on the wheat farm."

"But you probably worked all night sometimes."

"Oh yeah," he agreed. "Ready?"

"I am."

And she was also concerned about his distracted attitude. Should she ask?

No. She was there to ride fence, not to suss out her boss's personal issues. But Tanner didn't feel like a boss, and they'd made an agreement, which involved his personal life, so...

"Everything okay?"

He gave her a surprised look, as if she was infringing on his business, which in turn made her feel self-conscious. Whit didn't do self-conscious and the fact that she felt that way both irritated her and shut her up, so when he said, "Everything's fine," she turned her mind elsewhere.

Or tried to.

Definite change of energy between them.

She could live with that, but...she didn't like it. When she thought back to how many times she'd worked alongside difficult people on a project, the fact that she didn't like the shift gave her pause. It was almost as if she missed him.

A man she hadn't known for that long.

But with whom she felt an affinity.

There was no denying that, but maybe, as

Maddie had suggested, she'd misread him. Her perceptions were skewed by his business dealings with her dad and the fact that he was wickedly attractive. And he was fun when he played.

Today Tanner opened all the gates and Whitney let him. When they arrived at the turnaround point, they unloaded their horses in mutual silence. It wasn't a petulant silence or a punishing silence, it was more of a Tanner-getting-a-grip silence and she couldn't see how that could possibly involve her. In fact, when he caught her mid-stare, he gave a reassuring smile, telling her that whatever had made him go quiet wasn't personal.

Had he encountered more blowback because of who he was? Possibly so, because after riding the rutted road together for a mile or so, to the place where they'd both left off the day before, his expression relaxed as he lined out the plan for the day, which was pretty much ride fence, meet in the middle. No mention of not getting stuck to a tree.

She missed that. It made her want to… what?

Reach out and touch him? Reassure him? Instead, Whit touched the brim of her hat and she and Charley made a right-angle turn to head through the brush to the fence line half a mile away.

TANNER SUCKED IN a deep breath of pine-scented air. It was good to be on the mountain, feeling the echoes of his teen years. His taut mental muscles began to relax. He'd made two mistakes the previous day. The first was asking Whitney what motivated her and getting the last answer he wanted to hear, and the second was accepting the phone call from his brother.

Grant, being Grant, wanted the second payment Tanner owed him in return for keeping the ranch off the market. He had a business opportunity that he needed to jump on. Tanner had taken a long hard look at the books, and his savings, and figured he could scrape it together with the understanding there would be no more to come. And that Grant would stay off his back about it.

He wouldn't, but the deal would be done, and his brother would have no recourse.

He'd yet to answer Grant, but if he could swing the deal, he would and he would pray that he had no big equipment repairs and that the pivots remained operational, and

Len didn't hurt himself again, so that when Whitney signed off, he was paying one salary instead of two.

Clive picked his way over rocky ground, taking greater care than usual. If the gelding didn't watch himself, he was going to become a dependable mount. Usually when Tanner thought such things, Clive brought him back to his senses in short order, but the horse kept picking his way along the trail. Once they reached flatter ground, Tanner dismounted, giving the horse a break and stretching his legs. The fence, which had to have been a challenge to build in the rocky area, was in decent shape. Saints be praised!

Rose took advantage of the stop to find a nice boggy area to roll in and reappeared at his side sporting a faintly green tinge to her yellow coat. But a lot of the seedpods were now drowning in the bog, so he was good with that. And Whitney had no trouble allowing a smelly, muddy dog into her back seat, so all was well.

Except that part where he'd judged her.

If she was motivated by wanting nice things, as his dad had been, so be it. She'd given him an honest answer and it wasn't her fault that it touched a nerve. Money complicated things. But so did lack of the stuff.

He let out a breath.

Money concerns were controlling him at the moment, and he didn't like it one bit. He reached the end of the east-west fence line half an hour later and turned to the south. If things went according to plan—which wasn't a frequent occurrence lately—then he should run into Whitney soon.

As he did.

She lifted her chin when she saw him, smiled in a way that made him forget money worries and found himself nudging Clive to move faster over the soft earth of the trail. The gelding obliged and he and Whit reined up at the same time, the two geldings touching noses in greeting.

"Good day?" he asked.

"You have remarkable luck in fences. I replaced a bunch of staples, but there was nothing broken, no rotted posts."

He raised his eyebrows. "Did you just jinx me?"

She wrinkled her nose. "I did it on purpose."

They worked their way back to the dirt track that split the allotment and disappeared

over the mountain to another rancher's allotment on the other side of an official Forest
Service gate. He glanced at Whitney as she
moved past him to take the lead on the narrow,
rutted road. There was no getting around his
attraction to this woman who wanted what he
didn't have, and didn't really aspire to have.

If he could make enough money to hang on
to his property, he would be a grateful man.
He didn't need a lot of nice things. He simply
wanted peace of mind.

TANNER WAS MORE talkative on the ride back to
the trailer. They decided on a cross-country
shortcut, and as they left the trail, Tanner gave
a whistle. Rose did not appear. Tanner whistled again.

"That's odd," he said. He pushed back his
hat and scanned the area around them.

Whit had to agree. The Lab enjoyed explor-
ing, occasionally giving a squirrel or chipmunk a good chase, but she never went too
far from her human, since it was her job to
make sure he was all right.

"The last time I saw her, she was chasing
the ground squirrel around the big boulder
near the line shack." She'd made two circles

before the squirrel had headed off in another direction.

Tanner pulled Clive to a stop and whistled again.

Birds sang, a chipmunk scolded them, but there was no sound of a Labrador retriever crashing through the brush.

"This doesn't feel right," Tanner said.

There had been wolves spotted in their area, but surely they would have heard something had the sweet old girl gotten into a rumble.

"Let's head back the way we came," Tanner said.

Whit's stomach knotted as they turned the horses. Like Tanner said, this felt wrong.

The corners of Tanner's mouth were tight as he urged Clive back down the trail the way they'd just come. Whit followed behind as Tanner called Rose's name and whistled. They'd gone close to a half mile when a sound caught Whit's ear.

"Hold up," she said. Tanner's gelding stopped, the clatter of rocks beneath his hooves mingling with the low whimper.

Tanner dismounted, folding his reins over the gelding's neck. Clive lowered his head to shake off the reins and then stepped on one as Tanner walked to the edge of the deep gully behind the shack.

"Rose!"

Another whimper.

"She's down there," Tanner said before he disappeared over the side of the gully. Whit took a few seconds to tie Clive and Charley to sturdy tree branches, then jogged to the edge of the gully where she could see Rose at the bottom, struggling to get out from between two angular rocks where she'd gotten herself stuck. Despite his careful movements, Tanner's feet went out from under him on the steep slope and he skidded the last couple of yards. Pushing himself upright, he rubbed Rose's head, and she licked his hand.

"It's okay, girl," he murmured.

Whit swallowed as she watched the pair. It was obvious how much he cared for the dog and how much the dog cared for him, and Whit was a sucker for such things.

"She must have fallen," Tanner said before trying to get a hold on her to ease her out from between the rocks. The dog yelped and he immediately released his hold.

"Bruised or broken ribs, I imagine." Whit

started down the slope to join him, talus rolling beneath her feet.

"Yeah." Tanner analyzed the situation, sitting back on his heels as he stroked the Lab's head and told her things would be all right. "We need to move that rock. She's really wedged in."

Whit knelt next to the dog and gently felt beneath her. "I'll find a pry pole."

Tanner nodded and spoke to the dog again while Whit took off to find something to wedge between the smaller of the two rocks and the rock next to it. She returned with a sturdy windfall. Tanner took the branch, broke off a few lower limbs, then jammed it into place. The rock moved when he pushed down, then slid back into place.

"I'll hold it and see if you can get her out," he said.

"Let me hold it." She didn't want to hurt Rose and simply wasn't strong enough to lift an eighty-pound dog.

They switched places. Tanner got his hands situated and then said, "Go."

Whit used all of her weight to pull down on the branch. The rock moved and Rose gave a sharp yip as Tanner lifted her free.

He fell back on the talus, holding the dog on top of him as Whit let go of the branch and the rock settled into place. He ran his hands over Rose's side. She had an oozing wound where she'd torn her hide on the tumble down the hill, and she winced and cried when Tanner felt along her ribs.

"It's going to be tricky getting her back to the truck."

"I'll ride Charley back, unhitch the trailer, then drive up here."

"Windfall across the road," Tanner said. "We'll have to get her out on horseback."

Tanner carried Rose up the hill, no easy task with the loose scree moving under his feet. Whit mounted Charley, who was the more reliable of the two geldings, and Tanner eased the dog up in front of her, across her thighs. Whit gave the dog a gentle pat.

"She knows we're not hurting her on purpose," she said.

"Yeah." Tanner's features remained tight even though the first part of the rescue had been successful. He mounted Clive and they made their way down the mountain, following the rutted road that cut the allotment in two. When they got to the trailer, Tanner eased the dog off the saddle and laid her on the ground. Rose tried to get to her feet, but he put a gentle hand on her, stopping her.

"I'm worried about internal injuries if she broke ribs."

"Our ranch vet is good," Whit said. "I'll call her."

"Thanks," was all he said, but there was no mistaking how much his dog meant to him.

Whit headed to the truck to open the back door to allow Tanner to set Rose on the rear seat. The Lab closed her eyes, but her tail gave a few reassuring thumps before he closed the door.

Whit drove faster than normal as they headed for town, watching Tanner out of the corner of her eye as she drove. He stared straight ahead.

"I know she's going to be okay," he said to the windshield.

But she was hurting, and no one wanted to see that. Whit reached out to touch his arm and he shifted his gaze. She met his hazel eyes and felt a rush of compassion tinged with something deeper before dragging her attention back to the road.

"You might want to slow down," he murmured.

Indeed, the last wire gate was fast approaching.

"My brakes are good," she replied in the same low tone he'd used.

She sensed the look he gave her as she slowed the truck, but she wasn't setting herself up for another flash of discomfort. The guy put her off her game. She didn't want to react to him the way she was, but what could she do?

WHIT MADE IT to the vet's office in record time. The office had just closed, and the waiting room was empty. Tanner left Rose on the back seat of the truck where she was comfortable and followed Whitney into the clinic. Whitney greeted the receptionist by name—Callie—and then Dr. Leonard, a harried-looking older woman, came from the back and followed the two of them out to the truck. Rose lifted her head and thumped her tail again as the doctor ran her hands over Rose's sides.

"Let's bring her in, get an X-ray," she said.

Whit headed to the clinic door to hold it open while Tanner eased Rose off the seat.

A moment later, he surrendered his girl to a vet tech and then followed the canine gurney to the examination room. Whit hung back and Tanner wished that he could tell her it was okay to go, but she was his ride, and it wasn't like he could call an Uber or ask Len to pick him up.

When Tanner rejoined Whit half an hour later, he had what he considered good news. "Bruised and cracked ribs, no breaks. They suspect a concussion, so they're keeping her overnight for observation. They stitched up the gash, and other than being sore, she's going to be fine."

"Poor girl," Whit said as Tanner sat beside her on the hard wooden bench. "She's so sweet and trusting. You hate to see her hurting."

"It's tough," Tanner agreed. "She wants to go wherever I go, but she'll be ten this year, and isn't as agile as she used to be. But when I leave her at home, it breaks her heart."

"She'll be back on the trail before you know it," Whit said, leaning her shoulder into his in a reassuring way.

And wasn't it funny that it was a shoulder bump that made him realize how much he liked this woman?

She was fun, tough, empathetic. Ridiculously attractive. A ranch girl who'd made it in the corporate world and had every intention of going back. There was so much about her that he liked, which was why he needed to step back.

It was plain to see that despite this odd little interlude, with her helping him find a foothold in the community and his hiring her to work on his ranch, they had different goals and motivations. They had little in common in that regard. She was going to leave the area and land a high-powered job because she liked the security that money brought. There was nothing wrong with that. He, on the other hand, wanted to pull the place he loved out of debt and squeak by. Yes, that was about money, too, but he was willing to sacrifice financial security in order to keep his ranch.

He was about to speak when the receptionist said, "Mr. Hayes. I have some forms."

Whitney suddenly got to her feet, as if remembering something, then said, "I'll meet you outside."

When he stepped out of the building a few minutes later, he found her texting.

"Am I keeping you from something?"

Her head came up. "There's a meeting I was supposed to go to with my dad. I was just telling him what happened and that I'm taking you home."

"Is it important?"

"He should be able to hold his own." Tanner cocked his head at her dubious tone, and she explained, "It's a community board meeting. They're making plans for the Hearts of the West event and Dad's deeply afraid of being strong-armed into doing more than he has time for. He's kind of a pushover when it comes to these things and, unfortunately for him, people know it."

"I'll go with you."

"I don't think you know what you're getting into."

"How so?"

She let out a breath. "You're fair game."

"I don't understand," he said slowly.

"Go to this meeting with me and you will. When it comes to assigning tasks, the women who run the community board are... How shall I put this?" She folded her arms over her chest as she gave a quick glance skyward. "Like wolves stalking sheep. The sheep being the community members."

"They can't be that bad."

She studied him for a moment, as if giving him time to change his mind. Finally, she said, "I guess you can find out if you like. My dad will appreciate it."

Tanner jerked his head in the direction of the truck. "Let's go."

A faint it's-your-funeral smile curved her lips, making him wonder if he should heed her warning. But there was no way he could do that. Not after she'd helped him get his dog to the vet.

"If you insist," she said in a grim voice. "We'll consider it another step in the Hayes reputation rehabilitation."

CHAPTER SEVEN

THE LARKSPUR COMMUNITY HALL was located in the original Larkspur High School, a 1920s-era brick building that had been converted into offices. The gym now served as a meeting room and when Whit and Tanner stepped inside, the maple boards squeaked under their feet. Immediately, all eyes turned toward them—and, Whit noticed, her dad's eyes held a hint of desperation in their depths. Glancing up at the massive whiteboard behind the table where The Trio and their minions held court, Whit understood why. There was her father's name next to—Whit gave a mental groan—Prize Solicitation. What were The Trio thinking?

One look at Debra's face answered that question. They were thinking that Whitney was home and would take over for him. But what if she got a job before Hearts of the West, which was a month away?

Tanner and Whit took seats behind her dad, and Whit patted one of his stiffly held shoulders. "I'll handle it, Dad."

"You couldn't have saved me," Ben whispered over his shoulder. "I even said no. It didn't help."

"Whitney," Debra Crane said brightly. "Can we also put you down for the solicitation of prizes?"

"That won't work for me." The words came out sharply, but Whit didn't care, even though she'd clearly heard a gasp from the audience. She had had a day, and she wasn't about to be ramrodded into something she didn't want to do. Not when she could help with other assignments more efficiently. She was tired of allowing the fear that, if crossed, The Trio might resign the board, to allow them to continue to push people around.

Debra was in the middle of writing Whit's name on the board when she stopped and turned toward the room. "Excuse me?"

"I don't want to ask for donations and neither does my father. We'll help in another capacity." Whit spoke firmly, causing Debra's eyebrows to approach her hairline.

"I'm sorry, but we've already—"

"I'm happy to volunteer for the setup committee. It's closer to my skill set and certainly closer to Dad's."

Whit felt her father shift in his chair, but she didn't look at him, fearing that if she broke eye contact with Debra, the woman would finish writing her name on the whiteboard.

"It only makes sense to match people to their skills," Whit continued as if schooling the woman, which she was, in a public forum no less. But it was time to rein in The Trio. "We might hide it, but my dad and I are not public relations people."

"Obviously," Margo muttered from her chair at the front, but she spoke in a low enough voice that she could deny saying anything at all. Behind her, people were starting to murmur and Whit wondered if she might have started a low-key uprising.

"I appreciate all the work that the board puts into this, and I want to help," she said. "Please put us, my father and me, on the setup committee. You have openings."

Debra, obviously not used to having her steamroller tactics questioned, made a quick goldfish impression, opening and closing her mouth, then she turned to erase Whitney's and Ben's names from the prize solicitation committee with a slash of the erasing cloth. She then added them to the setup committee, forming their names with vicious strokes, and dotting the *i* in Whitney's name with a stab that flattened the marker head.

Margo let out a sigh and stood. She held out her hand for the marker, which Debra passed over before sitting.

"Would *anyone* like to procure prizes?" she asked. "Anyone here with that *skill set*?"

Whit let the verbal arrow bounce off her and was gratified to see that two people raised their hands, albeit tentatively. Both names were erased from other committees and added to prize solicitation.

And so it went for the next ten minutes, with people resigning from assigned committees and being added to others. The Trio was no longer having fun. People had struggled against them in the past, and a lucky few had gotten their way, but tonight had played out differently. Whit wondered briefly if they would abandon their positions, then decided that they loved power too much. They'd come up with other means of control.

Which they did in short order.

Margo's forehead was shiny by the time the committees were all sorted out. She let out a breath, drew herself up and turned a smile toward Tanner, whose chin came up, and when Whit glanced sideways, she saw a clear deer-in-the-headlights look on his face.

"Mr. Hayes, how nice to see you. We appreciate you volunteering for the setup committee. Can we also count on the usual generous donation from the Hayes Ranch?"

Whit guessed that Tanner had no idea what that donation might be, since she felt him shift in his seat beside her.

"The facility rental," she said out of the corner of her mouth. The community did not own the historic barn and grounds where Hearts of the West was held, and it was the only place suitable for the event, which had expanded every year.

"How much?" he murmured back.

"A few thousand, plus the insurance."

Tanner went still and Whit had to fight not to turn to him. He cleared his throat but before he could speak, Debra gushed, "We are so grateful for your family's continued support. It means so much to the community. When you didn't reply to our letters, I was concerned, so…again, thank you for showing up personally."

Whit's quick sideways look took in a stony profile.

Was he not a charitable guy? Or was it simply the way Debra assumed that the donation was a done deal that rubbed him the wrong way?

Whit decided to go with the latter. It certainly put her back up, even as she was basking in the afterglow of her victory.

"I owe you that chocolate cake you like so much," Ben murmured as they walked out of the meeting fifteen minutes later. Tanner had gone to speak with Debra, then caught up with them at Ben's truck.

"How long have those three been in charge?" he asked.

"Forever maybe?" Ben said.

"No one wants the job," Whit added, "so that allows them to go mad with power. They know they're bulletproof."

Ben glanced Whit's way. "Maybe you and Maddie and Kat should take over."

"That'd be grand, Dad." She mock-punched his shoulder. "I appreciate what Margo, Debra and Judy do. I would just like them to soften their tactics."

"I'd be careful," Ben said. "They'll be gunning for you next year." He turned to Tanner. "How's your dog?"

Tanner filled him in on Rose's condition, then said, "By the way, everything is squared away on the water lease. Stop by Harris and Sons offices anytime to add your signature. After that, I'll have Len handle the details of the diversion."

"Great." Ben smiled at Tanner, then turned to Whit as he pulled his keys out of his pocket. "Guess I'll see you at home?"

As Whit and Tanner headed to her truck and trailer, she murmured, "Sorry about that. I can truly say I didn't see that coming. I thought at worst they'd assign you to a committee that you were ill suited for."

"I ignored the letters. They're on my desk. I didn't open them, because I assumed they were for some community event I wouldn't partake in."

They stopped next to the trailer and Tanner climbed onto the running board to check the patient geldings waiting inside, then lightly jumped back to the pavement.

He looked down at Whit and said, "That'll teach me."

She gave a perfunctory smile.

The ride to the Hayes Ranch was accomplished in silence, but it wasn't the oddly uncomfortable silence that they'd traveled in that morning, when Tanner had been preoccupied. Apparently, he'd worked out whatever that issue had been, only to be presented with a new one.

When they arrived at the ranch, Tanner suggested that Whit leave Charley there rather than hauling him home and bringing him back again in the morning when they headed back to the mountain.

"Unless you need a day off."

"I do not," Whit said. She didn't want to kick around the house, waiting to hear from the recruiter she'd contacted the day before via email. Yes, she had to go back to work, but she wasn't in a hurry.

"I'll drive tomorrow." He gestured at the trailer where the horses were starting to shift restlessly now that they were on the ranch and familiar smells were coming in. "The boys can have a sleepover."

"Sure." Charley and Clive had bonded. They

weren't ready to share a feeder, but they could share a corral.

They unloaded the horses, and released them into a good-sized pen that already had sweet-smelling hay in the feeders. Tanner's mare was in a separate pen, so Whit felt secure leaving Charley for an overnighter.

When she headed back to her truck, Tanner fell into step with her but there was something in the way he carried himself, the energy he exuded, that told her something was up. Something beyond his dog and the results of the board meeting. Instead of opening the truck door, she turned to him. The night air was soft on her face and the breeze teased the wisps of hair that had escaped her braid. She pushed them back in an almost impatient gesture.

"Is something wrong?" It was more of a statement than a question, which Whit had discovered long ago usually gave her a quicker answer. Simply assume something is wrong and state it as a fact.

Tanner's chest rose as he pulled in a deep breath. His eyes seemed darker than usual in the artificial light shining down on them from the overhead pole fixture. Dark and troubled.

"I can't afford what they're asking for."

The stark statement sent a minor jolt through her. "You can't?"

If he had told her that he was flying to the moon that night, she wouldn't have been any more stunned.

"No." He dropped his chin, then shook his head and lifted it again almost immediately, as if he wasn't going to let life defeat him. "The ranch is in the red and I'm fighting to get it out."

"How?" Whit immediately regretted the question. "None of my business."

"Dad made some financial mistakes." His lips twisted in a cynical way as he said the last words. "And he was too proud to tell us." The twist became a full-on smirk. "Classic Carl Hayes."

Whit pressed her lips together. She couldn't find words. Didn't want to find words. So instead she lifted a hand to touch his face, causing a swirl of warmth to flood through her as she stroked the stubbled plane of his cheek before she casually dropped her hand.

His gaze had darkened at her touch, and he started to lift his own hand, only to let it fall again.

He was fighting something. Maybe reality. She had no way of knowing, but her heart, which she considered dependable in most circumstances, did exactly what she didn't want it to do. It started twisting. She wanted to be empathetic but…distant. Was that even possible?

This wasn't a dog she was dealing with. This was a man. So much more dangerous.

But when had she ever stepped back from danger? Except for that one time at the alligator farm…

"No one knows?" she asked.

He shook his head. "And they won't. Right?"

Whit's gaze snapped up. "If you don't trust me, then why—"

The look on his face stopped her cold. He did trust her, or he wouldn't have told her the truth.

"Okay," she said. "When are they expecting the check?"

"I put them off, told the tall lady that I had to talk to my accountant. I doubt that Dad funded them last year, because things were tight according to the books, but appearances meant a lot to him, so maybe he scraped the money together somehow. I don't know."

"Okay. Let me think on this."

"I'm not asking for you to get involved." There was a fierce note in his voice. He cleared his throat and said, "Since I asked you to help me with my reputation, I thought you should know that there's a reason for my apparent stinginess. And that you may soon be released from that duty." He spoke unironically, as if working for him had been a duty.

Whit cast about for solutions, as she always did when confronted by a problem.

"I don't need to be paid for helping you." It would have been nice to bring in a paycheck to help tide her over, but she had free rent, as her dad had mentioned yet again that morning, and when she was done on the Hayes Ranch, she could take another temporary job that paid. She wasn't going to cause her neighbor, whom she was beginning to like more than she probably should, additional financial difficulties.

Tanner had other ideas. "You will be paid."

She thought not, but she wasn't going to have an argument under a yard light that turned them both blue. Instead, she gave him the same look she'd given her dad upon finding out that they were in similar circumstances. "Thank you for telling me. It helps me understand a few things."

Like the moment on the mountain yesterday where she'd probably come off as money hungry and he'd clammed up all of a sudden.

"When you come to work tomorrow, I want things to be as they were this morning. In other words, I'm paying you."

They studied each other in the oddly blue light.

"We'll figure something out," she said softly.

"We?"

Her chin came up. "I took you to that meeting."

"But you are not responsible for what happened there."

She begged to differ. She was responsible for some people being more comfortable in their Hearts of the West work assignments. She was also responsible for bringing him into harm's way, and putting him into a situation he had no way of getting out of while saving face.

Tanner took a step closer, and Whit became aware of the fact that his nearness only made her want to close the space between them even more. Suddenly she wasn't thinking about paychecks or getting Tanner off the hook for the venue rental. She was thinking about the guy in front of her who smelled so good. Whose hazel eyes were searching her face for answers.

If only she knew the question.

Whit broke first, but probably not in the way Tanner expected.

"We've got to be unified on this," she said in her corporate team-leading voice.

He frowned at her. "In what way?"

"In a you and me way. You can use my help. You may as well accept that I'm going to give it."

"Okay." The word came out grudgingly. Tanner was not a man who was used to being forced into teamwork. And there was still something in his expression that part of her wanted to answer. When his gaze dropped thoughtfully to her lips, Whit knew it was time to de-escalate.

"We'll handle this together," she repeated firmly.

"I'm not—"

Whit put a hand on his upper arm, effectively cutting him off before rising onto her toes to gave him a quick, casual kiss. So casual that he had to get the message that she was putting whatever it was that they were feeling into the friend zone. If she was romantically interested, she wouldn't have given him such a chaste little kiss. And she wouldn't have stepped out of reach so quickly after delivering it.

At least she hoped that was the message she sent.

"The deal is sealed," she said as if she couldn't still feel the warmth of his mouth on hers.

He touched his mouth with the side of his index finger. "Good sealing," he said.

"I'll see you tomorrow." She walked the few steps to her truck and pulled the door open. "Take good care of Charley."

TANNER POURED HIS second cup of coffee at 5:30 a.m. to his surprise, he'd fallen asleep almost instantly the night before, then awoken at 4:00 a.m. and lain staring at the ceiling, worrying about his dog and wondering if he'd made a mistake telling Whit the truth about the ranch finances. Wondering if that quick kiss had been a gesture of understanding or pity or what. Or perhaps it was exactly as she'd said—a gesture to seal the deal. It wasn't the first time she'd touched him. He knew because he remembered every instant that she'd made contact. A hand on the arm, a pat on his cheek. A kiss on the lips.

Whatever had prompted the kiss, it had stirred a longing in him that rivaled his concern for his dog and his indecision as to how to make the community donation that was so obviously expected. The quick little kiss made him realize that he was alone, which was not a healthy state of being.

He turned his mind back to the donation. He could change his yes to a no. He may have to, although it would have to be soon, because at this point the community board was counting on him to provide the venue rental fee. He should have opened the letters from the board, but had considered them the mail equivalent of spam. He'd have to watch things more carefully in the future.

Say no or come up with the money?

Saying no was not going to help him get future plumbers and mechanics. It might not hurt, but he didn't know. That was the problem with returning to the small town he'd only known as a kid. He wasn't familiar with the players or the unspoken rules. Whit was guiding him.

Whit, who'd offered to work without pay. As if.

He got to his feet to pour a third cup of coffee. The light was on in Len's house, but that was not unusual. Sometimes Tanner wondered if the old guy slept with his lights on, but kept the thought to himself. Len was an efficient manager, but he wasn't exactly warm and fuzzy. He liked to be left alone, and frankly, Tanner liked leaving him alone. Unlike the foreman's relationship with Carl, which Tanner would have called a friendship of sorts, theirs was more of a professional relationship. Tanner had grocery shopped for the old man a time or two while he was recovering from his injury, but Len had recently told him that his nephew Kenny—a kind of squirrelly kid who seemed resentful of Tanner—had volunteered to take over the job.

But Len knew the ranch, and Tanner could depend on him. So what if he didn't want to be friends, too? Tanner had his own friends... who lived seven hundred miles away in the middle of Washington State. And it looked like Whitney might also qualify, if he could put his growing feelings aside.

After finishing his third cup of coffee, Tanner headed down the hall to shower, only to be stopped by the landline ringing—at 6:00 a.m. He reversed course and answered on the third ring.

"Is this the Hayes Ranch?"

"It is."

"Your steers are in my grain field."

"My steers—"

"Are in my grain field. I'd appreciate it if you'd get them out of there. Now."

"Where are you located?"

"I'm your neighbor to the east. Stevens Ranch."

"I'll get right on it," he said. Because his neighbor's next step would be to call the brand inspector, who would confiscate his cattle. He was kind of surprised that hadn't already happened, given the way his dad liked to fight with the neighbors. That would be a nice bit of payback.

He went to his room to change out of his sweats into jeans and the first shirt he put his hand on. He yanked on his socks, jammed his feet into his boots and headed down the hall. The house seemed empty without Rose showing him the way to the kitchen, but at least he knew she was in good hands.

He grabbed his jacket off the hook by the side door and headed to Len's house. The old man yelled for him to come in after he knocked, and Tanner opened the door to find Len seated at his table, an old-school game of solitaire laid out on the table in front of him.

"The steers are out. Stevens's property."

Len's head jerked back. "I thought you had that girl ride the fence."

"I did."

"Doesn't look like she did too good a job of it."

Tanner let the comment slide. "Right now, I just want to get the steers out of trespass." Thereby hopefully shoring up his relationship with the neighbors. Unlike his dad, he recognized the value of getting people on your side, which was one reason he was going to come up with a way to make the usual Hayes Ranch donation to the Hearts of the West event.

"I'll go with you."

Tanner shook his head. "Whitney should be here soon. I'll take her with me." Len looked like he wanted to argue, so Tanner added, "I want to check the fence with her. Find out what the problem was."

Len made a silent "ah" and then Tanner heard the sound of an engine in the distance. "She's here. I'll keep you posted."

Tanner went behind the barn to catch Clive and Charley. By the time he led the geldings out of the corral, Whitney had pulled up next to his truck and trailer.

"Change of plans," he said, tamping down the part of him that lit up upon seeing her. She might have given him an I've-got-your-back kiss, but she was still his employee and they had work to do.

"How so?"

"The steers are in the Stevens Ranch grain field."

A frown brought her eyebrows together as the realization struck that she'd ridden the fence the steers had to go through to get to that grain field.

"No way. That fence was tight." She spoke with such indignation that, despite having to spend the morning rounding up steers instead of doing the work on his agenda, Tanner found himself fighting a smile. Not that he was going to let her see.

"I guess we'll find out," he replied in a neutral tone.

"Guess so," she said. She set her hands on her hips and looked out across the field to where she'd ridden the first day, then brought her gaze back to him, a flash of challenge lighting her eyes. "If the fence was breached at one of the spots where I fixed it, I'll eat my hat."

"WOULD YOU LIKE ketchup for your hat, or will you eat it plain?"

They'd driven to the Stevens Ranch, spotted the steers in the grain field before the ranch buildings came into sight, stopped the trailer and unloaded the horses. The first step was to find the breach in the fence and see about pushing the steers back through it. The break was at Whit's repair.

She picked up the wire with the metal sleeve that had clamped the two broken pieces together still hanging on one end. One of the wires had slipped free.

She gave a defeated sigh and let her chin fall to her chest in a very un-Whitney-like way.

Tanner pushed back his hat. "The sleeve failed. It happens."

"Easy for you to say. You didn't get all egotistical about your fence-fixing abilities. Now I have to eat crow for the second time this month."

"The first time being...?"

"When I came to you to ask you to please continue the water lease with my dad after you messed up my car."

"Which as you now know, I would have done anyway because I need the money. You didn't need to eat crow."

"Argh." Whit raised her fists to the sky. "Wasted crow."

Tanner couldn't help but smile. He loved it when Whit did Whit, and if he wasn't careful, he was going to fall in love with this woman. Which in turn made him glad that they'd talked about what they wanted in life so that he wouldn't make any mistakes in that regard. Whitney wanted a comfortable life with nice things, and he wanted to hang onto a debt-ridden ranch. That put them firmly in the just-friends zone.

But with Whitney looking at him the way she was now, with that sassy smile on her lips, he had to admit that he wouldn't mind making a few minor errors with her.

"Let's push them through."

They remounted their horses and circled the steers, who were spread through the grain field, bringing them into a bunch, then pushing them toward the opening. Once the lead steer figured out where the break was, he dashed through, and the rest followed.

"I'll get the tools," Tanner said.

The steers began to scatter, working their way through the trees, seeking out the tender grass that grew in the sunlit areas. Whit guarded the break, in case one of the steers decided fresh grain shoots were better than young grass, but none of the cattle seemed interested in returning to the field.

Tanner fixed the fence the exact same way that Whit had, but he used two sleeves instead of one, crimping them with extra force. Maybe she wasn't the only one who was egotistical about her skills.

"By the way," he said conversationally, "I'm still waiting for you to out-cowboy me."

"Maybe that's already been done. Maybe you don't know defeat when you see it."

"That makes no sense."

She laughed, unconcerned, and started packing tools.

"Any news on Rose?"

"Not yet. I plan to call when we get back."

They rode back to the barn side by side through the uncut meadow grass. Tanner explained how he'd leased out part of his farming for the same reason he'd leased the water, but that he still had hayfields to tend to once his crew showed up.

"Until then, I'm hanging on as best I can. Len will be on his feet before long and then I should be able to spend time maintaining equipment and other fun things."

"You have corrals to clean," she pointed out.

"I know."

"I'm good with a tractor," she said as she leaned down to open the gate from her horse.

"Show-off," Tanner muttered.

"This is part of out-cowboying you. It's the small skills that win things."

"Yeah, yeah, yeah," he groused as he rode through the gate. "Stand back."

Whit did as she was told and was impressed that Tanner managed to maneuver Clive so that he was able to close the gate. The gelding jumped forward when Tanner tried to drop the latch, almost unbalancing him, but overall, it was impressive.

"Bravo," she said. "Clive is coming along."

She began leading Charley to the trailer, thinking they'd put some work in on the tangled stretch of fence on the mountain that Tanner had told her about, and be done with it, but he stopped her.

"It's late. We'll work around here today, go to the mountain tomorrow."

She gave him a sideways look. "If the steers don't get out, that is."

"Are you questioning my fencing skills?"

"Just curious to see if they stand the test of time."

Tanner seemed lighthearted today, which made her wonder if he was trying to distract her from his confession the night before. Deflection by banter.

The guy needed breathing room after telling her the truth about his ranch.

Maybe she did, too. Maybe banter was the way to handle their relationship from here on out. It would simplify matters, but it wasn't like they could banter their way to a solution for the venue rental issue. She'd meant what she'd said about being a team, but it was up to Tanner as to whether to enlist her help.

She thought about that as she unsaddled Charley and then released him into the corral. Tanner took his time with Clive, brushing him down before leading him to the pen. Whit rocked back on her heels, hands in her back pockets, waiting for orders when he returned to the horse trailer.

"Since you're good with the tractor, let's see what you can do with those corrals."

"Happy to," she said.

And so she spent the afternoon cleaning corrals and stacking the compost in piles to be spread on the fields after breaking down. It was a tiring job, and a dusty one, but she'd made some decent progress when Tanner waved her to a stop. And by some miracle she'd managed to spend most of the time thinking about her future—her real future. She needed to get busy with her job search, up her networking game and call her former coworkers to see where they'd landed.

Tanner appeared at the gate of the corral she was finishing and made a slicing motion across his throat, followed by a gesture to indicate that she should leave the tractor where she was working. Whit lowered the bucket, popped the lever into Neutral and shut down the machine.

"How'd you spend your day?" she asked as she joined Tanner at the gate.

"You don't want to know."

The grease marks on his shirt and arms told her that maybe she didn't, but she took a guess. "Baler?"

"When isn't an older baler fighting back?" He held up a bottle of water, damp with condensation, and she took it gratefully. "The vet phoned, so we're calling it a day."

She lowered the bottle from her lips and wiped the moisture off her mouth. "I can work without you, you know."

"Or you could come along."

"The vet already knows you're a good guy. She saw you with your dog."

"Right."

They continued toward the area where Whit was parked, walking side by side.

"About yesterday," Tanner said.

She took a stance, water bottle gripped in one hand. "We aren't going to argue about pay again."

There was something about the way he met her eyes that caused her to shift her weight. No. This wasn't about pay.

"You kissed me," he said simply.

That. Yes. Whit launched into a Crocodile Dundee impression. "That wasn't a kiss," she drawled. "*This* is a…" Her voice trailed off and her lips unconsciously parted as she met his eyes.

So much for deflection by humor.

"You were saying?" he asked in a much better Australian accent than her own.

She cleared her throat. "I was saying that was just a deal sealer." So much for her tactic of a casual kiss putting them in the friends lane.

"Okay." He glanced down, toeing the gravel with his boot in a thoughtful way. "My lawyer never does that."

Whit gave up trying to save face—as if she had a chance.

"You want a kiss?" she asked, expecting him to back off after she'd drawn her line in the sand.

"Wouldn't mind." There was a light of challenge in his eyes.

Whit rarely let a challenge go unanswered, so even though her heart was now pounding, she stepped forward to put her palms on either side of his face. She slowly drew his mouth down to hers so that there was no question of consent. He could step back at any time.

He did not step back.

Their lips met in a kiss that was warm and sweet and promising. Maybe a little too promising.

Whit's breathing was ridiculously uneven when she dropped her heels back to the ground. She met his gaze as if seeking reassurance that she wasn't the only one who felt that way, then found herself back in Tanner's arms as their lips met again in a deep, heady kiss. And when the kiss ended, Tanner gathered her against him in a way that felt so right that it was scary.

Really scary.

Whit jerked back.

"Whoa," she said.

Tanner moistened his lips. "Agreed."

"I can't afford to… I mean…" She cleared her throat and stopped with the embarrassed schoolgirl act. "That was hot."

Tanner nodded.

She shook her head. "We can't do that again."

"That might well be a mistake."

"Bad timing," she continued as if he hadn't spoken. "I'm job hunting. I work for you." *I'm*

not ready for another complication in my life.
She put her hands on her thighs and let out
a breath.

"Totally bad timing."

When she looked up at him, she could tell
that he understood. He was not insulted by
her retreat.

She could have kissed him.

She didn't.

He reached out and brought her in for a
gentle hug. A brotherly hug. Maybe if he gave
her a noogie, she'd believe it was truly brotherly, but it made his intentions clear without
having to hash things out. Thank goodness.
So much better than her own attempt to make
her intentions clear.

Whit stepped back and for a moment, they
considered each other from a safe distance.
"Yesterday was so serious," she said. "The vet,
the meeting, the…" She didn't have to say the-
ranch-is-broke-confession because he understood. "And now today—"

"Is a different day."

She gave a choked laugh. "Yes, it is." She let
out another whoosh of breath, then brought her
hands together. "What do you say we go get
your dog?"

WHIT DIDN'T KNOW who was happier during the reunion at the veterinary clinic—Rose or Rose's dad. The Lab's midsection was bandaged, but Dr. Leonard said she foresaw no issues now that the danger of concussion had passed.

"Take the stitches out in seven days," Dr. Leonard directed. "Call me if there's any change in behavior. She had a good dose of antibiotics, so the wound should heal just fine. You can take off the covering tomorrow. Keep an eye on it."

"Thank you." Tanner leaned down to stroke his dog's head inside the cone of shame, then straightened again as the door opened and Margo Simms from the community board came in carrying a lopsided cat carrier in one hand.

"Mr. Hayes." She beamed at him, but Whit knew that the beaming was all part of the control process. "I was going to call you."

Tanner gave her an uneasy smile.

"You have been generous in your support."

"It's a good cause."

"Indeed, and we have had a small hiccup."

"A hiccup."

She set down the carrier and the cat inside

gave a plaintive yowl as she took Tanner by the sleeve and led him to the side of the room, far enough away to make it look like she was seeking privacy, but not far enough away that Whit and Callie the receptionist couldn't overhear the conversation.

"Today we got word that the venue rental fee has increased," Margo said in a stage whisper. She gave him an expectant look.

"I'm sorry to hear that."

Obviously not the answer that Margo had expected. She waited for more, but Tanner remained silent. The message was clear, but Margo refused to accept.

"And your father *generously* footed the entire venue rental in the past, but I want you to know that we *can* cover the overage from the community fund." But it was obvious that Margo did not want to go that route.

Callie met Whit's eyes, her own widening at the little drama playing out in front of them.

"Right."

An awkward silence followed the single word. Tanner smiled tightly, Callie shifted her position, and Whit decided it was time to intervene before the receptionist made popcorn to eat as she watched the action.

"Tanner, I hate to interrupt, but I have that appointment. I'm going to be late if we don't leave now."

"When would be a convenient time to call you?" Margo asked Tanner.

"I'll be on the mountain tomorrow," he said. "No service." He made no offer to call her back, which wasn't going to help with his reputation rehabilitation plan.

"Tomorrow evening, then." Margo made it sound like a done deal.

Tanner nodded rather than reply and took the leash from Whit. They left Callie to deal with Margo and made their way to the truck. Rose whimpered when Tanner helped her inside, then licked his hand after curling up on the rear seat.

They drove out of town in silence, then Whit said, "Just because your dad footed the bill for Hearts of the West, it doesn't mean that you have to."

"I think it does. If I want to get help on the ranch, I need to follow through on the one thing that put my dad in good graces with the people of this town."

"Don't let pride—"

Tanner shot her a look.

"Okay. Do let pride stand in your way." Whit lifted her gaze skyward before refocusing on the road ahead of them.

"I'll figure something out," Tanner said. "We're good."

CHAPTER EIGHT

NO HARM, NO FOUL.

But no matter how often Whit repeated the mantra, she couldn't shake the feeling that she'd just started going down a slippery slope by kissing Tanner Hayes. It wasn't the first time she'd impulsively kissed a man, or shared a hot kiss, but it was the first time she'd done it with a man she worked for. Or a close neighbor. Or her dad's business associate.

So many reasons not to have done it, but while Whit questioned the wisdom of the kiss, she couldn't bring herself to regret it. Tanner Hayes had a way with his lips, so her only regret was that the man had enough worries without adding her to the list.

That said, what a kiss.

When she got home, her dad was still in the fields, so she retired to her command center at the dining room table, which was rarely used for dining, and pulled up her job search information. She wasn't settling for just anything, and between selling her car and living rent-free, she had time to find the best fit instead of taking the first thing that came along, as many of her colleagues had to do.

She skimmed the list of openings on several sites, answered an email from a recruiter, then put the laptop to sleep. But she didn't move away from the table.

Something was off. She'd been slow to start her job search, but that was because of the latent burnout she'd suffered, coupled with the shock of being axed. Honestly? She'd thought she'd be safe in a layoff situation.

She didn't want to find herself in that same situation again.

No guarantees. You know that. In other words, it was time to get it together and take her chances on a new job. Just as in the corporate world, things on the ranch could change on a dime, and she wanted her family ranch to have a security blanket. She wanted to be able to afford nice things. She didn't want to scrimp and make do, as she'd done for most of her life.

Did that make her shallow? Whit didn't think

so. She liked the life she'd built in Missoula. Liked having money to burn, and liked the prestige of her position. Taking a backward step, having her safety net pulled out from under her and moving back home had been difficult.

So why wasn't she actively doing more to find the perfect job?

Because she had the luxury of time, and because there was no real reason not to be momentarily distracted from her goal by doing some ranch work and hanging out with a guy who was unexpectedly witty and caring and—

Stop it, Whit.

It was time to stop thinking about Tanner Hayes.

She leaned back in her chair, stretching her arms over her head. The truth was that she didn't want to obsess over her future, as had been her practice in the past. There truly was no reason not to enjoy these early days of summer, because she'd have a job nailed down by autumn. She would work on the Hayes Ranch for a few more weeks, ride Charley in the mountains, help her dad set up for Hearts of the West.

But she wouldn't be sharing any more kisses with Tanner Hayes.

WHITNEY'S TRUCK PULLED into the driveway at exactly the same time as it had yesterday. And the day before. Whitney was punctual and serious in her work ethic, which were the traits Tanner told himself he would dwell on. Good employee traits.

He couldn't keep a straight face as he lied to himself. Whitney was a beautiful woman who would spend a few weeks in his life, then move on. She knew her own mind, made plans, stuck to them.

Rose lifted her head when Whitney knocked on the door.

"Got any coffee?" she asked after he called for her to come in.

"Always." Tanner felt a whisper of relief. They were post-kiss cool.

Whitney went straight for Rose, crouching down to offer commiserative words concerning the collar of shame and injuries. She gave the dog a few gentle rubs on her chest, probably one of the few areas that didn't hurt, then stood.

"Has Margo hunted you down yet?" she asked as Tanner set a mug on the table. It wasn't the tar she preferred; for that she'd have to wait a few hours.

"I turned off the ringer on the landline and she doesn't have my cell number."

"Oh. I gave it to her," Whit said innocently. "Was that wrong of me?"

"Not funny," Tanner said as he took his chair. "I have never ducked someone like this in my life. I hate feeling like a weenie."

"You were never in the sights of The Trio before."

"I'm calling Margo tonight and telling her that…" His voice trailed as he rubbed a hand over the back of his neck. "I don't know what I'm telling her."

"Tell her that you'll provide the venue."

His gaze came up. "I think you're missing the point."

"Hold Hearts of the West here. On your ranch."

"Here?"

She nodded. "Here." She leaned forward. "The idea came to me as I was driving over. You're not that far from town and I know for a fact that there are people who want to get a closer look at the place. Particularly this house."

Tanner realized that he was staring. So did Whitney. She smiled as if waiting for him to come up to speed, which he was.

"What do you think it would entail?"

"A few weeks of headaches—some major, some minor—but think about it. You would get yourself in solidly with the community—"

"And you wouldn't have to parade me around town like a prize sheep," he pointed out.

"No. I'm still going to do that." Whit gave him a reassuring pat on the arm. She met his gaze as she did so, as if to say, "See, we can touch in a friendly way."

She was setting the tone, helping to keep them in the friendship zone without things feeling weird.

"Do it," she urged. "Call Margo and give her your offer, and tell her that due to your finances being tied up after your dad's passing that it's the only solution that you can offer. You did put her off earlier by mentioning your accountant, so…"

"I wish you would have come up with that finances being tied up thing earlier." Why hadn't he thought of that simple solution?

"I was trying to save my own skin at that meeting. And back then, I thought you could afford to write a big check."

Strange how it felt good to have someone in

on the secret other than Grant. Even Len was in the dark, as far as Tanner knew. The only way the foreman would know that the ranch was in trouble was if Carl had told him, and Carl hadn't even told his own sons the true state of affairs.

"Well?" Whitney asked.

"I need more coffee." Tanner got out of his chair and crossed the kitchen to the island. He brought the pot back to the table, poured, then put the pot back.

"I've never been to a Hearts of the West event. What would it involve?"

"Okay. A little background. It started while I was in college. The money goes to the community fund, which does a lot of good deeds. They used to hold the event in February as a Valentine's Day celebration called Hearts of Winter, but after three blizzards in a row caused three cancellations in a row, they moved it to June and changed the name."

"It's a Valentine's event in June."

"They don't call it a Valentine's event, but they use hearts as a theme for everything. And it is a little romantic, what with the cow flop contest and all."

"Cow flop?" Tanner gave her an uncomprehending look.

"Surely you…" Whit looked at the ceiling as if he was hopeless. "They make a big grid on the ground with chalk, number the grid, people buy squares, then they turn out a cow and the square that she goes on wins."

"A cow poop contest."

"Exactly."

"I hope there are other events?"

"There are. That's the only one that involves a cow."

"Good."

"There are vendors, kids' events, dinner and dancing. It's lots of fun. And if you held it here, all you'd have to do would be tolerate people coming and going. Think of how many people you'd get to know again."

"I didn't know that many before I left. Just a few close friends." He could see now that he'd isolated himself during high school, with the exception of that small handful of friends he'd mentioned.

"Time to rectify that."

Tanner studied the table as he considered just what he was getting himself into. He loved the idea of not writing a big check. Loved the idea of changing the Hayes reputation.

He looked up at Whitney. "This won't get in the way of the ranch work?"

She shook her head. "Shouldn't."

"Are you going to lead me down this path, then get a job and abandon me?"

"It's a possibility."

He considered, then gave a slight nod as he came to a decision. "I'll call Margo."

Whitney touched his sleeve and gave him one of her fascinating slow smiles. "This will be fun."

"I'm glad you think so, because you will be my right-hand in this endeavor."

"I don't know about—"

"Right hand."

She smiled. "Got it."

"I LOVE BEING able to meet regularly." Kat stirred her cocktail, giving Whit a satisfied look. "All three of us. Just like old times."

"We're going to milk it for all it's worth until you take off on us again," Maddie added.

"It might be a while before that happens," Whit replied. Both of her friends perked up, and she let out a sigh. "I mean, I am getting a job elsewhere, but it won't be instantaneous."

Maddie stabbed her straw into her drink a few times, then she looked up with a cheeky grin. "I heard that you caused quite a commotion at the board meeting."

"That you broke the bonds of tyranny," Kat said.

Whit rolled her eyes, but had to admit to some truth to the words. "I got tired of cooperating with uncooperative people."

"I heard rumors of a statue in the town square," Maddie said in a hushed voice.

"If only we had a town square," Kat added.

Whit laughed and leaned back in her chair, giving a quick look around. The pub wasn't very full, so they could talk without anyone overhearing. Tonight she didn't have much to say, preferring to listen to Kat tell stories about the latest wild scheme her rambunctious brothers had come up with and the challenges of co-parenting a young toddler.

Maddie soon had them in stitches, telling stories of her guy, Sean, helping out at the bridal boutique.

"You're quiet tonight," Kat said to Whit.

"Nothing to report," she replied easily. Fixing a broken waterer wasn't news, and the actual news she had, she couldn't share until Tanner had firmed up the details of holding Hearts of the West on the Hayes Ranch. Once things were settled, they'd discuss.

Kat launched into a story about her fiancé Troy trying to shoe a noncooperative pony, and Whit had to admit that the affection in her friends' voices when they talked about their partners stirred a touch of envy in her.

It was a good kind of envy, she decided. The kind where you don't begrudge your friends, but hope you can have what they have someday. She'd like to eventually experience raising a toddler and coming home to someone dependable. She could see it happening in the distant future.

But at the same time, she liked the solo life she'd built. Liked providing for herself and having the security of her career. Yes, it involved a desk and computer rather than people and the outdoors. She may be missing out in some areas, but life had a way of balancing out. Her mother had shared that message many times when things in Whit's young life had taken an unfair turn, and she hung on to those words.

Things would balance out.

"Earth to Whit?"

Her chin snapped up. "Sorry. I was…thinking about Mom."

Kat tilted her head and raised her glass in a silent salute. Maddie followed suit and they all drank.

"I have a proposal for you," Whit said after a beat of silence. It was one of the reasons she'd suggested drinks tonight.

"Yeah?" Maddie pushed her glass aside.

"Given proper notice, would you like to help push Hayes's cattle to Old Timber Mountain?"

Kat raised her hand. "I would."

Maddie grinned at Whit. "A day on horseback? Count me in."

"I'm not sure when, but we've ridden the fence and it's almost ready to go."

"All you have to do is to say the word," Kat said, "and you'll have two enthusiastic day hands."

"It'll be like the old days," Maddie added.

Kat lifted her glass again. "To reliving the good old days." She gave Whit and Maddie a wicked grin. "So, you want to go tip some cows or something?"

"WHAT ARE YOU DOING?" Tanner asked Len. He'd knocked on Len's door after Whit had gone to work in the corrals and was surprised to get no answer because Kenny's motorcycle was parked outside. Then he'd heard the sound of a tool dropping in the shop.

Len gave him a guarded look. "I'm fixing the carburetor on the Weedwacker. I'm still useful around here."

"You are," Tanner said matter-of-factly. "Just don't push things."

"I was thinking that I could also maybe work on that float in waterer number 2. It's still high and I—"

Tanner shook his head. "Whitney will do it."

Len let out a frustrated breath and stood straighter, holding the wrench against his palm. "I'm just gonna ask. Is she a danger to my job?"

Tanner gave a surprised laugh. "No. She's here to help until she finds a job."

"And if she doesn't do that?" Kenny asked.

Kenny didn't seem to be a bad kid, if one overlooked his tendency to be as defensive as his great-uncle. His distressed jeans hung low on his skinny hips, and the oversize T-shirt had seen better days, but that was all just a fashion statement. The kid took good care of his uncle.

"She's not a permanent hire." Kenny and Len exchanged looks and Tanner asked, "Is there a reason you don't believe that?"

"I heard that she likes this job, which might make her want to keep it."

"News to me," Tanner said, and if Kenny had heard such a thing through the grapevine—well, he didn't put faith in grapevines. "Where did you hear this?"

The kid shrugged. "One of the guys who works for Joe at Clinton Automotive."

Gossipy Joe speculating. He met Len's gaze. "You have seniority. You will not be replaced."

He was also injured and may never be 100 percent again. It was easy to read the older man's concern.

"Len. You have my word."

"The word of a Hayes. Huh."

With that, Len went back to his carburetor and after a brief glance his way, Kenny joined him, leaving Tanner just this side of mystified. He almost asked why Len, who'd stuck with Carl Hayes until the end, would say such a thing, then decided he didn't want to know what might have gone on between Len and his father. If Len wanted him to know, he was free to tell him. If not, then he and Len would work out their own relationship over time.

Tanner left the barn and headed to the house to make that phone call he'd been dreading. He poured a cup of tar, turned off the coffeepot heater, looked up Margo's number and dialed. She answered on the first ring.

Tanner took a quick sip, grimaced, then said, "Tanner Hayes, Ms. Simms. I wanted to talk to you about a possible venue change…"

After outlining his offer, which would literally save him thousands of dollars he didn't want to spend, he was rewarded with a long silence. Knowing The Trio's contrary way of thinking, he half expected the offer to be summarily rejected.

"This would be a way to help introduce myself back into the community. To…give back." Tanner rolled his eyes. He did want to give back, but it sounded so hokey when he said it aloud.

"I can't speak for the board," Margo replied after a thoughtful silence. "But I can call an impromptu meeting to discuss."

Tanner used the opening to explain that after

his father's death, there were still some financial issues being ironed out and he couldn't be depended on for that big check.

Margo perked up like a bird dog on a scent when he mentioned financial issues.

"I'll get back to you," she promised.

"Do that," Tanner said. He hung up the phone thinking that no matter which way things went, he was in for some headaches. Either his reputation would suffer in the community because he'd broken his father's tradition of buying community support, or his ranch would be the site of a major event with lots of comings and goings, setups and cleanups.

Grumpy Len was going to love that.

Margo called that evening. The board had indeed held an emergency meeting and they would like to visit the ranch tomorrow to see if it would do for the event.

"That large meadow of yours would be perfect for the tent," Margo gushed, "and the views…"

They planned for a midmorning get-together the next day, which meant that Whit would be working alone, at least until he could catch up with her after the meeting. If this worked out, he would save face and he wouldn't lose money he couldn't afford to spend just yet. He wouldn't be the jerk Hayes Ranch heir who refused to continue his father's attention-getting traditions.

Next year at this time, he'd make certain he had enough money in the bank to pay for the usual venue, thus leaving his ranch in peace. And he would do it for the good of the community, not so that he could exert some sort of control over people.

He was a different kind of Hayes.

"How DID IT GO?" Whitney asked the next morning after arriving for work. The sun was just topping the trees when she pulled in, creating little streaks of sunlight across the driveway and encouraging the songbirds to give it their all as they greeted the day.

He pushed his boot toe into the gravel. "I'm not sure whether I'm delivering good news or bad."

"They approved."

"And asked for a tour of the house."

Whitney grinned. "Nosy, aren't they?"

"Curious. They did say that they missed Dena."

"I never knew her."

"She kept Dad in line. Her secret weapon was that she didn't care." Whit sent him a look and he explained, "She just ignored all the stuff that sent me over the edge."

"What kind of stuff?"

"Judgment, I guess. Let's just say it was hard to live up to his standards. And if I did—"

"He raised the bar."

"Yep."

"That couldn't have been easy."

"It made it easy to leave home," he said.

"That's sad."

"We made up later."

"For real?"

He hesitated, as if not wanting to address what was real and what wasn't. "As much as was possible. We pretended, hoping that if we pretended long enough, it would start feeling real."

Whit absorbed the words, but said nothing. It broke her heart, to be honest. She and her folks had been the epitome of land-rich, cash-poor as they scraped by year after year. That scraping had been the reason she'd given up her silly dream of becoming a horse trainer—not to mention buying the Hayes

Ranch—and gone into renewable energy production instead, a field where she could flirt with upward mobility.

She'd lived like a college student for the first few years of employment, funneling money into the ranch in return for a percentage of eventual profits. Thankfully, her dad managed to turn the ranch around. With Whit's help, he paid off the last of her mom's medical bills and was able to sink some money from his second job into the place. Now the Fox Ranch was holding its own, with a full crew and, surprisingly, more head of cattle than the Hayes Ranch had. The fields were in good shape, and thanks to the water lease, they would soon have more land under production.

At this point in time, the Fox Ranch was doing very well after two decades of struggle. The Hayes Ranch was not, but no one, save for her and the Hayes brothers and their accountant and lawyer, knew the true lay of the land.

Strange how things played out.

"Are you still on board to help me drop off my car tomorrow? Clinton Automotive called to remind me."

"How about I meet you in town?" he said, leaning back on his heels. Whit met his gaze, told herself not to be drawn into those hazel depths.

"Great," she said in an upbeat voice. "We can grab breakfast. My treat."

"I might not be able to afford a venue for a major event, but I *can* afford bacon and eggs."

She almost said something about receiving graciously, then decided that given the circumstances and personal pride, he didn't need a lesson in etiquette.

"We'll split the check."

Tanner rolled his eyes, but he didn't argue.

"I have good news," she said.

"Yeah? Shoot."

"Maddie and Kat are game to help move the cattle whenever we drive them to Old Timber, so one less worry there."

"I should pay them."

She gave him a *really?* look. "No. You shouldn't. That isn't how things are done and you know it." When neighbors helped neighbors, the only payback was the promise of reciprocation in the future. And maybe a big lunch or dinner on the ranch.

"I guess I'm used to more transactional relationships."

Whit shook her head as if dealing with a difficult student and took a slow, swaggering step closer to the man, with the intention of making her point—neighbors don't pay neighbors. The proximity effect was immediate. An instant recollection of how it had felt to be wrapped in his arms.

You're close enough, her small voice shouted.

Whit had to agree with her inner warning system. It would be easy to step out of the friend zone, to replay that hot kiss and really muck things up. She wouldn't do that. She might be impulsive, but not in the life plan area.

"You were about to say something?" he prompted. Whit could see that he was aware of her inner battle. Was it possible he was fighting the same fight? Because his hands were curled into loose fists, as if he was trying to keep them under control.

She lifted her chin and said, "Yes. I was about to say that if you're going to become part of this community, you're going to have to let that idea go. Transaction worked for your dad. It's not going to work for you."

"I'm going to have to take my chances being a good guy and hope that people notice?"

Whit nodded. "You're playing the long game, Tanner."

And she would keep playing it with him, until she found that she couldn't.

CHAPTER NINE

THE NEXT MORNING, Kenny rode his motorcycle into the ranch just as Tanner was heading out to feed the horses and do a few quick chores before meeting Whitney in town at Clinton Automotive. Kenny usually showed up in the afternoons with his deliveries to his great-uncle, so Tanner ambled over to ask why he was there so early.

"Taking Uncle Len to the Zoo. Doctor's appointment," the kid said as he got off his motorcycle. Len came out of the house and worked his way down the steps.

"Going to Missoula," he called to Tanner in a gruff voice, calling the city by its proper name rather than the Zoo.

"Hope you get good news."

"It might happen."

But Len didn't sound convinced that it would.

While Tanner was feeding Emily and Clive,

Len and Kenny drove away in Len's truck, leaving the motorcycle parked next to the foreman's house. Tanner hoped that Len heard something that would cheer him up, although it was possible that the guy was simply negative and morose by nature. That said, he was still haunted by that "the word of a Hayes" remark.

He was going to broach it, but he would wait until Len was less guarded. The way things were going between them, they might discuss the matter in a year or two.

He was due to meet Whitney in town at Clinton Automotive in forty-five minutes, which gave him time after feeding to open the gates and move the steers into another pasture. He headed out on the ATV, because it was fast. The steers knew the routine and followed behind. Tanner opened the gate, and a few minutes later, the leader, seeing an opening in the fence, began to gallop. His buddies followed and soon fifty Angus flew past Tanner, only a few of the fat, sassy steers feeling the need to throw a playful kick his way. He closed the gate, then glanced toward the waterer fifty yards down the fence line.

The thing was surrounded by a lake, created

by a leak at the back of the unit. He rode the ATV to the waterer and took off the cover to investigate. Not an obvious fix, so he'd tackle it later. That meant heading back to the shop to get tools to shut off the water supply, which was going to make him late, but he wasn't going to have water flowing for the hour or so that he would be gone. By the time he'd finished, he was wet and cold and had just enough time to change his jeans and make sure Rose was comfortable before heading to town.

"THIS IS A BEAUTY," Joe Marconi, the head mechanic at Clinton Automotive, said after Whitney handed him the key fob to her fully loaded Audi TT RS. "You're lucky that we were able to get the parts from the Billings store." His eyes strayed to Tanner, then to the damaged rear end, then back to her. "What a shame."

Whit gave a careless shrug. "These things happen," she said. "The important thing is that I'm able to get it fixed locally."

"I guess so," Joe allowed with another accusatory look at Tanner, who fought an exasperated look as he shifted his weight to his opposite leg. "This was a pristine vehicle."

"What's the time frame?" Whit asked, and after getting an open-ended answer—"depends on if we find other issues"—she turned to Tanner. "You said something about breakfast before going back to work?"

"It's on me." He gave her a *touché* look. "You're on the clock after all."

The guy was good. She hoped they didn't have to arm wrestle for the check after eating. She turned back to Joe. "I'm helping out on the Hayes Ranch while I look for another job in renewables."

Joe bounced a look between them. "I heard you were working there." The wheels were turning in his gossipy head. *Why* was she working there?

"Len's still healing from his accident, so it's neighbors helping neighbors, you know. And Tanner's a good boss."

Tanner cleared his throat, obviously concerned about Whit overplaying her part. "Everything is cleared with the insurance company?" he asked Joe.

"We're good," Joe said.

A few minutes later, when they were seated in his truck, Tanner turned to Whit and asked, "Do you think he suspected that he was being played?" Joe lifted a hand to wave as they backed out of the parking space, then turned to run a reverent hand over the hood of Whit's car.

"No."

"You're that certain."

"Yes."

"'Neighbors helping neighbors,'" he quoted. "Tanner is *such* a good boss."

"You can't be subtle with Joe. And I wanted to be sure he knew it was professional, not romantic. Therefore I emphasized the boss thing."

She was impressed at how offhand she sounded, because thinking about Tanner and romance was becoming a guilty pleasure. It wasn't going to happen. His reaction after the kiss assured her of that, so no harm in the occasional venture into fantasyland.

Especially because, *again*, it wasn't going to happen.

They found a parking spot on a side street and walked to the café across the street from Maddie's bridal shop.

Holly Freely, the red-haired motherly dynamo who owned the café, approached with a coffeepot. "Hey, you two."

And although Whit knew for a fact that Holly was not judgmental, she could tell she was curious about Tanner Hayes. Whit had been acquainted with Holly for a long time. The café had been a favorite high school hangout, and she and Kat and Maddie had their own favorite booth in the back, which was now occupied by an elderly couple.

"You know Tanner, right?"

"I haven't seen you since you were in high school," she said, pouring coffee in both cups. "I guess I did see you from a distance," she added musingly, holding the coffeepot in front of her, "with your brother and father, but I don't think you've set foot in here for a decade, at least."

"I was one for quick visits home. There and gone." He smiled, making Whit's breath catch. He wasn't holding back with Holly. "But I'm back for good, and you'll be seeing me on a more regular basis."

"That would be nice," Holly said in a tone that even Whit couldn't read.

"I'm working for Tanner while I job hunt."

"Well, isn't that nice?" Holly said. "You living close and all."

"It is." Whit beamed at the woman. "I get

to spend my time doing things I love while looking for a job…doing something else I love." Internally, she grimaced at that. She didn't love working in corporate. She loved the security it provided and the sense that she had the means to weather storms and to help the Fox Ranch do the same.

"So it all worked out," Holly said, adding, "Good for both of you," before continuing on with her coffeepot, checking tables.

Tanner pulled the menus out of the holder and handed one to Whit. She opened it, even though she knew the contents by heart. Little had changed since her high school years of eating fries and drinking cola and laughing until she was in danger of it coming out of her nose. She closed the menu and set it on the table.

"You know what you're having?"

"Fries and gravy."

He side-eyed her and she reached across the table to touch his hand. "Try it."

He closed his menu without seeming to notice that she'd touched him. Again. "Sold."

Whitney settled her hand back in her lap—but not before Holly, who was pouring coffee at a nearby table, noticed.

"JUST A COUPLE more stops," Whit said when Tanner tried to head to the truck after an excellent breakfast. She was taking this project thing seriously.

But, on the plus side, Holly at the café had treated him with more genuine warmth upon his exit than his arrival. She'd been all professional smiles when she'd seated them, but when he paid for the ticket, she'd made a little joke when handing him his change and her smile had touched her eyes. He had tipped generously and promised to come back soon.

He and Whitney visited several other businesses for minor purchases, with her introducing him at each one as if no one in town had ever heard of the Hayeses, then they stopped at the bridal boutique that her friend owned.

When they walked into the shop, the wedding march sounded, startling him, and a man sitting in a brocade chair looked up from his phone and grinned.

"Yeah. It just comes out of nowhere. You aren't the first to jump." He got to his feet and held out a hand. "Sean Arteaga. Proprietor."

Tanner gave Whitney a quick look. He'd been under the impression that Whitney's friend was Maddie, who'd been with her when he'd rear-ended her car.

"Sean owns half the boutique," Whit explained. "Long story."

"Maddie had errands, and no fittings until this afternoon, so I'm holding down the fort. I have a bride arriving in half an hour. Hopefully Maddie will show up before the bride does, but if not, it's all on me."

He spoke without irony, and Tanner fought a smile. He recognized Sean as a bronc rider he'd watched ride in some of the richer Washington State rodeos. Seeing him surrounded by tulle and lace and talking about meeting with brides was, well, interesting.

"I sold a prom dress a few minutes ago," Sean continued. "Lilac number." He looked at Tanner. "I'm supposed to be a silent partner, but every now and again I am called upon, which means I have to get my hands all gussied up." He held up his hands, which were nicked and scarred but clean as could be.

Tanner did the same and Sean gave an appreciative nod. "Same line of work? Ranching?"

Sean was not a local, and it was refreshing to meet someone who hadn't already formed an opinion of him. "Wheat farming before that."

"I'm heading off to diesel mechanics school in a few months, and after I graduate, I don't think my hands will be allowed in the shop."

"Good hand talk, guys, but since Maddie isn't here, I think we'll be on our way. No offense, Sean." Whit adjusted the two small shopping bags she carried on one arm.

"None taken." He gave Tanner a humorous look. "If you ever need a wedding dress, I'm your man."

Tanner laughed. "I'll keep that in mind."

And he didn't see it happening any time soon.

THE FINAL STOP before they were finally able to leave town was at the grocery store.

"What's it like to cook in that amazing kitchen of yours?" Whit asked Tanner.

"I don't cook a lot."

Whit gave him a disbelieving look. "That's criminal." She let out a breath. "I have no choice but to call the kitchen police."

"I've never been much of a—"

"Whitney! Mr. Hayes!"

They turned to see Dr. Leonard, the veterinarian, coming up behind them pushing a cart overloaded with paper products. "We go through a lot of paper towels," she said.

"I can imagine."

"How is Rose?"

"The stitches look good," Tanner said. "She's resigned to the cone. I don't think she'll disturb the wound, but I don't fully trust her."

Dr. Leonard laughed. "Labs are really good at appearing innocent. I'm looking forward to seeing her again at Hearts of the West. I heard you're hosting this year."

"I am. The committee thought it would be good to change things up this year."

"Test run," Whit said, as if the ranch would be up for hosting the next year if things went well.

When the vet turned her cart around and headed back the way she'd come, Whit said to him, "This hosting thing is gold."

"I'm just surprised how quickly the word spread."

"Are you?" she asked. "Really?"

He made a noise in his throat, acknowledging the speed of small-town grapevines. They could work for you or against you, and in this case, he was hoping for the better outcome.

They continued through the store with him throwing instant food into the cart and Whit rolling her eyes even though she was putting almost the same stuff in her basket. "For my dad," she said when he'd given her a particularly pointed look.

"Your dad likes Marshmallow Crunchios? He looks like more of a cornflake guy to me."

"Appearances are deceiving."

All in all, he'd had a decent day in Larkspur—much better than he'd anticipated—and he had enjoyed parts of it, like breakfast, and walking around with Whitney, being amused and sometimes touched by her insights into their former classmates.

The former star quarterback, now employed by the local service station, had gone the way of the cliché, peaking in high school, but Whit explained that he was better off for it. "His parents were so pushy that I'm surprised he didn't have a nervous breakdown. He's happy now."

Tanner wondered if he needed to look up former quarterback, Dakota Reese, and arrange to have a beer. It appeared they had something in common.

And then there was shy Amber Lee, a woman

who'd graduated a year behind Tanner and was known for spending every free moment in the library. She had, in fact, become a librarian, but she moonlighted as a mounted trick rider during the summer months, traveling from rodeo to rodeo.

"That's something I could see you doing," Tanner said.

She shook her head. "I was set on becoming a horse trainer."

"What happened?" he asked.

"That thing called life."

When they got to the ranch, Whitney set her groceries in his kitchen so they wouldn't get hot in the truck, then fired up the ATV and rode around the pastures, checking the waterers while Tanner worked on the flooded unit. His phone rang just after he finished the repair and was drying his hands on the shop towel he kept in the toolbox.

"Aiden. Good to hear from you." *Please don't tell me you can't make it this summer.*

"Hey, boss. Just checking in to give you a definite ETA. Looks like two weeks on the nose and Coop and I'll be there."

One less battle. Between him and the boys, he'd be able to keep the cattle managed and get the farming done on the acres he'd kept for himself. Whit would move on, and his ranch would be emptier without her, despite having his crew on board.

Such was life. His life, anyway.

He'd just do what he always did and push on.

"I'M NOT SURE how long the Audi repairs will take." Whit dug into her ready-made pasta bowl, twirling the spaghetti onto her fork. "When we left it at the shop, Joe said it would be about a week, but he couldn't say for sure. It depends on whether he finds other issues."

She and her dad had been discussing the wisdom of rebuilding the engine on the old hay truck as opposed to finding a "new" used truck, when Ben had brought up the matter of her car.

"Just make sure he doesn't charge you storage while he waits for parts." Ben smiled grimly. "I heard he did it to Carl Hayes once."

The townsfolk did have their ways of getting back at people who disrespected them.

"I'm hoping that by Tanner being there and being friendly, Joe might look at him through a different lens and not do things like that to either one of us."

"That reminds me," her father said, a slightly cagey note to his voice. "I heard a rumor while at coffee this morning."

"Imagine that. A rumor at the ranchers' coffee klatch."

"It's not a coffee klatch," Ben said gruffly.

Whit set her chin on cupped hands. "What rumor did you hear?"

"You and Tanner Hayes are dating." Her dad gave her an expectant look, and for the life of her, Whit couldn't tell if he wanted her to confirm or deny.

She denied.

"Crap." Whit closed her eyes for a beat, then sat back in her chair. "That was what I *didn't* want them to think."

"Because it's not true?"

"Of course it's not true." She scowled at the table. "I purposely made a point of saying that I was *working* on the Hayes Ranch. I mentioned it at every place we stopped."

"How many places did you stop?"

"Six or seven. I wanted to make good use of my time and I had things to pick up here and there." With Tanner tagging along, looking like a good beau. Had he been carrying bags for her?

Of course he had been.

Shoot.

"Then you aren't seeing him?"

"Are you really asking me that question?" Whit leveled a dark look at her father. "I mean, *when* would I be seeing him? I do my job there and then I come home." Surely her dad didn't think they were flirting with each other instead of working. He knew her ethic better than that.

"Right."

Whit bit her lip as she considered the situation. "Do me a favor?"

"What?" her dad asked warily.

"Tell your coffee kl…" She caught herself. "Tell the guys that we're not dating. Convince them that we're just friends and that I'm working for him."

"Telling and convincing are different things, but yeah. I'll make it a point."

"Just don't make too much of a point, so that they think you're covering something up."

Ben gave her a look. "Like I don't know how to manage my own crew."

"You can distract them by mentioning that Hearts of the West is being held on the Hayes Ranch this year."

"Everyone knows that."

"The Trio is coming to the ranch tomorrow afternoon to take a look. I'll probably be there, you know, to witness the event."

Her dad's eyes widened at this tidbit. "Really? Are you going to keep to the background, or give them what for again?"

"Background. Totally."

Her dad feigned disappointment.

"I did my part at the meeting. I think it's best to stand back for a while."

Ben got to his feet, ready to begin his evening of sports TV. "This reign of terror needs to end."

"You could always run for the board this fall. Bump one of The Trio off her throne."

Ben gave her a wide-eyed look. "Are you out of your mind?"

Whit laughed. "I've got to go job hunt, Dad. I'll see you later."

"THANKS FOR THINKING of me, but it's not what I'm looking for."

Whit ended the call from a recruitment contact who excelled at finding jobs that were below her experience level. Her cell signal disappeared, and she tucked the phone in her front jacket pocket.

"Not a good fit?" Tanner asked conversationally. The call had come just before Whit and Tanner turned onto the road to Old Timber Mountain on their final day of fence repair, following a scramble on the ranch proper as they made it presentable for the all-important visit from Margo, Debra and Judy. The ranch looked good; now the real business of cattle grazing was back on the agenda.

"Nope. And I'm not going to waste anyone's time." Particularly her own.

It was the second offer for an interview that Whit had turned down. She'd worked her butt off to get to the level she'd achieved at Greenbranch Renewable Energy, and she wasn't going to take a position that was several rungs down on the ladder. Not unless she got desperate, and she didn't see that happening, since she'd had several pings already about potential jobs. She'd agreed to one interview the following week, but so far none of the other jobs had met her parameters.

"I'm not taking just any job." He gave her an ironic look and she added, "*This* job doesn't count. I'm doing this as favor to a neighbor."

"Who has a contract with your dad."

"That might have gotten me into this, but it isn't what keeps me coming back."

"What does?"

There was something in his expression that made a red flag go up, but just a little one, so Whit continued. "The scintillating work environment, of course."

"I hear that the boss is an okay guy." He gave her an amused side-eye.

"So some say." She side-eyed him back. "I'm not necessarily one of them."

He growled and she laughed. The guy who people avoided because of his dad made her feel good.

"I'll give you this," she said as she swung the truck and trailer in a big arc at the last gate. "I didn't laugh as much at my old job. It was a put-your-head-down-and-work environment."

"That sounds…efficient."

"I laughed after hours. When I was at work, I worked." Which was why she'd gotten the promotion that had ultimately been her downfall when the buyout occurred.

They unloaded the horses and led them through the wire gate. When Tanner mounted,

Clive stood still, even though the reins were loose on his neck. A big change from the first mount she'd witnessed weeks ago.

"I've been working with him," Tanner said as he picked up his reins. "Don't want to embarrass myself in front of your friends."

Maddie and Kat had agreed to help move the cow-calf pairs to the grazing allotment in a few days' time. "They've seen their fair share of gnarly horses," Whitney assured him. "And we've all hit the ground a time or two."

"Clive isn't gnarly. He's…calculating."

Whitney had to agree. The gelding seemed to wait for the most opportune moment before indulging in an act of control, such as sidestepping or shying at nothing. But lately Clive seemed to be feeling mellow. He followed Charley without bumping him with his nose as they rode the trail, and despite working his tie rope loose when they'd stopped for lunch after fixing the final stretch of downed fence, he'd stayed put instead of disappearing into the timber at a gallop.

Yes. Clive was being a good boy and he continued his good behavior on the ride to the trailer—right up until the grouse flew up out of the underbrush at his feet. He was several yards ahead of Charley when he took to the sky, and Whit had to give Tanner credit for riding him out through a series of serious bucks and crow hops, as the horse took advantage of the clearing where the grouse assault had taken place.

Charley snorted and danced, but trusted that Whit would keep him safe from horse-eating birds. Clive gave one last buck, landed spraddle-legged and blew snot with a loud whistle. Tanner held his position, sitting deep in the saddle, shoulders back, waiting for the gelding to give an encore, then a crash sounded in the underbrush behind Charley, and Whit's trustworthy gelding reached his breaking point. He launched himself sideways at the unexpected noise and went down in the muddy bog just off the trail.

He hefted himself to his feet, leaving Whit sitting in the muck, then gave a full body shake, flinging mud in all directions. Whit wiped the muddy splatters off her face as Charley started picking his way out of the bog, his feet making gross suction noises.

Whit looked over her shoulder to see Tanner standing on the bank, holding Clive's reins. He offered Whit a hand and she took it, allowing him to pull her to her feet.

"Thanks," she muttered.

"What is it about you and gooey substances?" he asked.

"I'm only muddy from the waist down. It could have been much, much worse."

"I'll give you that." The words were barely out of his mouth when Clive hit Tanner with his nose, sending him stumbling forward. He let go with a colorful curse, but somehow managed to keep his feet as he windmilled his arms and sank into slimy mud up to his knees.

He gave Whit a weary look, started to take a step, then stopped abruptly. "My boot is coming off."

Clive started to amble away, his duty done for the day, but Whit snagged his loose reins. A moment later, after Tanner had made it to dry ground with both boots still on his feet, she solemnly handed him the reins.

"I need a new horse."

They walked the last half mile to the truck, water sloshing in their boots. After loading the horses, they made their way to the cab. As soon as Whit sat on the protective canvas seat cover, her pants felt even wetter. She wrinkled her nose as Tanner reached for the key.

"This stuff smells funky," she said.

"And could present a laundry challenge." Tanner put the truck into gear, then glanced her way. "Is this the kind of stuff you were trying to avoid when you said no to full-time ranch life?"

"Not at all," Whit said on a surprised note. "This was the part I liked."

Tanner lifted his eyebrows in a questioning expression. "What part didn't you like?"

"The part where I felt guilty whenever we had to spend a penny. Even a school field trip could be a challenge."

"The ranch wasn't doing well when you were young?"

"My mom got sick just before I went into middle school. Cancer, and the medical insurance was bare-bones. We were squeaking by before her diagnosis, but after...it was awful, and it stayed awful long after Mom passed away."

Tanner didn't say anything, and she appreciated the way he waited until the lump that always formed when she talked about her mom gave way, allowing her to speak normally again.

"I hated going into crisis mode every time something went wrong, and you know how often something can go wrong on a ranch. We had to sell most of the cattle to meet expenses, and we got to the point where we weren't even close to breaking even while I was in college. Dad took on a side job, and he thought he was going to have to sell, which was really hard because the land has been in the family since the turn of the last century."

"That's rough," Tanner said. When she glanced his way, she understood that recent events in his own life made it possible for him to relate to what she was talking about. So she went on.

"I decided that I wasn't going to live like that. If my refrigerator blew up or I needed a car repair, I wanted to be able to handle it without figuring out what to give up. I didn't want to scrimp for the rest of my life, so I said no to ranching, no to horse training and went into something where I could indulge in the occasional luxury."

The result was that when her fridge had broken down, she ordered a new one. She had a closet of nice clothes, a suite of stylish furniture that was now in storage and a great car. The car was going, but she'd get another. Someday.

"Your ranch is doing better now."

"I helped save it," she said matter-of-factly. She gave Tanner a quick warning look. "Don't ever say that to anyone. I don't want my dad's pride hurt."

"I know something about keeping a secret," he replied easily.

Touché.

She directed her gaze forward, watching the clouds move over the mountains across the way. "I lived bare bones in the beginning of my career, funneled cash into the ranch, and we eventually got to a place where we were earning money instead of bleeding it and Dad was able to quit his side job and go back to ranching full time. That's why I don't have as much of a savings cushion as I would like." She let out a breath. "I thought I was safe careerwise and had time to build my savings. I was not."

"Which is why you're selling the car."

"Even though the ranch is doing well right now, all it takes is a couple bad seasons in a row, a few disasters and it could be right back where it was."

Tanner frowned at her, and she realized how doom-and-gloom her attitude sounded, but that was indeed how she felt about ranch life. She loved the work, loved the outdoors, but the risks were not worth the reward.

"I won't live that way," she concluded.

"You mean the way I'm living now?"

"No offense."

"None taken."

But she had apparently given him something to think about because he was quiet for the remainder of the drive home…or maybe he was thinking about Debra, Margo and Judy, who were due to arrive an hour before Whitney went home for the day.

Her dad would be disappointed that she had nothing to report on The Trio's Hayes Ranch tour, but her clothes were a wreck, and she wasn't about to borrow some from Tanner.

TANNER HAD BECOME oblivious to the scent of decaying organic matter and mud by the time he drove under his father's fancy archway, and his wet jeans had warmed to body temperature, but he was pretty excited by the prospect of cleaning up. Whit had at least another half hour before she'd be able to get out of her muddy clothes.

Tanner took the turn off the drive that led behind the barn, and as he did so, he caught a glimpse of a sedan parked in front of his house.

"What the…?"

Whit craned her neck as the barn blocked her view. "I'd say that Debra, Margo and Judy are an hour early. I wonder if they've been in the house?" she asked in a thoughtful voice. "At the very least, they've looked in the windows."

Tanner glanced down at his muddy, funky-smelling jeans and boots. "When you show up early, you get what you get."

"No apologies," Whit said firmly. "If they sense weakness, you're toast."

"Agreed. Two against three. Can we take them?"

"We have to try."

Tanner held up his fist and Whit bumped it before they simultaneously reached for their door handles.

They debated about unloading the horses, decided that it could wait until they were done with The Trio, then made their way through the barn to the main driveway, where three women wearing neat mom jeans and cardigan sweaters were waiting near the front walk.

"Mr.—" Debra's voice faded as she took in Tanner's appearance. Then she swept her gaze over Whitney and her eyebrows inched even higher.

"We had an incident," Whit said calmly.

"We thought we had time to shower," Tanner said, then realizing the way the woman's expression changed, amended his statement. "I thought *I* had time to shower. Whitney is going home."

She gave him an *I am?* look. He nodded.

She turned back to the women. "Yes. I'm going home to shower and do laundry. I'll see you tomorrow morning, Tanner."

Sending Whit on her way was not easy, because Tanner, who could face down an angry drunk in a country bar, was at a loss as to how to handle these three fiftysomething women.

Whit headed for her truck, little clumps of mud coming off her boots as she walked.

"Would you like a moment to change?" Margo asked Tanner.

"I'm good if you are."

"We are perfectly fine," Judy said. She cast a sweeping view around the property. "This will actually be quite lovely for the event. We have to rent a large tent for the dinner, and we were hoping that perhaps, if finances were not *too* tied up…"

"I'll spring for the tent. The one thing I can't do is to spend a lot of time here managing setup because I am running a ranch." Shorthanded, at that.

"That's perfectly fine, Mr. Hayes." Debra sniffed. "It seems that Whitney has that skill set."

"And I'll have my foreman Len Anderson keep an eye on operations while she's working."

"Len Anderson?" Margo said, as if she wasn't aware that the man was employed by the Hayes Ranch.

For a moment, Tanner thought that the ladies might change their minds. They exchanged glances, made a few unusual faces at one another and then, without a word being spoken between them, nodded in unison. The silent exchange was borderline spooky, and the opening scene of *Macbeth* shot into his head.

Tanner pushed the thought aside and said, "Great. Perhaps we can meet and discuss liability and those types of issues."

"That sounds marvelous, Mr. Hayes."

"Tanner." He held out a muddy hand, then pulled it back again. "We'll have to pretend," he said.

Judy's smile was genuine, and he thought maybe he'd made a breakthrough.

"We'll be in touch, Mr.—Tanner," Margo said before leading the way to the sedan. The women climbed inside and a moment later drove away.

The dust from Whit's truck was still settling when they left, because she'd lingered near her truck for a while before pulling out. It slowed the ladies down, but Tanner waited until they were out of sight before letting his muscles relax. Those women had a gift for putting people on edge.

He stood in place for a few more seconds, debating whether to tell Len about his new duties—which he truly hoped the older man would agree to—then decided to clean up instead.

Rose came out from under the porch, where she'd been sleeping and perhaps hiding from the community board, and greeted him by pushing the edge of the cone she still wore against his hand. Tanner ruffled her fur, apologized for not being able to take her with him that day and noted that she'd made a trip to a faulty waterer. Her underbelly was almost as muddy as his clothing.

He'd chase that down after he changed his clothes.

When he went into the house, he instantly noted little bits of mud that hadn't been there when he'd swept the floor that morning.

No wonder the ladies, who'd been curious before, hadn't asked for a tour. It appeared that they had welcomed themselves into his home, or at the very least had opened the door. Rose had joined them, flaking mud as she went.

"Yeah. I watched them," Len said when Tanner visited the man a half hour later, with his hair still damp from the shower. "They just opened the door and kind of yoo-hooed. Only one of them went inside and it wasn't for long. Your dog followed her in." He gave a small snort that might have been a laugh. "She had a hard time getting her out again."

Which explained the scrape of mud he'd noticed on Judy's slacks.

"So they didn't riffle through drawers or anything?" Tanner was being facetious, but he had to admit he didn't think such a thing was impossible.

Len considered. "I don't think they had time." He gave Tanner a sideways look accompanied by an almost smile, and Tanner sensed his second breakthrough of the day. He hated to ruin it, but he did, by explaining to Len that he would soon be the grand overseer of the Hearts of the West setup.

"Me?" Len scowled. "And why here?"

"Community relations," Tanner said. "Dad burned so many bridges that I have to do something."

"He did do that," Len said.

Len had worked for his dad for longer than anyone, but apparently had no warm feelings for the man.

"I don't want anyone screwing things up," Tanner said.

"Yeah. I can keep an eye on things. It'll feel good to be useful again. Doctor said it'll be a bit until I can operate a clutch."

"Len, if you handle the community board, you don't need to worry about clutches."

In fact, if Tanner had any kind of windfall in the near future, he'd give the man hazard pay.

CHAPTER TEN

BEN WAS STUFFING jeans into the top-loading washing machine when Whit let herself into the mudroom. He did a double take, then said, "Tell me you weren't trying to catch ducks again."

"I haven't tried to catch a duck since I was ten." She grimaced as she looked down at her filthy jeans, stained with black organic-rich mud.

"It smells like you were in the duck pond."

"Nope," she said cheerfully. "It was a bog on the mountain. Charley dumped me."

"Charley?"

"There was a lot of excitement at the moment." She motioned toward the door, indicating the need for privacy. "I'll finish loading your clothes and throw my stuff in."

"No. I don't want that nasty mud all over my clothes. Leave yours on the floor and we'll do them later."

"Fine." Her dad had always been better at laundry.

He finished loading his clothing, started the machine, then left the mudroom, pulling the door shut behind him. Whit grimaced again as she kicked off her boots and water dribbled out, then she eased out of jeans that insisted on clinging to her skin. Gross, gross, gross.

But again, all in a day's work. Things like this were *not* the reason she didn't want to go partners with her dad and work the ranch. It was her outside job that allowed her to infuse enough cash to become a silent partner owning 20 percent of the ranch. Twenty percent of the ranch profits wasn't going to support her, and even if it would, she didn't trust that the operation would remain solvent. Her dad was a rancher to the bone and accepted the whims of markets and weather as the price he paid for living the life he loved.

You love it, too.

She did. But she was a realist. Not everyone got to combine their job and lifestyle. It was better to go with the sure thing: a monthly paycheck instead of semiyearly lump sums at sale time, company-paid benefits, a retirement plan.

Then why aren't you hitting the job search harder?

Because she was being picky. She had that luxury at the moment, and although she had yet to flesh out Life Plan Number 3, she knew what she didn't want. So far that had been everything the recruiter had thrown her way.

When she went into the kitchen, wearing the chenille robe she kept in the mudroom for emergency strip-downs, her dad was sitting at the table with a printed spreadsheet in front of him.

"I got some donations for Hearts of the West," he said proudly. "Not by myself, but I was there."

"What? Really?" Whit sat across from him and turned the spreadsheet so that she could read it. Sure enough, there were businesses marked off. She gave him an incredulous look. "I fought to get you onto the setup committee."

"And don't think for one minute that I'm not grateful. Harold got put on prize procurement because he missed the meeting, so the guys and I had mercy and went with him. He needed moral support."

Whit went over the spreadsheet, dragging a finger down the first column. "Let's see. L&M Construction. Good one. Daisy Lane Daycare. Okay. Walt Stenson." She raised her gaze, then read on. "Littlegate Farm. Uh-huh." Whit looked up again. "Gee, Dad. Did Kat help you?"

Because every one of those businesses had a link to Kat or her fiancé, Troy Mackay.

"Troy joined our ranch meeting group."

Definitely not a coffee klatch.

"He comes a couple times a week while Kat watches the baby. It's good for his farrier business to make contacts."

Whit nodded at the spreadsheet. "Did Troy make that?"

"Harold got it from Margo. Anyway, I thought I'd let you know that I sucked it up. It's easier when you don't have to do it."

"I'm proud, Dad. It's good to expand your skill set." She grinned as she mocked her own words. "Just keep it secret, okay?"

"I'm not foolish. I know what would happen if you-know-who found out." Ben folded the spreadsheet in half and put it on top of the stack of papers near the landline. "What do you do on the Hayes Ranch?" he asked.

"Today I bog surfed."

Her dad didn't even crack a smile. "And…"

"I'm still riding fence and checking waterers. I dug out a ditch the other day. After we put the cows on the mountain, I may do some range riding. Tanner is going to have to get busy in his fields in a bit. First cutting is coming up, so I'll handle things until his crew arrives in a few weeks."

"Do you like what you're doing?"

"Well enough," she said, recognizing the potential for a fatherly ambush.

Her dad knew not to push when she spoke in that tone, but he wasn't able to keep himself from saying, "You seem happier. More relaxed."

"It's the mud baths, Dad."

He pressed his mouth flat, his way of acknowledging a touché, then slapped his cap on his leg. "I gotta head out. Dinner is every man for himself."

"My favorite kind," Whit replied.

Ben put on his hat at the door, then stopped and turned back. "The Hayes Ranch is still pretty nice?"

"You'll get to see for yourself when we set up for Hearts of the West."

"Guess I will." Ben drew in a breath. "What made him do it? Hosting the thing, I mean?"

"Community relations. Tanner is trying to overcome his dad's reputation."

"He doesn't want to control everyone with his checkbook?"

Whit felt guilty as she said, "I think he would prefer to have people respect him because he's a decent human being."

Ben's gaze became thoughtful, then he said, "Looking forward to seeing the place."

With that, her dad stepped outside, closing the door after him, leaving Whit to wonder if she really was more relaxed. If so, what had she been like before?

Stressed from work.

Who wasn't? She managed her stress just fine, thank you very much. She'd simply have to make an effort to leave the job, whatever and wherever it might be, behind when she visited her dad in the future.

THE NUMBERS WERE not looking good.

Tanner leaned back in his chair and closed his eyes. He'd been laying out hypotheticals and yes, he'd squeak by this year and the next, as long as they got rain, paying off the debt as he went, but would he be able to bring the place out of the red in three years, in order to avoid having to sell?

It was going to be nip and tuck. If cattle and hay prices held…he set the pencil on the table and rubbed his eyes, then stilled as he heard a noise outside. It was daylight, but too early for Whitney to arrive for work. He got to his feet and went to the window. It was quiet outside except for the early-morning bird songs, and he was cognizant of an empty feeling as he went back to the table where he had his calculations spread out.

The ranch felt better when Whitney was there. He didn't want to think about what that meant, because frankly, it was threatening to his peace of mind. He didn't trust easily, didn't get attached and when he hit a point in a relationship where he had to bare his soul, he stepped back. Always.

Yet he'd told Whit about the ranch being insolvent.

Different kind of trust, he assured himself. It would hurt his pride if people knew what shape the ranch was in, regardless of the fact that he hadn't been the one to put it there. But it wouldn't ruin him emotionally.

Different kind of trust.

Whit understood his issues because she was allergic to scraping by, and would eventually take a job that gave her the security that was so important to her. She needed a secure job. He needed his ranch. He didn't care if it scraped by as long as he had it. He would rebuild it. Make it his. Pay his brother a yearly dividend.

Maybe burn down this house.

He regarded the beautiful room in which he worked and wished that his dad and Dena hadn't sunk so much money into renovating the house. Poor use of resources, but appearances were all-important to Carl Hayes.

As they are to you, or you wouldn't be keeping the finances a secret.

Maybe he was like his dad in that regard. No one wanted to be seen as a loser. He might have inherited his losing hand, but he found himself unable to share his father's guilty secret—except with Whitney Fox.

WHIT WAS PEELING a hard-boiled egg for her Sunday lunch when her phone pinged with a notification for a video call. She quickly rinsed her hands and pushed Accept when she recognized the name on the screen. Her relationship with Rob Ketchum had been close to love-hate. The guy had great ideas but was terrible when it came to execution. As he'd laughingly put it, he was the brains and Whit was the brawn. He never seemed to notice that Whit never laughed at his joke.

"Hey, cowgirl," he said with a laugh when Whit came on the screen.

"Hey, yourself. How's the new job?"

He gave her a coy look. "That's why I'm calling. They have an opening at Tullamore Wind and Solar and they've yet to fill the position. If you're interested, they'd be happy to interview you. I sang your praises."

"Would I be working with you?"

"We're a great team, you and me. I'm the—"

Whit couldn't handle hearing that she was the brawn yet another time, so she cut him off. "Is it in New Mexico?"

"Albuquerque."

She liked Albuquerque.

"I'm gonna cut to the chase," he said in an upbeat voice. "Are you still in the market for a job, and would you like to interview for TWS?"

"Tell me more about the position."

Whit took a seat at the table and jotted down notes, then asked Rob to send her the details via email.

"So, should I tell them you'll do an interview?"

"I'll take a look at the information you sent, and I'll get back to you tomorrow. One question, though—will I be working under you?"

His tone grew serious. "We might have the occasional project together, but this place is set up differently than Greenbranch. This is a great opportunity, Whit. Excellent people. A real team environment."

"I'll let you know after I look everything over."

After ending the call, Whit went to the sink and continued peeling her egg, then rinsed it, salted it and took a bite. She smiled as she chewed.

A job had just come looking for her.

"WHAT'S UP?" Tanner asked as Whit waltzed into the shop where he'd been blowing the dust out of the riding lawn mower Len had made good use of the previous day, preparing the big lawns for the Hearts of the West setup.

"I have an interview."

His stomach sank, which was silly. And telling. "Do you need time off?"

"It's a video interview. I could do it here between chores."

"Is it a job you'd consider?"

"It's a good one," she said. "It's in New Mexico."

"That's a bit of a distance."

"The company is working on some serious renewable energy opportunities and needs someone with my expertise in federal regulations and permitting. The pay is good, the potential for advancement is good. I could keep my car. One of my former colleagues landed there and recommended me."

"Sounds promising. New Mexico is beautiful." It was the most positive thing he could think of to say. It wasn't like he could say that losing the closest thing he had to a confidante was going to leave a hole in his life, but the truth was, he was going to miss having someone to talk to. He was going to miss Whit.

You knew this was coming.

He did. And it hammered home the fact that he was about to be alone. Ally-less. His brother wasn't on his side regarding the ranch. Len was about as warm and fuzzy as an iguana. He'd become dependent on Whit to bounce things off of.

"I went to the hot-air balloon festival in Albuquerque a few years ago and could totally see myself living there."

"Good."

An awkward silence fell, then Tanner said, "When is the interview?"

"Tomorrow. Short notice, but my former colleague just got wind of the position and managed to get me into the system."

"Sounds like a good friend."

Whit laughed. "I did a lot of his work for him. I did it so that I wouldn't look bad when we worked together, but now it has paid off, I guess."

"If they hired someone who slacked, they'll hire you."

"He looks really good on paper. Not at all like the slacker he is. And I do owe him a solid for this." She glanced at the table where he had his papers spread out. "Taxes?"

"Ranch math."

"And?"

He was struck by how easy it was for him to say, "It's going to be a nail-biter."

"Ranching can be that way." She spoke flatly, as if reminding herself of why she was job hunting. "Unpredictable."

"You're making the right move."

"Why did you just say that?"

He hesitated, then spoke his mind. "Because you're questioning yourself."

"Not at all." He lifted an eyebrow, and she tightened one corner of her mouth. "You're right," she confessed. "I am. And I shouldn't be. Other than the distance from home, this is exactly what I'm looking for." She held his gaze. "You'll keep my secret?"

"The interview?"

"The doubts." She pushed her hands into her hair. "I hate doubts. I fought them in college and thought I was done."

"Come here." He motioned with his head as he spoke, indicating that she needed to come closer, just as he'd said.

"Do I look like I need a hug?"

"Totally. And I happen to be in a hugging mood."

"Aren't I the lucky one?"

"Yes, because I don't hug just anyone. Only those people who can do something for me. I'm a transactional hugger."

Whit let out a choked laugh and moved closer, even as a small, cautious part of her warned against following instinct. But the instinct was strong, and Whit didn't feel like fighting. She felt like filling her lungs with Tanner's scent and feeling his heart beating beneath her cheek.

"You do know how to sweet-talk a girl," she said as she came closer, feeling a touch awkward.

"Years of practice." He folded his arms around her, and she breathed deeply, thinking she'd never encountered a guy who smelled better than Tanner, and then laid her cheek on his chest, closed her eyes and listened to his heart.

"Doubts are normal. Healthy, even."

She wasn't thinking about doubts any longer. She was thinking about the trouble she could get herself into if she stayed. The need to settle herself, to get back into the professional groove, was strong.

But what if she could grow something meaningful with this man?

His lips touched her hair in a light kiss and Whit shivered. *Do not fall in love. Don't do it.*

He nuzzled her ear, brushed her neck with

his fingertips, and when she raised her head to look at him, to try to get some clarity as to what the situation was between them, she found herself without words. So what could she do but kiss him?

And kiss him she did. Short, sweet kisses. Long, deep kisses. Lose-herself-in-the-moment kisses.

Finally, she eased away from him, but kept her hand on his chest as she said, "What are we to each other?"

"Allies." He watched her as he spoke, gauging her reaction.

She didn't know if she believed him, but appreciated that he knew what she needed to hear.

"I like that," she said softly. "Allies."

"NEW MEXICO IS a long way away." Maddie closed the back door of Spurs and Veils, and a moment later the muffled sound of the UPS truck starting up drifted into the room.

"I haven't made the cut yet." But the interview had gone well, and she'd know if she would be asked for a second interview in two days. Whit picked up a box and headed back to the steaming area. The biweekly dress unpacking was an excellent opportunity for the friends to bounce things off one another, only today Whit was doing all the bouncing.

"You will." Maddie put her box on the one Whit had just set on the ground.

"How are things going on the Hayes Ranch?" Kat asked as she lugged in the last of the UPS delivery through the back door and set the box on top of the other three.

"They're going good." Whit waited for Maddie to open the top box and then start moving plastic aside.

"You're dating the man, you know." Maddie gave Whit a solemn nod when she raised a disbelieving gaze. "I have it on good authority."

"Bridal shop rumors?"

"My clients are all about happy endings," Maddie said, shaking out a short cocktail-style dress in a delicate apricot color.

It was Whit's turn with the steamer and again her hair was frizzing up.

"Keep me posted. I'm curious as to what Tanner and I will be up to next." Maddie laughed and Whit looked at her over the top of the steamer head. "He really is a good guy and I hope that the community comes to understand that before I leave."

"You sound pretty sure that you'll get this job."

"Nothing is ever sure, but I have a ton of experience and I was recommended by someone they've already hired from my old firm."

"It's just too bad that it's so far away."

"The company has a generous vacation plan. I'll be able to come back several times a year." She'd spoken to her former colleague the previous evening. Her sense that he wanted her there to help him with his job grew stronger as they talked, but everything else about the job met or exceeded her parameters.

"So other than labor issues, Tanner is doing okay?" Whit frowned and Maddie explained, "Gossip. After they decided to change the venue from the Gallagher Barn to the Hayes Ranch, people are talking. And there's been rumors that he can't get help because he can't afford it."

Whit willed away the guilty flush that threatened to give her away. She never lied to her friends and rarely kept anything from them, but she'd promised Tanner, which meant that for all intents and purposes, she knew no more than her friends did about the Hayes Ranch. The secret was in the vault.

"He can't get help because his dad was a jerk and people assume he is, too."

"But he's okay to work for?" Maddie asked.

Whit thought she'd made that clear, but maybe she hadn't.

"I have no complaints," she said.

"Well, you are dating," Kat pointed out.

Whit made a face and went back to steaming. "I like working there. I like Tanner. We're allies."

She ran the steamer head over the dress as she spoke, giving extra attention to a stubborn crease until she realized that her friends had gone quiet.

"Allies?" Kat asked.

"It's hard to explain, but it's not romantic."

Why had she mentioned romance?

Better question—why did she feel so cagey about having said the word *romantic*?

Confession was good for the soul, and keeping things from her friends was not her style, unless it involved other people's finances.

"We've kissed a few times." She gave a casual shrug. "Twice. Three times if you count a quick brush of the lips."

Whit looked up in time to see her friends exchange looks, then quickly busy themselves.

"It's nothing." When her pants didn't spontaneously catch on fire, Whit continued, "The man has a force field around him. He's not the trusting kind."

He had trusted her with certain secrets, but only after they'd shared some trauma and he realized that they had stuff in common.

Whit handed the silky apricot dress over to Maddie and took another, in the same color but a different style. "I know his limitations and he knows mine." They were allies.

"I did hear that things weren't great on the Hayes Ranch after his mom and brother left."

Whit met Maddie's gaze. "How so?"

"Bill Monroe—you know, the deputy on the scene of your fender bender—and I were standing in line at the bank and got talking about the accident. And the Hayes brothers. He said that Tanner changed after his brother went to college. Kept to himself more and more."

"That sounds like he's an emotional abuse victim," Kat murmured.

The steamer head spit as Whit held it at the wrong angle, but no water spots appeared on the dress. She righted the head and continued steaming. "I don't think his dad treated him well, but Tanner fought back. Left home as soon as he could, established a relationship with his dad on his terms. He might have suffered emotional abuse, but he isn't a victim."

If her friends were surprised at her flat statement, they didn't show it. Of course, Whit didn't look at them, either. Tanner had become a touchy subject with her.

Not a good sign, girl. You need to do something about that.

CHAPTER ELEVEN

PUSHING THE CATTLE to the grazing allotment on Big Timber Canyon would have been a much shorter trip if Tanner's neighbors to the east had allowed him to move through their scrubby pasture, but when he asked, he got an unequivocal no.

Good old Dad.

He wanted to ask what Carl Hayes had done to them, but decided against it. The less time the neighbors spent thinking about Carl, the better for him. He just had to somehow convince said neighbors that he was different, and that was where Hearts of the West came into play.

There were already people visiting his ranch, taking measurements, scoping out locales. Everyone seemed pleased with the new venue, and he'd had to give a total of four house tours. People may not have liked his dad, although they seemed quite fond of his checkbook, but that didn't keep them from wanting to see what Dena had done to the place.

Everyone, including The Trio, who finagled the first official tour—not to be confused with their unofficial tour led by Rose—told Tanner how lucky he was to live in such a house.

He was. Now all he had to do was hang on to it.

The cattle filled the county road from ditch to ditch as they headed toward new grass.

A hundred cow-calf pairs were not that big of a cattle drive, and other than the occasional car or truck needing to slowly work its way through the herd, which was blocking the road, it was a quiet trek to the first wire gate.

Len's leg and hip had healed to the point that he could straddle the four-wheeler, and he'd agreed, with a surprising show of cooperation, to allow Rose, who was now cone-free, to ride on the rack on the back. Tanner had worked up a box with low sides so that she wouldn't tumble off when Len gunned the engine, and the Lab was quite content riding drag with Len at the back of the herd.

Maddie Kincaid and Kat Farley rode flank on one side of the herd and Whitney and Tanner rode flank on the other.

Tanner opened the gate and held it while Len pushed the cattle through and Whit brought Charley to stand near him, out of the way of the herd.

"Don't let them spread," Tanner called, and Kat and Maddie expertly brought the cattle back into a line.

"I have a good crew," Whit said.

He smiled at her. "So do I."

She pressed her hand to her chest in a gratified way, and he grinned at her.

After closing the gate, Tanner remounted Clive, who was becoming more trustworthy by the day. But he still swung his head back and hit Tanner in the knee. Tanner moved him forward and Whit fell in next to him. The cattle were no longer trying to spread, so they were able to ride side by side.

"I made the cut for a second interview," she said conversationally. After receiving the call that morning, she'd been alternately excited and uneasy. She needed a job. This was a good one. She wasn't ready to leave. She liked being closer to her dad and—she shot a quick look in Tanner's direction—she was going to miss working with this man.

"Congratulations."

"It's not a done deal and the one caveat *if* I get offered the position is that I'm staying with you until your mini crew arrives."

"Aiden and Cooper will be here early next week."

"So I can just…leave?"

"I'm in no hurry to see you go."

There was something in his tone that caused her to give him a sideways glance, but he kept his profile to her. In fact, he appeared not to have spoken at all.

"I'm in no hurry to go," she replied. "But life happens."

They rode in silence, the only noise being the beat of the cows' feet and the *putt-putt* of the ATV behind the herd.

As was customary, Tanner fed his crew after they'd ridden home from the cattle drive. Len waved off his invitation, saying that he needed to rest his leg, but the old guy was pleased with how much he'd been able to do that day. Tanner spent a pleasant hour with Whit and her friends, eating takeout from Holly's Café and being entertained by the three women telling tales of their high school days.

He learned that Whit and Maddie had not started out as friends, but instead had been the youngest at a riding camp and grudgingly paired up for mutual protection, which is how they ended up being lifelong friends. Kat had been Maddie's friend and had also bonded with Whit, and they'd become a solid trio from middle school on.

"This is a beautiful house," Maddie exclaimed as she and Kat helped clear the table.

"Only the best for Carl Hayes."

He spoke matter-of-factly, because it was the truth, and Whitney's friends took it that way. Carl had loved nice things, and that love had ultimately been his downfall. Whit liked nice things, too, but not in the way Carl had. And the woman was not afraid to work hard and get dirty. Or gooey. The incidents with the pitch and the bog still made him smile. She was so easygoing about things that might set other people off.

Whit saw Maddie and Kat to the door, then after her friends had driven away, she crossed the room to where her sweatshirt lay over a chair.

"I should go."

"One drink to celebrate interview number two?"

She considered it, then said, "Why not? Got rye?"

He got up and poured, then handed her a glass of WhistlePig.

Whitney sat in a custom-made oak chair and held the drink on the arm. "I could get used to only the best," she said.

"There used to be more artwork, but Dad sold a lot of it before his death."

"Trying to make ends meet?"

"He pretended he was tired of looking at the same old stuff, but it was one of our first inklings that all was not well. Each piece of art was like a treasure hunt to my dad. I couldn't see him letting his finds go to someone else."

"But he did."

Tanner nodded.

"Did he have to mortgage the place?"

"He secured a private note with a business associate, which allowed him to keep operating." Tanner swirled his drink. "I'll be paying on that sucker for a while. Dad was also in the process of trying to get a friend to invest in the ranch, despite having the loan. I found the rough draft letter outlining the idea, but it never got off the ground."

"It must have been shocking to find out that your inheritance had been compromised."

"I suspected, but Dad was tight mouthed about it. I'm sure he thought he could pull the ranch out of the red. He was Carl Hayes, after all."

Whit's mouth curved as she regarded her drink, but she wasn't smiling. "Life plays out in funny ways."

"Amen to that."

Rose padded into the room and fell to the ground at his feet, letting out a sigh as she rested her chin on his boot. Tanner smiled down at his girl, then looked up in surprise when Whit came to sit beside him on the sofa.

"Ally time," she said.

"Yeah?"

"Your financial issues, my job search…yes. Time for some mutual moral support."

"Your job search has taken a positive turn," he pointed out.

She sat close enough to him that it felt natural to slide his hand along the back of the sofa as he spoke. When his fingers brushed her shoulder, she moved even closer, leaning her head against his arm. It felt companionable and right and when she said, "So why aren't

I more excited about making it to the next interview level?" His arm tightened around her.

"You don't want to be that far away from your dad?"

"That's part of it. He's not getting any younger."

"And of course, there's me." He meant it to sound facetious, but it came out sounding way too serious. Whit shifted the position of her head to look up at him.

"Which kind of boggles the mind," she murmured.

His lips twitched and so did hers—just before they met. He could get used to this, cuddling with a beautiful woman with his dog at his feet.

"You know what?" Whit murmured.

"Nope."

"I could get used to this." She pushed herself to a sitting position, unaware that she'd just spoken his thoughts aloud.

A half dozen responses sprang to his lips one after another and he choked every one of them back. Whitney was a special woman, but he wasn't that special a guy. He had trust issues that had obliterated every serious relationship he'd attempted to embark upon.

Sometimes a guy just had to accept reality, and his reality was that he'd protected himself for so long that he didn't know how to stop.

"I'm not going to get used to it, however. We made a deal."

"I must have been absent that day."

"We agreed to help each other out and I don't think complicating our lives falls into that category."

"You classify me as a complication?"

She got to her feet, downed the last of her drink, then raised the empty in a toast. "More than that, Tanner Hayes, you are a danger."

He wanted to point out that from his standpoint, she was a threat, but there was no sense arguing about who was more dangerous. They knew their paths forward and all they had to do was to keep to them.

WHIT WAS IMPRESSED with how she sounded like she had the whole attraction thing under control before parting company with Tanner. Like she had a choice about the matter. She didn't. She didn't want to be drawn to the man, but she was. An ally was a good thing. One that disturbed one's equilibrium, not so much.

Yet she kept kissing him.

New Mexico will save you.

Yep. She could run and hide in the name of financial security, and no one needed to be the wiser. But her plan took a hit later that evening when she got a phone call from Lacy Tom, a friend who, along with her husband Buster, had been laid off with Whit.

"Have you guys landed anywhere yet?" Whit asked.

"I did. Right here in Missoula. The accounts department in the hospital. Buster is looking, and he's found a job that he might be able to do remotely, so fingers crossed we'll be okay."

"Great to hear."

"How about you?"

There was an edge to her friend's voice that made Whit reply cautiously. "I'm helping a neighbor with his ranch while I job hunt." She wasn't going to jinx her new job possibility by talking about it.

Lacy stopped being coy. "Rob called Buster trying to track you down." She hesitated. "Rob doesn't have your contact information?"

"Not since I turned in my company phone and quit using my work email." She'd wondered how he'd found her.

"He told Buster that you guys were the best

team and that he's really hoping to welcome you aboard at his new company."

"Really?"

"Rob is a charming work leech and he needs you to leech off from." Whit knew that was a danger, but he'd assured her during the interview that if they worked together, it would only be on the rare occasion.

"He told me he didn't think we would be working together that often. Just the occasional luck-of-the-draw project."

"He told Buster that he'd been given the opportunity to bring someone on board as his second."

Whit pressed a hand to her head and muttered a few words she didn't say in front of polite company. It would have come out eventually, because Whit did not go into things unaware, but the fact that Rob had tried to blatantly misrepresent their professional relationship fried her. She wasn't that naive, and it ticked her off to have Rob think she was. And it ticked her off that she'd been so excited about the job possibility.

"Lacy, thanks for the heads-up. I could work for the same company as Rob, but there's no way I'm putting myself through the stress of working *with* him again."

"Glad I could help," Lacy said. "If Buster finds something, I'll let you know. There might be something else there for you."

"Thanks. Actually, I'm doing okay now. And thanks to you, I've dodged a bullet."

"WHAT'S HAPPENING HERE?" Aiden Book asked as he got out of his car. Tanner had seen his help's distinctive orange Ford Ranger from the barn where he'd been working on the swather, and emerged to meet the kid before he was swept up into the crowd and put to work.

The Hayes Ranch was buzzing with activity as the community board and various committee members milled about the place, placing stakes that Tanner had been admonished to be careful of and arm waving as they decided how best to use the area.

"I'm hosting a community event," Tanner said. "Good to see you." As in really, really good. It'd only been a matter of two months, but it looked like Aiden had grown at least an inch in that time. Tanner hoped he could afford to feed him.

"Young man," Judy called as she hurried over. "Please move your vehicle. We have a delivery coming in."

Aiden met Tanner's gaze and Tanner nodded. "Behind the barn is good. I'll show you." Tanner got into the car and directed Aiden around the granary to the place where he parked out of the way.

Aiden parked and then spent a few seconds taking in the fields, the pastures and the mountain that rose up at the far edge of the north field. "Nice place. How's the fishing?"

Tanner pointed to the creek that cut through the pasture. "It had fish when I was a kid. You can check it out later." He jerked his head toward the house. "I'll help you cart your stuff in. I assume Cooper's not far behind you?"

"Girlfriend issues. He'll be here in about an hour."

Aiden pulled two duffel bags and a computer case out of the trunk and Tanner took the last grip bag. They walked through the barn and out the open bay door, then crossed the driveway to the flagstone walk leading to the house. Rose emerged from under the porch and gave Aiden a joyous greeting.

"What happened to you?" he asked. "I heard you had an accident."

Rose made happy whining sounds and shifted her weight from side to side as she gave Aiden a big canine grin. He ruffled the hair between her ears, then stood back up.

"She recovered okay?"

"She did, but her feelings are hurt when we go without her, so I'm letting her come along next time."

"Holy…cow…" Aiden stopped just inside the door, gaping as he took in the interior of the house. "And you voluntarily lived in a single-wide instead of working out of this place?"

Tanner never mentioned his family to his friends and coworkers at the wheat farm.

"My dad and I didn't see eye to eye."

"My dad and I get that way sometimes." Aiden spoke with the assurance of a kid who knew that even if he got sideways with his dad, things would work out.

Tanner smiled and then led the way down the hall to one of the many guest rooms. It was going to be good to have some company around the place. "Your room. Coop's room."

"Good. We can stay up all night giggling."

"Right." More likely they'd be up all night cutting hay.

"So tell me about this event."

"Not much to tell. It's a fundraiser and their original venue didn't work out, so I volunteered my place."

A knock sounded at the door and Tanner instantly tensed, hoping it wasn't Judy again, only to relax again when Whit called his name.

"Come in!" he yelled.

When he and Aiden emerged from the hall leading to the bedrooms, she was standing in the living room.

"Whitney Fox, this is Aiden Book."

"Someone else in the single syllable surname club."

Aiden grinned appreciatively. "Are you part of this community event thing?"

"In a small way. I'm also part of the ranch operations for now."

"Aiden, meet my range rider."

"Nice to meet you," she said.

Tanner could see that Aiden was as impressed with his range rider as he'd been with the house.

"Nice to meet you," he echoed.

Whit turned to Tanner. "Len is having a bit

of a meltdown out there. I didn't feel like intervening."

"Right." He turned to Aiden. "Settle in. The fridge is full."

"Excellent." Aiden gave Whitney a polite nod then headed back down the hall.

"He worked for me for two summers. This is probably his last. I'm glad he could come."

He and Whitney headed across the lawn to the sound of raised voices. They rounded the corner of Len's small house and found him facing off with an older blonde woman dressed in creased jeans and a starched long-sleeved pink oxford shirt.

"You were a pain in high school and you're still a pain," the woman said to Len as they approached.

"Now listen here—"

"No. You listen—"

Tanner stepped between Len and a woman he didn't know, something he wouldn't have normally done, but both parties were getting red-faced. He turned to the woman. "Is there a problem?"

She pointed at Len.

Tanner gave Len a look and the older man said, "You told me I was in charge."

And since telling him that, Len had been in a better mood.

"You are." He turned to the woman, thinking that since hosting this event was an exercise in bettering community relations, he needed to tread lightly. He didn't know who she was, but she seemed to think she was in charge. "Perhaps you could—"

"We are setting up the tent there." She pointed to where a corner stake had been driven into the ground.

"It'll block my morning sun."

Tanner refrained from rolling his eyes, but it took effort. "It's temporary."

The woman gave a victory sniff. Tanner needed Len to understand—he needed the community to believe he was a good guy.

"We have to set up the vendor booths there." She pointed. "And the flattest, largest spot for the tent is there and it allows us to hook into the power source."

Tanner gave Len a help-me-out-here look and the old man scowled deeply, then broke.

"Fine, Leticia. That looks like a great place for the tent."

Leticia gave him a smug look and strutted

back to the group that was staking out sites and arm waving.

"I hate letting her win. She was always pushing the envelope, that one." Len glared after her and Tanner rubbed the side of his head. Apparently, age didn't change mind-sets.

"If there are any other problems, I'll be servicing the swather. I'll introduce you to the new crew later."

"About time we got that hay down."

Len limped off. Tanner watched him go, then turned looked at Whit, who shrugged. "I have to fix some windbreak boards."

"Aren't you and your dad supposed to be part of all this setup?" Because she hadn't said a word about it, instead working her usual hours on the ranch.

"Only on the morning of. We're doing all the last-minute stuff, setting up games and helping vendors. I had another talk with Judy, and I must have made an impression at the meeting, because she agreed."

She gave him a quick smile then, before heading off in the direction of the corrals.

He and Len might never be friends, but he found that he didn't mind the guy. If he and his dad had had the same conversation, it would have ended entirely differently. But Len seemed to accept that he wasn't going to get his way and move on.

No wonder the cranky old guy was growing on him.

SMALL CREWS SHOWED up on the ranch every couple of days, and after the first visit, Tanner told Margo Simms that the volunteers didn't need to check in, but if they felt that they had to, then Len was the man to talk to.

He did his best to steer clear and let the workers do their jobs, so he was surprised when, as part of his steering clear, he went through the barn to saddle Clive for a quick fence check while Whit mowed ditches, and found a middle-aged woman studying his horses through the rails of the fence.

"Oh. Hello," she said when he appeared from the back of the barn. "I was just admiring your Rockies."

He smiled, then she floored him by saying, "That gelding was supposed to be mine, you know."

Tanner gave the woman a surprised glance. "Clive?"

She nodded. "I owned the stud he's out of.

Your father and I had a deal. In exchange for the stud fee for three mares, I got the pick of the get. Your dad had great mares." She pointed to Emily. "Good example there. Anyway, after the foals were born, I picked Clive. Your father changed the deal and insisted that I take one of the two fillies. He wanted the gelding for himself."

The word of a Hayes.

Len's odd statement shot into his head.

"I'll trade you back," he said.

The woman laughed. "The filly worked out just fine. I have a new stud and she threw an excellent little stud colt last month."

"Are you *sure* you don't want him?" Tanner asked. "I could have Clive's bags packed before you go."

The woman gave him an appraising once-over. "You look like your father…but I'm sensing you're cut from different cloth."

"There were things we didn't see eye to eye on." He wasn't going to bad-mouth his dead father, but he wanted the woman to know that they were different. "And Clive here… he's headstrong. You came out on the better end of the deal."

She smiled. "I was angry at the time because I wanted a gelding to ride, but I've heard rumors that he wasn't the mount your father had been hoping for."

"Sounds like karma was at play here."

"I think so." She held out a hand. "Mary Bledsoe."

He did the same. "Tanner Hayes. Nice to meet you."

WHIT HAD JUST parked the tractor and was thinking about heading home for the day when the phone rang in her pocket.

Rob Ketchum.

She stepped into the shop through the open door, saw Tanner working on the ATV and quickly stepped out again before he saw her. The phone buzzed again as she opened the main door of the barn and stepped into the cool interior.

Her mouth flattened before she accepted the call and said simply, "Rob."

"Whitney. I just got word that you canceled your second interview. Did you get a better offer?"

"No."

"Then what happened?" Rob sounded affronted.

"I decided that I want to work closer to home. My dad isn't getting any younger, and I need to be nearby."

Besides that, she'd rather get tossed into a bog than "team" with Rob again.

"You're not going to find a better job. I went out on a limb for you, and with a little finessing we can still schedule the second interview. It's not too late."

"Rob, I appreciate you thinking of me, but I'm not going forward."

Rob put forth another sputtering argument, but Whit cut him off and hung up the phone. She leaned back against a grain barrel. One bridge burned.

"You plan on working here full-time?"

Whit nearly jumped out of her skin when Len's gruff voice sounded. She turned to find the man standing at the door to the tack room.

"Why do you ask?"

"Because I won't have you pushing me out." He made a frustrated noise as he moved closer. "You'll tire of this place and leave, and I have nowhere else to go."

Whit studied the man as a thought took root. "Is this why you're so cranky with Tanner?"

Len gave her a startled look, as if he thought

he was the only guy on the ranch allowed to speak freely. "I'm worried about my future. I got lied to by one Hayes, and it's going to take me a while to trust the other." As soon as he finished speaking, he let out a harsh breath and turned to go.

"Wait a minute."

The man slowed. Turned. Gave her a malignant look that held an edge of…fear? And despite herself, Whit felt for the guy.

"We need to talk to Tanner."

"Don't go pushing your nose into my business."

"You're the one who opened the can of worms. Are we going to see Tanner, or do I have to bring him over here?" When the old man didn't reply, she called Tanner's name. She had good lungs, and he wasn't that far away.

The alarmed look on Len's face concerned her; she didn't want him having a heart attack or something, but he'd started this, and she was going to finish it. For his own good. She didn't for one minute believe that Tanner would push him out, and it seemed the guy needed major reassurance.

Tanner opened the barn door, looking alarmed,

as well. His expression shifted to bemusement when he saw Len standing a few feet away from Whit.

"Len has a concern. I think you should hear it."

"A concern." Tanner hooked a thumb in his belt as he waited for his foreman to speak.

Len swallowed, looking patently uncomfortable.

"Tell him," Whit urged the man.

"I had a deal with your dad."

Not what Whit had expected. She'd brought Tanner in for job reassurance. Now she was a witness to something different.

Tanner's face instantly tightened. "What was the deal, Len?"

"I had a job offer from an old friend a few years back. Good job, too. Your dad told me that if I stayed on here, that I would always have a place. And if he passed on before me, that I would inherit that five-acre plot near the main road."

"Do you have anything in writing?"

Len gave his head a shake. "He told me he'd made an addendum to his will, but when the time came, there was no mention of me."

His father had named neither son to be executor of his will, tapping his attorney for the job. The bequeathals had been straightforward—a fifty-fifty split between sons. There had been no amendment made for Len.

"Word of a Hayes?" Tanner asked softly.

Whit frowned, but Len simply nodded and then his mouth flattened. "He even told me he had the plot surveyed."

"I'm not selling the ranch, Len. You have a home."

"Until your brother forces a sale."

"I'm not going to let that happen."

Len's expression remained mutinous, as if he was afraid to believe the truth.

"I'll have my lawyer work something up. We'll sign it." Tanner held the older man's gaze until he looked down.

"No need."

"There is if you have issue with the word of a Hayes."

Len lifted his gaze. "Your dad was good to me in a lot of ways, but this hurt."

Tanner shifted his weight. "I'll have papers drawn up, and we'll agree to some terms. I think you deserve that and we'll both sleep better knowing we have a deal."

The older man didn't reply, but Whit read

the relief in his face. He needed the papers and Tanner understood that. Tanner was a good guy, and if he continued as he was, he would be fine with the community. He didn't need her help, even if he thought he did.

Whit had fulfilled her commitment to the ranch, and to him.

So why was it so hard to think about leaving?

CHAPTER TWELVE

IT'S TIME TO MOVE ON.

Whit reached into the soapy dishwater and pulled out a coffee cup, hoping to lose herself in a mindless task, but failing as the events of the day continued to play on a loop in her head.

She needed to move on, because Tanner Hayes had her thinking about *not* doing that.

Life plans were important, and surprisingly easy to forget when the guy warmed her heart by guaranteeing an old man that his living situation was secure. Or when he wrote "Wash Me" in the road dust on the back of Judy Blanchard's otherwise pristine car. Or when he did a hundred other small things that made her laugh or squeezed her heart.

Camaraderie, she told herself as she scrubbed a bit of baked beans off the plate her dad had used at lunch.

Baloney, her small voice answered.

But she would continue to play that game.

She would be Tanner's sounding board and workmate, while at the same time keeping her emotions under control.

She'd try, anyway.

She put the plate in the drain rack and reached for the skillet.

It was time to put new energy into finding a job—one that did *not* include Rob Ketchum. The guy had almost played her and that ticked her off. Had she gone soft during her time at home? She knew better than to fully trust the guy. She'd had a few blips of doubt, but had brushed past them.

Just like you're brushing off your attraction to Tanner. Except in that case it made sense. If she couldn't play the long game, then it wasn't fair to anyone to play at all.

After she'd finished the dishes and wiped down the counters, she stood for an uncertain moment, listening to the reassuring sound of the baseball game playing on the television in the living room. Her dad was probably asleep.

On with the job search, but her first move was to call her former workmates, Lacy and Buster, to let them know that their insights about Rob had been dead-on.

This time Buster answered, and Lacy was out.

"Thanks for giving me the heads-up about Rob," Whit said as she walked into the kitchen so as not to disturb her dad. "He did indeed plan on us having another one-sided partnership."

"Are you—"

"I am not."

Buster hesitated, then said, "FYI, I hear there have been issues with our former company and the merged positions. Rumor has it that they may be contacting former employees in the near future. Sounds like they got pink-slip happy and shot themselves in the foot and ended up with their own employees in roles they aren't prepared to handle. Typical case of thinking they knew what they were getting into, but didn't."

"Interesting."

"Would you go back?" he asked.

Whit closed her eyes. Thought for a moment. "They'd have to make one heck of an offer to compensate for laying me off."

"I don't know what I would do, either. I tried to tell them that a guy trained in human resources wouldn't be able to do my job, but they assumed I was just trying to keep my job. Which I was, so…"

Whit gave a small laugh. "I hope they do contact you, and I hope you get double your old salary."

And what was she going to do if they contacted her?

THE HEARTS OF the West crew had finished setting up for the day, but there were still a few stragglers loading tools into their vehicles as Tanner and Whit sat on the steps of his house sharing a beer before Whit headed home. It had become something of a routine for them over the past week. Work on fences, check the cattle on the mountain, feed the steers, have a beer before parting company.

"Big day tomorrow," Whit mused.

"And won't it be grand when it's over?" he said. Whit nudged him and Tanner made it a point not to smile. He was not looking forward to having his space being invaded more than it already had been, but he approached the matter with good humor, because he wanted to forge better relationships with his neighbors. Rebuild some burned bridges.

He wasn't certain how well that was going, but no one had keyed his truck or anything, so maybe it was going okay?

The frame tents were up—one for dining, one for games—and the generators to supply electricity for the food booths were in place. The area for the kids' activities was decked out, and the dance floor was in position. There was a slight chance of rain that evening so the folding chairs had been left in their racks, and the raffle committee members had yet to draw the chalk grid inside the panel enclosure for the cow flop contest.

"Last one," Whit said as a pickup with a lumber rack pulled out of the drive. "I'd better follow."

He didn't want her to go.

It'd been that way for the past few days. Whit would say she was leaving, and Tanner would feel a stab of disappointment.

Aiden and Cooper were still on tractors, mowing hay. Tanner could hear the faint drone of the engines in the distance. They'd be back in an hour or so, and then the house wouldn't be as lonely, but what really bugged Tanner was realizing that he'd never felt lonely like this before. Alone was his state of being. Alone was his protection, his strength. He didn't fear it.

But he no longer embraced it.

You're setting yourself up for a fall.

He got up and offered Whitney a hand. After pulling her to her feet, their fingers clung for a moment, then drifted apart, and they walked down the flagstone path to the low stone wall. Rose lifted her head from where she still lay on the porch, loath to move from her spot of early-evening sun, but wanting to keep a close eye on Tanner, just in case he needed her assistance.

"You get the day off tomorrow."

"Thanks." She gave him a wry smile.

"You're coming to this thing, of course."

"If I don't, who are you going to hang out with?"

Tanner smiled. "I'm glad I'm only the venue guy. I don't think I could handle running this thing."

"You ran a major farm."

"Where Margo, Debra and Judy were not employees."

"Len has had a great time bossing them around."

"But he steers clear of Leticia."

The old guy had met his match there. Leticia, whom Tanner had discovered via Margo was in charge of the layout committee, won the tent location contest and several other minor skirmishes.

"I think he enjoys doing battle," Tanner said as he set his beer aside. "Speak of the devil…"

Whit raised her gaze to see Len crossing the gravel drive, his cane slipping every now and again as it came down on a larger piece of gravel.

"Can you help me out?" The words came out in a burst as he stopped a few feet in front of where they stood at the gate.

"Of course," Tanner said.

"It's Kenny." Len's face hardened as he spoke, as if he expected an instant backlash when he said his nephew's name. But Tanner said nothing, and after a brief hesitation, the old man continued. "He was on his way out here with the groceries and had some kind of wreck. His phone kept cutting in and out, but as near as I can figure, he can't get his motorbike out of a gully."

"Is he hurt?" Whit asked.

"I don't think so. He kept talking about the motorcycle." But the worried look on the old man's face made Tanner's insides twist. Had his dad worried about him that way? He didn't know. Would never know.

"Any idea where the gully is?"

"I'm guessing that it's the one on the big corner past the Fairfield Ranch."

"I'll go take a look."

"I'll go with you," Whit said. "My truck or yours?"

"Mine's hooked to the horse trailer. In case we need to load the bike."

"Yours it is."

"I appreciate this," Len said gruffly.

"It's what people do for one another," Whit said. She glanced over her shoulder at Tanner, then started for the truck.

She made a good point.

"LEN'S HAVING A rough spring," Whit said as they drove over the cattle guard, the empty trailer rattling behind them. "Do you think your dad intended to alter his will to give him the five acres he promised?"

Tanner gave her a weary look before fixing his gaze back on the road. "I'd like to think that he did. That he treated other people better than family. Especially the guy who remained loyal to him."

Whit thought of the few times she'd seen Carl Hayes out and about. He'd been a handsome silver-haired man with a ready smile that didn't reach his eyes. He drew people in with natural charisma, then surprised them by turning cold when he no longer needed them. She'd heard her dad and friends talk about the man and how they avoided dealings with him. But he'd been a steady source of revenue for the community, giving generously and writing it off on his taxes. *He has more money than he knows what to do with*, was the common refrain.

Come to find out he didn't.

"There are only a few corners," Tanner said, punching the gas after they turned from the driveway onto the county road. They sailed along the washboard road, then Tanner slowed as they approached the first big corner. He stopped the truck and Whit got out to take a look. The creek ran close to the road there, but it was slow and lazy. The gully wasn't deep. She called Kenny's name, then got back in the truck.

"Not here."

The next corner was less than a mile away and as they approached, a solitary figure came into sight, walking along the edge of the road.

Kenny.

Tanner pulled up beside him and the kid gave them a mutinous look.

"We're here to help. Your uncle sent us. Where's your bike?" Tanner asked.

The kid jerked a thumb over his shoulder and Tanner said, "Let's go get it."

Kenny got into the back seat of the truck and Whit turned to give him a quick once-over. He had scratches on his face, but other than that seemed no worse for wear.

"It wasn't that bad a wreck," Kenny said stiffly, wiping a hand over his cheek. "The bike's too heavy for me to get up the bank."

"What happened?"

"Gravel got me."

Whit almost said, "You need to drive more slowly," but held her tongue.

The motorcycle lay on its side at the bottom of the gully, which wasn't so much deep as steep-banked on the roadside. After skidding down the bank, with the dirt and gravel shifting easily beneath their boots, Tanner and Whit made a plan to roll the thing down the creek until they came to a place where the bank was more manageable and secure.

"Just around that corner," Tanner said as he and Kenny started pushing the bike. Whit climbed back onto the road and turned the truck and trailer around in a nearby field. By the time she got to the low spot Tanner had pointed out, Tanner and Kenny were trying to wrestle the heavy motorcycle onto the road.

"I couldn't have done that alone," Kenny said after the bike was on the road. He swallowed. "Thank you."

"Can you start it?"

He tried, but the engine wouldn't take hold, so Whit backed the trailer to a low spot, and between the three of them they managed to load the motorcycle, setting it on its side.

The ride to the ranch was quiet, until they turned onto the driveway.

"My uncle was worried that you were going to replace him," Kenny said abruptly. He didn't need to explain who the "you" was, even though he didn't speak directly to Whit.

She exchanged a quick look with Tanner, then said, "I'm not."

"We know about that," Tanner said. "Len and I talked."

Kenny blew out a breath. "He's, like, all proud, you know."

Whit watched as Tanner met the kid's eyes in the rearview mirror. "Listen carefully. I'm not letting Len leave the ranch unless he tells me he wants to go."

The kid's chin came up. "Really?"

"As long as I have the ranch, your uncle has a home."

"Okay."

It might have sounded like an inadequate response on the surface, but Whit heard the relief in the kid's voice. She gave Tanner a sideways glance, but he kept his gaze straight ahead, then his chin came up.

"Are you kidding me?" he muttered.

Kenny took hold of the seat back and pulled himself forward to get a look at the Land Rover parked in front of the gate where no one ever parked.

"This keeps getting better," Tanner muttered.

"Your brother?" Whit asked as they drove past the Land Rover to the turnaround area.

"Appears so."

Tanner pulled behind the barn and turned off the engine. "Grant can cool his heels. I'm going to see Len." He looked over the seat at Kenny. "First I'll help you get your bike on its wheels."

"I'll entertain Grant," Whit said.

Tanner gave a curt nod in response, and after getting out of the truck, she heard Kenny say to Tanner, "You don't like your brother?"

"I like him fine," Tanner said as they walked to the back of the trailer. "We just don't agree on some stuff."

"Like what?"

Whit headed into the barn before Tanner could answer, but she had to admit that she wanted to hear what Tanner said to the kid. Ironically, he, the community pariah, seemed to have a knack with people.

Although he wasn't so much of a pariah anymore. The people working on the Hearts of the West setup were treating him like any other community member, not like a guy who might stab them in the back at any minute, just because he could. They were moving closer to trust.

Would Tanner ever be able to trust others back?

WHIT HAD ALREADY ushered Grant into the house by the time Tanner got done talking to Len, explaining once again that no matter what, the guy had a home there.

"More business in the area?" he asked as he came into the kitchen.

"I'm talking to the folks on the Fairfield Ranch about insurance. But I have some disturbing news and thought it would be best if I delivered it in person."

Grant seemed to have a lot of disturbing news of late. Tanner sank into a chair across the table from his brother. "Shoot."

"Bert Wallace had a heart attack."

"I'm sorry to hear that," Tanner said. Bert was one of their father's oldest acquaintances, and possibly the closest thing to a real friend that Carl had, because they were cut from the same cloth. Appearances and money were numbers one and two in their lives. Relationships a distant third. He'd given Carl the personal loan to keep the ranch afloat, but he hadn't done his friend any favors when he'd set the interest rate.

"He's okay?" Tanner asked.

"So they say. He's in the hospital in Billings," Grant replied offhandedly, before leaning forward and asking, "What if he sells the note?"

The private loan Carl had taken out to keep up appearances until he recouped losses could be sold. All Bert Wallace had to do was to give six weeks' notice to allow an opportunity for refinancing. Until this point, Tanner hadn't worried about the note. But now that Grant was on the job, all bets were off.

"Isn't that exactly what you want him to do?"

Grant blinked at him. "I'm here to warn you that trouble may lie ahead."

"Okay." Tanner wasn't certain he believed him.

"Selling the ranch makes sense, Tanner." Grant spoke adamantly, then seemed to remember that Whit was there, and changed his tone. "I want top dollar. I don't want to be scrambling to sell in order to get out from under this debt." He tapped the table with his index finger, emphasizing the words as he said, "That kind of knowledge tends to bring down prices."

"I'll worry about the note when and if it comes due. It's *my* worry, Grant. For the next two years and nine months it's my worry. So…do you want to spend the night?"

Grant got to his feet. "I have a room in Larkspur."

"I can offer you a drink or—"

"Thanks, no." Grant picked up his hat from where he'd left it on a chair back and held it with both hands. "I need to head back. I have a late dinner meeting with another client. What kind of circus are you setting up here?"

Grant knew exactly what the circus was, but Tanner explained what he assumed his brother already knew, since he was doing business in Larkspur. "I'm hosting Hearts of the West."

"So you don't have to write a big check. Brilliant." Grant sounded sincere.

Tanner walked his brother to the door while Whit hovered near the table. He was glad she wasn't taking this as a cue to leave, because for once in his life he felt like talking. He poured two whiskeys, handed one to Whit, then sat on the cream-colored leather sofa. Rose immediately moved from where she lay to settle at his feet.

"And this is where I am," he said to Whit. "My brother is not my ally."

She perched on the sofa arm next to him and ran a hand over his tense shoulder muscles.

"He pointed out a legitimate concern," she

offered. "The guy selling the note after a health scare. He might want to have more ready cash."

"It is a concern, but I'm guessing that this was my brother's way of warning me before he goes to work on the guy, trying to talk him into selling the note."

"You think that he would do that?"

"I think that he wants more than yearly profits from this property—once I start turning a profit, that is."

"You need to buy him out."

He gave her a *duh* look. "You think?"

Instead of being insulted, she smiled and ran her hand over the back of his neck. Her fingers were warm and soothing and just what he needed—a momentary distraction from the reality of his life. "We need to think outside the box."

"Uh-huh." He noted the way she'd said "we" and the way it made him feel. Like they were a team. Allies. Like someone had his back and not just for a convenient moment.

"Did I sound like I just came out of management training?"

He pulled her down onto his lap and wrapped his arms around her. "You did."

"Mr. Hayes," she said in a prim voice, but

she leaned into him instead of easing away. He felt her let out a soft breath and he settled his cheek on her hair, no longer worrying about what was right or wrong. Whit would keep them honest.

He wrapped his arms around her more tightly, holding her close and breathing in the fresh scent of her hair. There were so many things he wanted to say to her, things he wanted to discuss. Things he was half-afraid of discussing because he was fully afraid of the answer.

"Whitney—"

The sound of the front door opening interrupted him, followed by the noise of two teenage boys entering the house. Boots and other things hit the floor, then the fridge door opened and one of them called, "Dibs on the potato salad!"

Whit eased herself off Tanner's lap. He started to speak, but she touched her fingers to his lips to silence him.

"Let's leave things as they are."

The faintly pleading note in the voice of a woman who rarely pleaded was enough to decide him. Whitney had to make the next move.

The question was, would she?

CHAPTER THIRTEEN

BECAUSE BUSTER TOM had warned Whit about the possibility of a call from the Greenbranch human resources department, she was mentally prepared when it came. One of her former bosses had already returned to the company, which green-lighted Whit's return if she so desired. The fact that Shandra Johnson was willing to risk a second go with the newly formed Greenbranch-Lowell Renewable gave Whit reason to hear them out. Which she did.

She liked what she heard, but after ending the call, the wave of uncertainty hit, and she had to talk herself down. Her dad didn't need her on the ranch. That had been proven a dozen times over since her return. Unlike in years past, she wasn't called up for emergency fence repairs, or to take her turn on the tractor in the hayfields.

And as Len continued to heal, and with his

temporary crew now at work, Tanner didn't really need her, either.

What *she* needed was to get back out there and start focusing on her career again. The Greenbranch-Lowell HR representative had laid out all the possibilities for advancement in the newly formed company, and although Whit still had a bad taste over being let go to begin with, she understood that the way things looked on paper and the way they played out in real life were often miles apart. She could have told the Lowell executives that coming up to speed on federal regulations was no easy task, but why bother after getting booted?

As it turned out, they'd figured it out on their own and they wanted her back. The offer included a bonus and a raise. A new title.

And, she assumed, the long hours that went with that new title.

Her dad was going to think that she was a fool to leave the ranch and go back to a desk, and she could see his point, but she appreciated the security of her career. She'd worked hard to build it, and had received many perks because of it.

Once her bank account was back up where

it belonged, and she had poured enough into her retirement fund to feel secure, she would be in a position to rethink her options. She had a feeling that she would stay right where she was, working with people she knew and a company that appeared to be better because of the buyout.

Life Plan Number 3 was taking shape.

She only wished it wasn't making her chest ache as she chose practicality over dreams that wouldn't pan out any better than Life Plan Number 1.

"Let me get this straight." Ben frowned at the paper Whit laid down in front of him with the offer that had come in less than two hours after the call from Shandra. "The company that bought your old company wants you back?"

"The person whose position merged with mine isn't working out. They need someone who knows the ropes, fast."

"You'll be in Missoula."

Whit set a hand on her dad's shoulder. "That's the bad news…they've moved their executive operations to Portland. But it's closer than New Mexico."

"Still a distance." He gave her a long look. "There's more to life than money, Whit."

"I'm not chasing money, Dad. I want security. Don't forget that you might have lost the ranch if it wasn't for the money I earned at this same job."

"And if I had lost it, I could have dealt with it."

"Really?"

"It would have eaten at me, but that's how life works, Whit. Doors close and open. The only reason we have the ranch to begin with is because your great-great-grandfather's business in Butte went bankrupt and he decided to try his hand at ranching. I bet it killed him to lose his business, but he found something that made him happier." His voice gentled. "You have been happier."

"These past several weeks have been like a big vacation. That's why I'm happier."

"Or maybe you're doing something you like better than clacking away at a keyboard all day."

"That clacking provides security."

"I can't deny that. But…"

Ben obviously had more to say, and Whit wanted to hear it. "Life goes by fast, Whit. I don't want you to wake up one morning and realize that you've sacrificed good years to a career that doesn't let you see real sunlight as often as you should."

"I'll take vitamin D."

Ben didn't crack a smile. "Why are you really taking this job, Whit?"

He knew. He knew that she was running scared. When was she going to learn not to make jokes when she was afraid? It was her tell.

"I'm taking this job because I'm afraid to stay here."

And there it was. The honest truth that she had been dodging.

"Does that have anything to do with Tanner Hayes?"

She flattened her mouth and let her dad draw his own conclusions from her silence.

WHIT KNEW THAT she'd done the right thing taking the Greenbranch job.

She was occasionally impulsive in her personal life, but she always made safe and sane career decisions, which was what she'd done when she'd said yes to Greenbranch.

So why did she feel so torn about leaving the ranch, and Tanner, behind?

Do you really have to ask yourself that question?

As much as she tried to convince herself that what she and Tanner shared was the equivalent of a short summer romance, her heart begged to differ, whispering that she should take a chance, stay on the ranch and pursue the life she loved. Then her brain stepped in to complicate matters by bringing up financial security and adult responsibilities. The battle between logic and emotions had kept her up for a good part of the night, so when she rose in the early morning hours to drive to Hayes Ranch for the Hearts of the West event, she drank two cups of coffee in an attempt to jump-start her tired body.

Her dad walked into the kitchen just as she was about to head out the door.

"You're already leaving?"

"I have to help with final details. The event starts at ten, and you know something will explode or somebody will melt down before then."

"Last year the cow went AWOL."

"And I promised Debra that wouldn't happen again."

"Good luck with that," her dad said. He crossed the room to the coffee pot, then shot her a curious look when he saw that there was only about a cup left.

"I didn't sleep well," she admitted. Whit was not a huge coffee drinker, so by almost emptying the pot, she'd given herself away.

But her dad had mercy and didn't ask questions. Instead he said, "Making a big life move is never easy, even when it's just going back to your old job."

Whit smiled, then crossed the kitchen to give her dad a kiss on his weathered cheek.

"I appreciate that you understand why I need to go."

"I may not understand the why," he said, gruffly, "but I can see you have the need."

Whit took what she could get and headed out the door to start the old ranch truck she was driving that day.

When she got to the Hayes Ranch it was abuzz with activity. Someone called her name and soon she was on the chalk machine, making the squares for the cow flop. The cow was corralled nearby, so there would not be a repeat of last year's, "Has anyone seen the cow?"

She spotted Tanner after she'd finished the grid, standing near a vendor's booth, deep in conversation with Len. For once the older man did not look defensive. It was good to see the two of them conversing freely after everything that had gone on between them, thanks to Carl Hayes's empty promise. Tanner was going to be all right. He had his summer crew, his foreman was now on his side, and the community was warming up to him.

Her job here was done.

You have to tell him you accepted the offer.

She would and she didn't need to feel shifty about it. They'd laid out parameters, and one of those was that she could leave at any time to take a job. That was exactly what she was doing.

The vendor booths had just opened for business and the local musicians were tuning up when Whit found Tanner standing near the barn, watching the stream of cars pulling into his ranch. High school kids in orange vests directed the parking in a newly mowed hayfield. When he heard her approach, he turned, his expression reminding her of a cartoon of an expectant father.

"Nervous?" she asked.

Tanner's cheeks creased as he smiled, and Whit's heart did a little stutter. Was she ever going to stop reacting to that smile?

Not today, apparently, which made delivering her news all that much more difficult.

"I am nervous," he confessed. "I'd like the event to go well." He shifted his weight as he looked over the vendors' booths. "I feel like if it doesn't…" He made a slashing motion across his throat.

"This isn't on you." Whit came to stand in front of him so that the toes of their boots were a few inches apart. "All you did was to graciously let the community use your property."

"I feel responsible."

"You shouldn't."

"Says who?" he asked in a mock challenge.

Whit tossed her hair and moved a half step closer to the man. "I do."

He settled his hands on her shoulders, fixed her a long hard stare. Whit made a face at him, and his challenging look melted away.

"People are being friendly with me. I owe you for that."

"They're getting to know the real you."

"I am pretty awesome."

His smile was infectious, and Whit felt the corners of her mouth tilt up. She needed to tell him that she was leaving, but she wasn't ready to see that gorgeous smile fade from his face. He looked so open and relaxed, so totally different than when they first met. So much had happened since he'd rammed her car from behind and she felt a bond with the guy that went beyond a few shared kisses.

Were they more than allies?

Yes, her small voice whispered.

But she wasn't going to put a name on anything. What was the point when she was about to leave?

Tanner's grip tightened on her shoulders, and she sensed that he was about to kiss her, right there in front of anyone who happened to look their way. And she wasn't going to stop him. Instead it was Kenny who stopped him, calling Tanner's name from where he stood behind a vendor's booth with a cartload of folding chairs.

"Better go and make a command decision,"

he said, reluctantly releasing her shoulders from his warm grip. "I'll see you later."

"Yes, you will." Whit brushed a few wind-blown strands of hair from her face.

I have news.

She let out a breath as she watched him walk away. Telling him that she was leaving was going to be harder than she'd thought.

TANNER WAS ENJOYING the Hearts of the West event more than he'd expected, although he had to admit that he was looking forward to having peace and quiet on his ranch again. He was also looking forward to having some time alone with Whit.

She'd been on the property since early that morning, managing the final setup and tweaks of the game and vendor areas. Then she'd volunteered at the children's games and for the cow flop contest—both morning and afternoon sessions. She'd also lent a hand with the pet scramble, a favorite with the kids as they scrambled to catch ducks, chickens, piglets and baby goats that they were allowed to keep. If he didn't know better, he would think that she was dodging him. But that wasn't Whit's modus operandi.

A steady stream of music drifted from the gazebo where local musicians took turns playing, and a few people were taking advantage of the portable dance floor that he was assured would be crowded by the late afternoon.

A hand touched his shoulder and he turned to find Whit standing behind him. He tried to ignore the fact that his heart rate bumped up at the sight of her, as it always did, but it was getting harder and harder to do that.

"Another three hours and you'll have your ranch back." She handed him a beer as she spoke. "I thought you could use one," she said when he took the cold bottle from her. "Hosting can be exhausting." She tilted her head as she surveyed the people milling around the vendor booths, sitting on the grass listening to music, playing various games. "Even when it is going remarkably well."

"Actually," he replied slowly, "I haven't minded hosting." When she looked at him incredulously, he added, "Okay, the days leading up were rough, and I was nervous earlier, but like you said, it's going well. And it's nice to have people talk to me, instead of glaring because of something Dad did to them."

"They like you, Tanner. You've proven yourself."

"Maybe I can get some help on the ranch after my summer crew leaves." He raised his chin in the direction of his new hire who was in the process of chugging a liter bottle of Pepsi in front of an admiring crowd of teenage boys. "Besides Kenny."

"You hired Kenny?"

"It seemed like the thing to do."

Now that Whit was about to leave—with a paycheck, whether or not she wanted one—he'd started thinking about the kid, and wondered if he might like to work closer to his great-uncle. Come to find out, he did, so now Tanner had someone on the payroll who knew how to deal with Len's impatience.

"Nice," she said. "I'm sure you'll be able to find day hands when you need them. I've taken great pains to let people know that the Hayes Ranch is a good place to work."

Her speech sounded oddly perfunctory, and the smile that followed didn't bring the usual light to her eyes. When Tanner gave her a curious look, she fixed her gaze back on the crowd. Whit was not acting like Whit. Tanner wasn't a body language expert, but he could read trouble.

"Tell me," he said.

She turned to him and let out a breath that made her shoulders drop a good inch. "I'm going back to work for Greenbranch. The new incarnation."

The abrupt announcement surprised him, but then again it didn't. "I guess we knew this was coming." But now that it had, he realized how much he'd been hoping that Whit would decide that she wanted to stay in Larkspur.

"You understand, right?"

The fact that she'd asked that question meant that what he thought mattered. So he spoke a simple truth.

"Frankly, I don't want you to go."

She opened her mouth to reply, just as Judy and Margo waved at them, then crossed the front lawn to join them. "We just want to thank you for volunteering your ranch," Margo said. "We've had our largest turnout ever."

"Glad to help," Tanner said.

"We'll have to talk about next year." Judy gave him a coy look, then a jet of fire at the barbecue caught the ladies' attention.

Margo took hold of Judy's arm. "We'd best see what's happening over there."

"Have they never seen a barbecue flare?" Tanner asked once they were out of earshot.

Whit said nothing and when he looked at her, he could see that telling her he didn't want her to go might have been a tactical error. But it was also the truth.

"You know that I have to go," Whitney said, as if they hadn't been interrupted.

He nodded, not trusting himself to speak just yet. His thoughts were jumbling, and he didn't want to say something he regretted later.

"I *like* being with you," she continued. "I can't deny that we share something." She let out a soft huff of breath. "Something I did *not* see coming."

"Join the crowd," he muttered, torn between agreeing that Whit needed to follow her original plan for her sake, and confessing that his feelings for her were growing stronger by the day. He'd known that this was coming, but had hoped it wouldn't. And in an odd way he felt betrayed—by his own heart.

"Maybe after I…" Her voice trailed as if she didn't want to continue the thought.

"Get more money in the bank?" he asked.

Her gaze flashed up to his face. "There's that."

Part of him regretted uttering the words, but another part pressed on.

"How much, Whit? How much before you can let yourself take a chance?"

"I don't know," she said in a stony voice.

"Gotta stick to those life plans."

"They've kept me secure so far."

And security was important to her. Her job had helped her save the family ranch and she was afraid of not having the means to stave off another emergency.

Which meant that she had to leave. And that he needed to be understanding even if it was ripping his heart out.

"I care for you." He chose the word *care* because it was safer than saying that he was falling in love with her. He didn't want to risk Whitney's reaction to a sudden declaration.

"I know." She whispered the words, as if they were a guilty confession. "I care for you, too."

Tanner became aware of the sound of an altercation near the gazebo. Someone had started yelling, but he kept his gaze pinned to Whit's face.

"You don't want to do the scrape-by thing, and that's what you'd get if things grew between us."

Whit's chin jerked up. "Being poor wouldn't stop me from loving someone."

His mouth opened, then he closed it, feeling like she'd just hit him square in the chest. Finally he said, "I guess that's my answer."

"Tanner!"

Whitney jumped at the unexpected voice, and they turned together to see Grant heading toward them, walking with a rolling gait.

"I didn't know he was here," Whit said in a low voice. Neither did Tanner, but it would have been easy to arrive unseen given the crowd and the parking situation.

"Tanner!" he yelled again, even though he was only two or three feet away from him.

"I'm right here." Tanner winced at the smell of alcohol on his brother's breath.

"I've been talking to people."

"I'm sure you have."

"And the consensus is that you should *sell* this place. You're broke and everybody knows it."

Tanner simply stared at his brother, then a

moment later he became aware of Whit putting a reassuring hand on his sleeve.

"How many people have you talked to?" Tanner asked, setting his beer on the porch rail next to him and steadying his brother, who was listing from side to side.

"He's going to pass out," Whit said. "I worked at a bar in college. I know the signs."

So did Tanner, and he didn't want his drunk brother ruining the Hearts of the West event. He put a firm hand under Grant's elbow and Whit took hold of his other arm.

Together they led him up the steps, having to stop once because he almost sent them over backward. "I can take it from here," Tanner told Whit when they'd made it inside.

"Are you sure?"

He met her gaze. "Positive."

"I thought that…" She lifted her chin. "Fine. I'll leave you to it."

"ARE YOU OKAY?"

Whit's gaze jerked around as Kat touched her shoulder from behind. She was headed toward the food booths and hadn't realized that her friend was following her, shaken as she was by the double whammy of Tanner saying he didn't want her to leave and his brother announcing the ranch's financial status to the world.

"I'm not." Now that her friend was near, Whit allowed herself to feel the full impact of what had just gone down.

"Troy has the baby," Kat said, pointing to where her fiancé stood with his little daughter near the petting area, allowing Livia to watch the action. "Let's duck out."

"Let's," Whit agreed.

Somehow, Maddie caught up with them before Whit opened the barn door, and they stepped into the cool interior. A giggle from the dark told them that they weren't alone, and Whit called out, "This building is off-limits." Because apparently teens couldn't read the neat sign on the door.

Four middle school-aged boys appeared from behind the straw bales, and then sheepishly marched to the door.

"Is that all of you?" Whit asked.

The last boy mumbled an affirmative just before the door closed behind him.

"That was something," Kat said, and Whit knew she wasn't referring to middle school boys.

"Did Tanner's brother make a major scene?"

Whit asked as she sank down onto a straw bale, glad to be away from prying eyes. She'd heard the ruckus begin while she and Tanner had been talking, but had been so focused on their conversation that she'd ignored the yelling until Grant accosted them.

"It was pretty spectacular once he got rolling. He was shouting about Tanner being a fraud and the ranch being broke."

"Poor guy," Maddie said, obviously referring to Tanner. "I mean, you know how many ranches are in the red, so that's not a big deal."

"Except that it's the Hayes Ranch."

"Yeah, that is a big deal. How the mighty have fallen and all that." Maddie blew out a breath as she sat beside Whit. "But I was thinking more about the embarrassment factor of having your own brother turn on you in front of everyone."

"Yes." Whit was certain that stung as much as having private business aired publicly.

Kat took a seat on a different bale, pulling it around so that it was at an angle to Whit and Maddie, and then the three of them sat in silence, allowing Whit to gather her thoughts.

No easy task.

"Tanner will have to deal with this matter without my PR skills," she said. "Such as they are."

"Why is that?" Kat asked, her gaze narrowing shrewdly.

Whit attempted an upbeat look. "Because yesterday I accepted a job at my old company. I'm leaving soon."

"Whoa," Maddie said. "Your old company?"

"It's a real opportunity." Whit explained about the restructuring and her hope that she could once again start climbing that corporate ladder and make the final jump to management.

Except her heart wasn't in it. Her voice was stiff, but other than a quick exchange of glances, her friends didn't call her on her forced enthusiasm.

"I was going to take you guys out for drinks and announce."

"Congratulations," Maddie said. Kat nodded and patted Whit's knee. "You can owe us the drinks."

"Here's the thing…" She swallowed and rather than giving them a big lead up, simply said, "Tanner doesn't want me to go."

"Okay," Maddie said, her tone gently encouraging Whit to go on.

"But I have to." Whit spoke the words in little more than a whisper. She did, right?

Kat left her bale to squeeze in on the one that Whit and Maddie shared, so that the three sat shoulder to shoulder to shoulder.

"I'm glad you're taking the job," Maddie said. "It'll give you some distance. Help you settle on what you really want in life without being distracted by…" Her voice trailed off as Whit met her gaze, then she forged on. "Distracted by a hot guy who's a pretty decent person."

"He is a hot guy. And I am distracted."

She made it sound like a minor thing when it was anything but. She told herself that she already knew what she needed and wanted— the security of her career—but the truth was that she had just enough doubts to make her uneasy.

"I need time to get a perspective," she admitted, then she gave Maddie a sharp look. "What did you mean by *what I really want*?"

Maddie hesitated, then said, "I mean that you've been glowing since you came home. You love the life here. I know that your career is important, but I'm wondering if once you get back to it, it'll seem *as* important as it did before."

"I agree with Maddie," Kat said. "But if you stay here, you'll always wonder if it was because of the hot guy. And maybe your career *will* be exactly what you need once you get back to it."

Whit raised her eyes to the ceiling high above them. A small bird was perched on the rafters, looking down at her and she felt a pang of envy. What a simple life, flying, eating, drinking, nesting. She looked back at her friends.

"You guys figured things out. Your lives, I mean." Whit smiled wistfully. "But we don't all need the same thing, do we?"

"We—you—need whatever makes you happy," Maddie said.

"Right." Whit got to her feet. "I love you guys."

"Are you going somewhere?" Kat asked.

Whit nodded in the direction of the door. "I'm going to see how Tanner is faring with his brother."

"Are you sure?" Kat wore a concerned look as she stood up.

"I want to talk to him before I leave for the day."

"You're going home early?" Maddie also stood, absently brushing straw from her jeans.

"I am. I'm done here. My commitments have been fulfilled and I want to go home."

Where she would not be forcefully reminded of things she was choosing to leave behind.

"Do you want us to wait around until after you talk to him?" Kat asked.

Whit shook her head before holding out her arms to hug her friends. "If I need support, I'll ping you guys, but I think I'll be fine." She attempted a smile. "Thank you for talking me down."

She and Maddie and Kat exited the barn, only to find another group of kids considering possibilities there. "Off-limits," Kat said sternly, and the kids scattered, laughing as they ran.

"Good luck," Maddie said to Whit. "Sean and I will also be taking off soon. If you *do* need to talk, any time day or night—"

"Thank you." Whit gave her friends another quick hug, then turned and headed for the house, having only a vague idea of what she was going to do once she got there.

If Tanner and Grant were talking, she'd slip away. If they weren't, she'd wing it.

Her heart started beating faster as she mounted the steps to the wide porch, and when she looked in through the tall windows of the double doors, she saw Tanner standing near the stone fireplace and his brother's boots resting on the arm of a sofa. Grant appeared to have passed out.

Time to wing it.

Screwing up her courage, Whit knocked and Tanner's head came up. His expression barely changed at the sight of her, but he waved her in. She stepped into the beautiful house, hesitating on the threshold as the door closed behind her, muffling the sounds of the festivities.

"It's okay," Tanner said with a glance at his brother.

It probably wasn't, but she crossed to where Tanner stood near the leather sofa where Grant Hayes lay with an arm over his eyes, gently snoring.

She was both curious and concerned as to how matters had played out between the brothers, but wasn't about pry into Tanner's family affairs. Not when things were so shaky between them. To her surprise, he answered the question she wasn't going to ask.

"I think my brother and I understand each other," he said with a grim twist of his lips.

"What do you understand?"

"That he has no hold over me. No way to make me sell the ranch. People know the truth now. I don't have to pretend."

"Will the truth bring in the real estate people?"

"I imagine I'll be dealing with some unsolicited offers. I'm good at saying no."

"And the private note?"

He smiled humorlessly. "If it comes in, I'll start leasing out the house and grounds for short stays and events, like say, the one going on now."

"You don't want to do that."

"I'd rather stick a fork in my eye, but a fork in the eye is better than having to sell."

Whit propped her hands on her hips, glancing down at the expensive wool rug at her feet.

"Sometimes," he continued, "we have to make temporary sacrifices to keep the life we want. I want this ranch."

She understood.

"There's other things I want, too." The look he gave her left no doubts as to his meaning. "But if it's not the right time—"

"Tanner…"

"Then it's not," he said firmly. "I jumped the gun. I'm not certain about my feelings, either. I guess I thought if you were, then we could figure things out, but now it's a moot point."

Whit's instinct was to argue, even though it was counter to her goal. Like Maddie said, she needed time, and she needed distance. So did he.

"Kenny is going to start work immediately," Tanner said.

An indirect way of saying he didn't need her any longer. Whit ignored the painful twist of her heart and brought her hands together.

"I have to see about renting an apartment in Portland."

Grant stirred on the couch, and they simultaneously glanced his way. He settled again and Whit took advantage of the moment to say, "I should go."

Tanner nodded, but he didn't say goodbye, and Whit didn't move. She couldn't leave things as they were. She studied the rug for a brief moment, then met Tanner's gaze.

"What I said about being poor not stopping me from loving someone…it didn't come out as intended." She pushed her hair back from her forehead. "That said… I need time to think."

"We both do."

"Right."

He hooked his thumbs in his pockets as if trying to keep from reaching for her. Whit knew the feeling, but if she gave in now… she couldn't.

Time and distance.

"Goodbye, Whitney." Tanner's voice was rough, but firm. "Good luck in Portland."

"Goodbye, Tanner."

She swallowed as she turned. Stupid tears burned the corners of her eyes as she crossed the room to pull open the heavy door. She stepped outside into the sounds of celebration. The community members were having the time of their lives indulging in food and music and games, thanks to Tanner. He was now part of the community, thanks to her. Everything had worked out as planned.

Except for the things she hadn't planned.

She glanced over her shoulder as the door swung shut, but it was too late to catch a glimpse of the man she might very well be in love with.

The latch caught with a quiet yet definitive click.

This part of her life, the fun easy days on the Hayes Ranch, was over.

CHAPTER FOURTEEN

TANNER WOULDN'T LET his mind linger on Whitney, or the fact that his life had a pretty good-sized hole in it now that she was gone. That was the plan, anyway. They'd had fun, they'd grown close. She'd been his ally and his sounding board. He'd fallen in love; she hadn't gone that far. That was something he had to learn to live with.

Kenny was working out well as an employee, helping his uncle get around and lending a hand when Len needed it. He was familiar with Len's short fuse and knew when to hand him a tool and when to let the man get it himself. In fact, Kenny was pretty impressive in that regard. And he had a genuine fondness for Len.

Tanner just hoped he'd be able to continue paying Kenny and Len if the note came in. Just in case he couldn't, he'd talked to his attorney about fulfilling his dad's promise to Len. There were issues to work out, but Len would get his parcel of land.

After coming to that decision, he'd taken yet another hard look at his finances—or lack thereof—and had come up with a plan that wasn't optimal, but was probably inevitable, since every bank he'd approached for a loan had turned him down due to the money already owed on the property. If push came to shove, he would turn his house into a glorified bed-and-breakfast, or whatever they called the short-term rentals, but while it was a good bluff with his brother, further research had shown that it wouldn't bring in enough to handle the note.

Still, good bluff.

Property was gold in Montana, and he could get some gold by going against his gut and selling off a parcel, something his attorney told him he had the right to do, as long as he split proceeds with Grant. He hated to sell anything, especially since a neighboring ranch had done the same the year before, and it was now a cozy subdivision advertised as country living at its finest, but he also hated wondering if Grant's announcement at the Hearts of the West was going to result in people looking to take advantage of his circumstances. There were plenty of vultures out there and Grant was trying to send them his way.

He had to do something, and the only piece of property he could reasonably carve out to sell was next to the five acres that his dad had promised Len. The problem there was that it contained the diversion point for the water he'd leased Ben Fox.

He could change the diversion, but it would take time and he needed to alert Ben. He'd given the man his word that he'd have water for the next three years and he was standing by that.

When he pulled into the Fox Ranch later that afternoon, intent on explaining to Ben that even though he was going to list a piece, it would not affect the water lease, he had to slow to avoid the chickens that had been pecking in the gravel, filling their craws. Rose remembered her roots as a bird dog and pressed her nose against the passenger-side window, whining her desire to show Tanner exactly where those birds were.

"I see them," he said as he pulled to a stop in front of the house.

The Fox Ranch looked prosperous with its

freshly graveled driveway and neatly painted outbuildings, and if he hadn't known better, he would have assumed it was always so.

Ben Fox came out of a shop-like building as Tanner got out of his truck, after rolling the windows down so that Rose would be comfortable. "Do not get out of the truck," he said to the dog, who gave him an easy canine grin. In her younger days, she might have sprung out the window, but her old bones couldn't handle much of that anymore.

"Hey," Ben Fox called.

"Hey. Sorry to drop in unannounced." He'd tried to call the landline, but it had remained busy, so finally he decided to stop by on his way to town and the county assessor's office, where he would inquire about plat map changes. "I'm looking at changing some things, and wanted to give you a heads-up."

"Come on in and have a cup, and you can tell me about it."

Five minutes later, Tanner was seated at the kitchen table, with a deeper understanding of why Whitney liked her coffee like tar. Ben casually tossed out the fact that she was coming home to pick up her car in a week or two, and Tanner asked if she was doing well in a polite kind of way that had her father giving him a speculative look.

"She likes the changes in the company."

"Good." Tanner sipped his coffee without grimacing and then explained that he was thinking of parceling off some land to sell. "I will make absolutely certain that your water lease is not affected, but frankly, this is my only option in case of the unexpected."

"Yeah. I heard about that unexpected," Ben said. "Your brother puts on a good show."

Tanner didn't mention that he half suspected that his brother might be in contact with Bert, urging him to call in the note.

"Do you want to sell the piece?" Ben asked.

"No. I'll lose production and I'm afraid of chipping away at the place." Total honest truth. It felt good not to hedge.

Ben thought for a moment, then said, "I think you need to talk to the rancher crew."

"I don't understand."

Ben focused on a tattered patch on the knee of his coveralls. "No one would do business with your dad because there was that possibility of being burned."

"I had the same experience."

"Things are different now," Ben said. "Stop

by Holly's Café tomorrow morning. It won't hurt, and some of the guys are pretty creative when it comes to getting out from between a rock and a hard place."

Tanner gave him a dubious look. "Okay…"

Ben gave Tanner a stern look. "But be warned."

Always a catch.

"Yes?"

Ben grinned. "You may find yourself becoming a regular."

GREENBRANCH-LOWELL RENEWABLE was a different animal than Greenbranch Renewable had been. Whit returned to work her first day ready to hit the ground running and dive into the backlog of work created by her predecessor's lack of knowledge and practical skills. It was shocking to discover then that employees were discouraged from working overtime. Being chained to one's desk was not considered a positive. Calling in sick was encouraged when one was actually sick.

She had security. Her new salary allowed her to keep her car, which she had yet to retrieve from Montana. She lucked into an affordable sublease on an apartment. She was working with some familiar faces that Greenbranch-Lowell had brought back. Shandra wasn't her boss, but she was in her department. She felt valued.

And secretly miserable as she battled an emotional state of flux. Why couldn't she settle?

You know why.

"Are you okay?" Shandra asked over Friday drinks on Whit's one-month work anniversary.

"I'm still getting used to working a sane number of hours," Whit said, leaning back to allow the server to place a glass of rye in front of her—a drink that reminded her of Tanner.

Everything reminded her of Tanner.

"But since I'm not being interrupted at every turn with an emergency this or that, I'm actually catching up during normal working hours."

Shandra lifted her drink, her bracelets sparkling against her dark skin. Whit used to wear jewelry to work, but she'd yet to unpack hers. A lot of her belongings were still in boxes, and she knew how telling that was. One day soon, she'd hang pictures, put out mementos, make her little apartment a home.

"I was wary, too," Shandra said. "I didn't think this new model would work, but it does."

"It seems to." Whit ran her fingers over the condensation on the side of her glass. "Why did they cut so many positions in the first place?"

"They made a mistake—the new broom sweeps clean, and all that—but you have to give them credit for realizing quickly what was and wasn't working, rather than persevering with a bad decision out of pride."

"Yes. Persevering out of pride." Whit was persevering, but she could truthfully say she wasn't doing it out of pride. Nope. She was all about security. But what good was security if she wasn't happy?

Whit drew in a breath to speak, then changed her mind.

"Go ahead," Shandra said.

She was getting as bad as Tanner when it came to discussing personal matters.

You're worse. Tanner started letting things out and you started shutting them in.

"I left a cowboy back home."

Shandra's chin dropped and she studied Whit from under perfectly shaped eyebrows. "Why would you do such a thing?" Whit was about to reply when Shandra added, "Seems to me that an unsupervised cowboy could get himself into a lot of trouble."

Whit laughed even as her stomach twisted. Tanner might get himself into trouble, but she wouldn't be able to stop that.

"He needs to come here, where you can keep an eye on him."

That wasn't going to happen.

Whit gave her former boss a weak smile. "It felt like a holiday thing. I was only going to be home for as long as it took me to find another job. That was my mind-set. Then I got a job and I left, and I miss him."

"Okay."

She opened her mouth to say, *But, of course, I have my priorities straight and I know the feeling will fade.* Instead, she said, "I really miss him."

"And he's not the kind to move here?"

"He has a ranch there. Responsibilities."

Shandra put a hand on top of Whit's. "I don't know what to tell you."

"Tell me that it's smart to stay with a company that's doing so much to create a great work environment for their employees."

"There's that, for sure."

"Tell me that it's important to build retirement and sock-away savings, because you never know when you might have to pump money into the family ranch."

"Okay."

"*If* I went home and got a job there, where I'm closer to…"

"Your cowboy?" Shandra said.

"I'd make half of what I'm making now. If my dad's ranch got into trouble again, I wouldn't be able to help." He'd made noises about accepting the loss, and figuring out a way to forge a new life, and Whit had no doubt that he could…but why would she let that happen if she could help avoid it?

Shandra swirled her drink, her bracelets catching the light. Then she looked up and said, "If."

Whit blinked at her.

"What if the ranch *doesn't* get into trouble?" Shandra continued patiently. "Being here because of what *might* happen when you'd rather be there seems kind of…dumb?"

Whit had to agree, but there were things that Shandra didn't know—like the trauma of almost losing the ranch. Having difficulty affording books when she went to school. Little things that carved deep trenches of worry back in the day.

"We barely squeaked by for a lot of years. I don't want to experience that again."

"How old were you when this went on?"

Whit frowned. "It started when I was in middle school and continued through my college years until I got the job with Greenbranch."

"Frontal lobe." Shandra lifted her glass to emphasize the words.

Whit also lifted her glass. "Frontal lobe to you, too."

Shandra smiled as she set the glass down. "Your frontal lobe doesn't fully develop until your early twenties. Your amygdala is hanging on to the bad memories. Creating a fear reaction."

"Is there a cure?"

"Conscious thought and logic." Whit raised her eyebrows at the seemingly simple answer and Shandra leaned forward, setting her palm on the table. "You need to overcome the thought patterns that are sabotaging good decision-making. When Lowell took over Greenbranch, they got rid of everyone above a certain level because they *thought* that the current employees wouldn't be amenable to change."

"They had a point."

"Then they realized they had a problem, and changed course, carefully bringing back people who could benefit the company."

"That is a good model, but—"

Shandra shook her head. "Lowell didn't start out with that plan. They *changed* to that plan, hoping for the best. They took a chance and it worked. People were starting new, instead of shifting gears and grumbling about change. They had a fresh attitude."

"You're saying…?"

"I'm saying that maybe you should take a look at your reality. What's steering your course, and are you going in the *right* direction for the *right* reasons?"

"Are you trying to get rid of me?" Whit asked, only half kidding.

"Never. But I want you to be happy." Shandra's expression was very, very serious as she asked, "How can you get to that place? Is it a matter of time? Or a matter of change?"

"OVER HERE, TANNER." Ben Fox raised a hand as Tanner walked into Holly's Café, as if he might miss the two tables pushed together, surrounded by six people wearing flannel and canvas.

Tanner lifted his chin in acknowledgment and started across the room to the empty chair next to Ben. He'd gotten there at 6:15 a.m., fifteen minutes after opening, and judging from the coffee cups closest to where he'd taken a seat, most of this crew was ready for their second cup.

"Tanner, I think you know everyone?" Ben then went through brief introductions, just in case. "Martin Fairfield," a neighbor that Tanner knew by reputation only, "Joe Johnson, Liz Forgone, Walt Stenson, Max Tidwell. Troy couldn't be here."

Tanner smiled and nodded, feeling very much as he had during the brief job interview phase of his career. He'd only participated in two interviews before he landed the wheat farming job, so the feeling wasn't a comfortable one.

After Holly gave him a warm hello and topped off everyone's coffee, talk centered on how to get the county commissioners to grade an unimproved road, and if they could not manage that, whether the volunteer firemen would offer their water truck if they were able to rent a grader.

Tanner started to relax as the road maintenance talk continued. He didn't know what he'd expected, other than the usual—to be snubbed or lambasted for the sins of his father, despite making headway with the townspeople since he'd teamed up with Whit.

But Ben Fox hadn't invited him to the klatch to be lambasted. Logically, Tanner knew that, but knee-jerk reactions were hard to control, and his nerves jumped when Max Tidwell, owner of a local guest ranch, abandoned the topic of road maintenance and turned to him. "Ben tells us that you're in need of some creative solutions to a problem."

"Yes." Succinct, and the sum total of what he was willing to put out until he understood his audience better. He assumed that they were there to help, but why?

"Can you tell us what you're facing?" Walt Stenson asked in his gruff voice.

I don't want to.

Tanner sucked in a breath and fought against his ingrained instinct to handle his issues on his own. To not put himself out there to be judged.

"The ranch is in debt. There's an operating loan and a private loan. I'm concerned that the private note will be called in, and I'm looking for a solution that doesn't involve selling off land that I need to operate."

Tanner studied the faces of the ranchers after he'd finished, trying to read reactions and wondering if he'd just made a huge error in being honest with them. It was a relief to no longer have to guard his secret, but he'd just let out information that opened up the possibility of people using it against him. People who wanted to profit from his bad luck.

"Welcome to the club," Liz Forgone muttered, and then gave him a weary smile. "These guys helped me out two years ago."

Tanner felt a small surge of hope. "How?"

Max spoke again. "We don't want to see viable farmland taken out of production. A parcel here, a parcel there, it adds up, and agriculture takes a hit as houses spring up on land that could still be growing crops."

Tanner agreed, but instead of speaking he waited, expecting red flags to crop up at any moment.

"If you want to talk in a more formal setting, bring us the numbers, what you owe,

your projections for the future and all that."
Max gestured at those around the table. "If
it looks doable, we can help you refinance."

"You're kidding."

The words popped out before he could
stop them. He'd been expecting offers to buy
pieces of his ranch, or perhaps lease opportunities, but not to get out from under the note
that his brother wanted to have called in so
that he could force a sale.

"We're serious," Ben said. "We work with
the Cattleman's Bank."

"They already turned me down. The ranch
has a traditional loan in addition to the note."
His dad had covered all of his borrowing bases.

"But they won't turn us down," Martin said.

"Why do you say that?"

Joe Johnson chuckled. "Because I'm the
president of the bank and I trust these guys."

"We have a lot of money in Joe's institu-
tion, including an emergency fund that we
use to make loans," Martin said. "We put this
together a few years ago, when Lizzie here
needed some help, and the fund has grown
nicely thanks to decent investments and interest, of course."

"Refinancing is the first step," Max said.

"And we can help you find a crew that sticks with you," Walt added, "if you want to go back to full operations. I know that your dad cut back in recent years." He made a tsking noise. "I just didn't know why."

Tanner looked around the table. "What do you get out of this other than saving farmland?"

"Satisfaction," Liz said. "It could happen to anyone."

Half an hour later, Tanner left the café feeling dazed. He had neighbors who were going to help him. Granted, they were going to get their money back and interest to boot, but the offer alone was enough to humble him.

He walked with Ben to his truck, which was parked near Tanner's.

"I don't know how to thank you for this opportunity," he said to the older man.

"It's not a done deal, but I have a good feeling about it."

Ben got into his truck but before he pulled the door shut, he said, "You're not your father, and I think you've hit a point where you don't have to keep proving that."

"I'm beginning to believe it."

"I think my daughter has feelings for you."

Ben tossed his bomb, then waited for Tanner's reaction.

"I think we both know that she's not coming back to stay." Tanner tipped his head to the side as a thought struck him. "If your ranch got into trouble, you obviously have some options for help."

"As long as the fund isn't being used."

"Does Whitney know this?"

"Yes. I'm no psychologist, but I think her career is her way of dealing with the aftermath of her mom's death. She had no security during that time other than me and her two best friends. We almost lost the ranch. Now she makes her own security in the form of money in the bank."

Tanner glanced up as two women walked past on their way to the café, the only business open at this hour. One of them smiled at him and he smiled back, thinking that it felt good to no longer be an outcast, before turning his attention back to Ben.

"Next moves?" Tanner asked, referring to Whit rather than the loan. He guessed from Ben's expression that he got the drift.

"We wait."

CHAPTER FIFTEEN

LIFE PLAN NUMBER 4 was shaping up in an open-ended kind of way. Whit had left it that way on purpose, even though it was a tad unnerving not to have all the i's dotted and t's crossed. Every now and again she had to pause and assure herself that open-ended was fine. Sticking to an obsolete plan out of fear was not.

Life Plan Number 3 had served her well. It had helped her save the ranch. It had put money in the bank and allowed her to buy nice things.

Now, thanks to her weeks with Tanner, she was in a been-there-done-that frame of mind.

She didn't need the security her corporate job provided any longer. She liked it, because it allowed her to be impulsive in other areas, but she didn't need it. She'd get by.

Shandra had asked if getting to a place of contentment was a matter of time or change.

The answer had come so much more rapidly than Whit had anticipated. Change. It was a matter of changing her outlook, of reassessing what security really meant. Of knowing that she could scrape by if necessary, and that if she was scraping by with a guy she loved, it would be a shoulder-to-shoulder venture.

Structure and money had been her security, but she was strong enough now to take risks. She'd been strong enough before, but hadn't recognized the fact. Deep down, she'd been the frightened teen who'd given up so much, only to lose her mom. She'd equated lack of money with loss, only to set herself up so that pursuit of money meant loss.

Loss of a possible relationship with Tanner.

But that loss was not carved in stone.

She hoped. They hadn't parted company on the best of terms, and they hadn't been in contact. She told herself she was brave enough to do this, to give up everything she'd thought she wanted to head back home and start a new life.

Maddie and Kat would probably laugh if they saw brave Whit shaking in her shoes, so she wouldn't. She would head home, get a job, live on her ranch and see if it was possible to salvage things with Tanner.

If not, then they'd be neighbors. And it would hurt to see him, to know what she'd given up in a mistaken effort to keep herself and her family ranch safe and secure.

She'd be lying if she said she wasn't nervous about the whole situation, but she also had no intention of changing her new course.

Not unless she was forced to. The only person who had that power was Tanner.

THE LOAN WAS in the works. Two weeks after the coffee klatch meeting, papers had been signed and the check was being sent directly to Bert Wallace, much to Grant's chagrin. Now he had no choice but to wait to see if Tanner could pull things out of the red.

Tanner was going to do just that. As he'd once told Whit, he was good at making ends meet, and now that he had some breathing room, he needed to see about finding a used cultivator to replace the one that was now beyond repair due to simple wear and tear.

He scrolled through the community marketplace on social media, hoping to find what he needed, flipping past furniture, tools, trailers, cars—

He abruptly reversed the direction of his thumb and went back to the car he'd just scrolled by.

Whitney's car.

As in, the car she was supposed to have picked up that weekend. He'd spent Saturday and Sunday jumping when the phone rang, then being disappointed when it wasn't her calling to ask about his new business deal with the coffee klatch ranchers. Maybe her dad hadn't told her.

Maybe if he wanted her to know, he had to tell her himself.

He read the listing, then sat back in his chair. She was selling the car after all.

It could mean nothing.

Or everything.

He reached for the phone and dialed the number on the ad. A few rings later, Ben Fox answered.

"Hi, Ben. Tanner Hayes. I see that you have a car for sale."

"Then let me hand you off to the owner." Tanner's heart rate bumped up as he heard Ben walking through a room, his footsteps echoing. A moment later he was back on the line. "She's not here."

"Would she want to talk to me if she was?"

"I can't answer for her, Tanner. I can just tell you that she's gone, the car's gone and the dust is settling in the direction of your ranch."

TANNER WAITED A good hour for Whitney to show, then decided that Ben was wrong. She didn't want to see him. If she did, he would have known that she was back in the area. Selling her car.

Why was she selling her car?

He went to the barn and started the tractor, warming the oil so that he could change it. Cooper was supposed to service the tractors, but Tanner felt the need to keep busy. If he focused on the ranch and rebuilding, he spent less time thinking about what he wished could have been.

Actually, he was going to do more than wish.

While the tractor idled, he readied his supplies, then after ten minutes he turned off the machine and reached for his phone instead of the wrench. He wrote a short text and pushed Send. His head came up a split second later when a texting chime sounded from outside the shop.

No way.

The door opened and Whitney stepped inside. "So much for surprises," she muttered.

"How much of a surprise did you want to give me?" he asked, somehow managing to get words out of his tight throat.

"I was going to stand outside the door for a bit while I gathered my courage," she muttered. "I got all of five seconds before your text came in."

Tanner's heart started thumping against his ribs. Slow, steady thumps that still didn't seem to be getting enough oxygen to his brain.

Whit lifted the phone with his text message on the screen. "Apparently, you'd like to meet?"

"I thought I'd have time to prepare."

"That would make two of us."

Barriers were rising on both sides and Tanner knew that he couldn't let his barriers get in the way yet again.

"If you were willing to try…" He looked past her to the door she'd just come through, trying desperately not to screw up.

"Try…" she echoed.

His gaze shifted back to her as she started toward him with slow, measured steps, her boots echoing off the walls of the barn.

She stopped just out of touching range and pushed her thumbs into her front pockets. "I quit my job."

"Whit—"

She cut him off with a look, which was just

as well, because he had nothing other than a flickering sense of hope.

"It's been a rough month."

"On the job?"

"In my head." She studied his boots as he studied her. "I've never been in love." She lifted her gaze. "Not like this. It's ripping me up, but it's also making things so much clearer."

She loved him. His heart swelled, but he waited for her to continue. He needed to know everything she was thinking. Every problem she had with them being together so that he could counter it.

She let her gaze travel around the interior of the barn. "Maybe I wasn't so far off the mark with Life Plan Number 1."

"The one you made in middle school?" The one she'd told him about when they were riding on the mountain.

"When my mom was sick, yes. Maybe I was meant to be on the Hayes Ranch, training horses. Or a horse." She gave him an unreadable look. "Clive is still a menace."

"Not as much of one as before."

Everything in Tanner's being cried out for him to take this woman in his arms. Hold her. Tell her how much he needed her in his life.

Instead, he found the strength to say, "I got out from under the private note."

"I know," she said quietly. "Dad is very proud of that."

"I still have a lot of financial worries."

She lifted her chin. "Here's what I think about financial worries." She closed the distance between them, took his face in her hands and kissed him. A long, slow kiss that melded into another long, slow kiss, which ended with Tanner backing her across the barn floor until she came up against the tractor tire. Then he kissed her again.

When he finally lifted his head, he pushed his fingers into her hair, then dropped one last light kiss on her beautiful mouth. "Since when don't you care about security?"

"Since I started doing battle with my amygdala."

Tanner blinked at her. "Uh…"

"Long story. Bottom line, I'm facing my fears. And then I'm beating them into submission. I was trying to do that outside the door when your text came in."

He laughed and pulled her closer. "You're really quitting?" He wasn't sure how he felt about that, knowing how important her job had been to her, but maybe some of those reasons no longer applied.

"First, I'm going to give the powers that be a pitch about working remotely. This company doesn't have a policy in that regard, so I'm hoping to force them into making one. If they say no, then I'm quitting. I own part of the ranch next door. It may not support me, but I'll have a place to stay while I find a local job." She frowned up at him and he realized he was staring at her as if expecting her to say, "April fool."

"What's wrong?"

He smiled. A genuine, nothing-to-hide smile. "Everything is right."

She touched a finger to his lips, and he kissed it. "Get used to it. With me around, things are going to go right a lot."

"You think?" he asked, dropping his hands to link behind her waist and pulling her closer.

She gave him a sassy smile. "I don't think. I know."

EPILOGUE

"FOOD'S NOT READY YET." Tanner settled on the grass beside Whit, stretching out his legs and leaning back on his hands.

"How long?"

"According to my stomach, too long."

Whit laughed and leaned into his shoulder. The summer had flown by, and it was time for Aiden and Coop to return to college for the fall semester, so Tanner had arranged a going-away party, which was now in full swing. Len and Whit's dad sat at a picnic table, playing cribbage. Kenny, Aiden, Coop and a few of the local ranchers were playing volleyball, which was something of a spectacle. Whit had to admit that it was amusing to see some of the guys in their go-to-town clothes instead of dusty jeans and plaid shirts. They'd brought wives and kids, and the summer picnic on the Hayes Ranch was shaping up to be a good time for one and all.

Tanner's stomach growled and Whit gave the hard muscles a pat.

"Good things come to those who wait," she said, turning her attention to little Livia, who was toddling around the lawn hanging on to Kat's finger. Her friend was a natural-born mother and after a quick elopement—she was afraid of having a real wedding due to the tendency for unexpected things to happen during Farley events—she and Troy were now trying for a brother or sister for little Livia.

"I don't want the kids to be too far apart in age," Kat had confessed to Maddie and Whit.

"How many kids do you want?" Maddie had asked.

"Open-ended," Kat had replied, and then been mystified when Whit laughed.

The volleyball sailed their way and Whit slugged it back into the game.

"Good one," Tanner murmured.

"I have skills," she said.

"Next you'll be saying that you can out-volleyball me."

"In a heartbeat."

He smiled into her eyes. "In your dreams."

She raised a hand to his cheek and smiled into his eyes before he took her lips in a quick kiss.

"Deflection will not work," he growled into her ear.

"Experience tells me otherwise," she replied, turning her attention back to the action.

She had to go to work the next day at her new job with the Natural Resources Conservation Service. She wouldn't be buying sporty roadsters, but she didn't need one. What she did need was the man sitting beside her. The man who'd sworn he'd love her forever.

"I'd like to get married someday," she murmured as she watched Maddie set out plates with her fiancé, Sean. Her friend looked so happy, as did he. She and Tanner had discussed the big step, even though they were only months into their relationship. Discussed it, tabled it. And now Whit was bringing it up again.

"To me?" he asked.

She ran a critical gaze over him. "I don't think I could do better."

His smile made her forget to breathe for a moment, and the next thing she knew her hair was touching grass as he leaned over her, kissing her deeply.

A wolf whistle sounded, and they pushed themselves back to sitting positions with sheepish grins, then Tanner stood and held out his hand.

"I like your plan," he said as he pulled her to her feet.

"It's Number 5."

Tanner laughed and pulled her close. "That might soon be my favorite number."

* * * * *